LOOKING FOR ANDREW McCARTHY

Jenny Colgan was born in 1972 in Ayrshire. After Edinburgh University, she worked for six years in the health service, moonlighting as a cartoonist and a stand-up comic. Her first two novels, *Amanda's Wedding* and *Talking to Addison* were bestsellers, and film and TV rights in all three of her novels have been sold. Jenny now lives in London and is working on her fourth novel and a TV series.

For more information about Jenny Colgan, visit her website at www.jennycolgan.co.uk.

From the reviews of *Looking for Andrew McCarthy*

'Colgan is on top form with this, her latest outrageous romp.'

Cosmopolitan

'Jenny Colgan is one of the leaders of the pack . . . and this, her third novel, will delight her legion of admirers. Fast-paced, funny, poignant and well-observed it reads as a pastiche of the movies she loved . . . If a time capsule were buried to capture the world at the turn of the 21st century, this would be a candidate for inclusion: her sense of time and place are that authentic.'   *Daily Mail*

'Looking for Andrew McCarthy will strike a chord with anyone who did their growing up in the 80s. Wonderful, warm and resonant for anyone who ever wondered what happened to teenage dreams.'

Hello

'*That's Life* meets *This Life*, with *Once in a Lifetime* thrown in, all talking heads, witty one-liners and angst-ridden relationships . . . Did I like this book? Well, d'uh! Do hedgehogs have quills? A pure belter of a novel'   *Glasgow Herald*

'Colgan's enjoyable new bestseller investigates the notion that having it all can sometimes mean having precisely nothing at all'

Marie Claire

'Colgan's *Looking for Andrew McCarthy* is sharp, well-observed and hilarious'   *New Statesman*

JENNY COLGAN

Looking for
Andrew McCarthy

HarperCollins*Publishers*

HarperCollins*Publishers*
77–85 Fulham Palace Road,
Hammersmith, London W6 8JB

www.**fire**and**water**.com

This paperback edition 2002
1 3 5 7 9 8 6 4 2

First published in Great Britain
by HarperCollins*Publishers* 2001

Copyright © Jenny Colgan 2001

Jenny Colgan asserts the moral right to
be identified as the author of this work

A catalogue record for this book
is available from the British Library

ISBN 0 00 710553 3

Typeset in Garamond 3 by
Palimpsest Book Production Limited,
Polmont, Stirlingshire

Printed and bound in Great Britain by
Clays Ltd, St Ives plc

Acknowledgements

Thanks to Ali 'the super' Gunn, Rachel Hore and Fiona McIntosh – all as supportive and fantastic as ever; Jennifer Parr, Yvette Cowles, Venetia Butterfield, Esther Taylor, Nick Sayers, Adrian Bourne, Martin Palmer, Jane Harris, Stephen Page, Julia Cass, the reps and all at HarperCollins; and Nick Marston, Doug Kean, Carol Jackson and everyone at Curtis Brown.

Also: Mum, Dad, Rob and Dom; Sandra, Shappi and Susan; Lisa Jewell and Andrew Mueller for their help in Kansas City; Henry Donne; Wesley Moody, who knows what the best thing to have is; the real Andrew McCarthy (incidentally v. difficult to track down, so not recommended), and Bliggers and Bedlamites everywhere.

HOSS Rocks!

This book is dedicated to the girls
I first watched these films with, particularly
Queen Margaret's finest: Katrina McCormack,
Karen Murphy and Alison Woodall. (I was going
to include some *Nightmare on Elm Street* stuff,
but I reckoned we'd get too frightened.)

The passion runs deep.
Strapline, **St Elmo's Fire**, 1985

The laughter. The lovers. The friends. The fights.
The talk. The hurt. The jealousy. The passion. The pressure.
The real world.
Strapline, **Pretty in Pink**, 1986

Bernie's back – and he's still dead!
Strapline, **Weekend at Bernie's II**, 1993

Contents

Less Than Zero

'HEY! HEY! HEY! HEY!'

Simple Minds. Ellie nudged it up with her foot, still concentrating on whitening up an extremely old pair of stilettos, and joined in with gusto.

'Wooohhwoooahh!'

The phone rang and she turned the music down reluctantly.

'Hedgehog!'

'Oh, hi Dad.'

'HAPPY BIRTHDAY!!!'

'Yes, yes, yes.' Ellie tried to sound embarrassed, but was actually pleased.

'Did you like your present then?'

'Dad, it's a beret.'

'It'll come in handy, though, won't it? For skating?'

Ellie hadn't been skating with her father for sixteen years.

'Uh, yeah.'

'So, are you all set for tonight then?'

Ellie looked around the room. One of the problems of having an eighties party, she mused, was not quite having the resources to rip out your entire flat and redesign it to look like the set of *Dynasty*. So she'd hung lots of old Brat Pack and Duran Duran posters on the wall, left lots of *Jackie* annuals lying about and bought a bunch of pink and black striped napkins. Later on, she was planning on spraying around some Anaïs Anaïs.

'Hmm, pretty much,' she said.

'Is Julia coming?'

Ellie raised her eyes to heaven. 'Dad, she's my best friend. Of course she's coming.'

'I bet she'll look nice.'

'Yes, well, I think it's enough every male my own age I've ever known fancying Julia without you as well, okay?'

She could hear her dad shrug over the phone.

'She's very pretty.'

'Dad, you've know her since she was five. Stop being disgusting.'

Ellie stared in the mirror next to the phone and squinted at herself, trying to see if she could get her hair to lie down simply by leaving her hand on it for a long time. Ellie didn't quite fit into the 'very pretty' category. She might make 'very perky' on a good day, with her ridiculously curly hair, which went in every direction, snub nose, and generous sprinkling of freckles. At least her eyes were nearly black, usually with mischief.

'Yes, well,' he said, changing the subject. 'Thirty, eh, darling? Leaving your wild, carefree youth behind you.'

Ellie contemplated a much-loved picture of Limahl and wondered if her youth had been quite wild and carefree enough.

'Ehm . . . something like that,' she said, trying to manipulate sellotape, poster and phone at the same time. 'I stole a traffic cone once. Anyway. What did you do for *your* thirtieth birthday?'

'Don't you remember, Hedgehog?' he said. 'You were the one who wouldn't stop biting the waitress.'

'I was *there*?'

'There? You were practically at school. Couldn't go back for another black forest gateau for years. Then we went to the garden centre in the afternoon and you weed behind the fountain.'

'That sounds terrible,' said Ellie, glancing at the piles of old twelve inch Howard Jones singles she was planning to use as the major form of entertainment.

'No, actually, it was lovely,' her father said, nostalgically.

3

Ellie examined her face in the mirror again. It was a Nik Kershaw one she'd found at a boot sale.

'Wrinkles *and* freckles? That can't be right, surely,' she thought to herself.

'Huh?' she said.

'Nothing. Just have a nice time.'

'I will. I'm just going to pick Billy up from his rehearsal.'

'Oh, right.' Her dad conveyed by those two simple words exactly what he thought of Billy, Ellie's latest paramour. Ellie thought it was because he played saxophone in a band. In fact, it was because her dad had been a policeman for thirty-five years, and had a pretty good idea what a rogue looked like.

'Okay. See you soon.'

'See you soon, darling.' He paused. 'And – have a *happy* birthday, sweetheart. You know? I just want you to be *happy*.'

* * *

'Now what the hell did he mean by that?' thought Ellie to herself, instantly upset as soon as she put the phone down. She started unpacking the bags of Wham bars, Spangles and Space Dust and gazed at the dusty box of Bezique she'd extracted from a rather shocked looking off-licence assistant.

'I'm completely happy,' she thought to herself.

Particularly now she'd bribed her evil landlord with several boxes of nasty cheap continental lager to get himself out the house.

She hauled herself out into the chilly October air to head round the corner to Wandsworth Town Hall where Billy would be making a racket and pretending to be Steve Norman. She dug her hands deep into the pockets of her duffel coat.

'I *am* happy,' she thought. 'Well, apart from my job, which is shit. And the flat of course. Which is also shit.'

She turned the corner. 'And I'm having a party. And I have a cake in the shape of Dangermouse.'

'Bought by me for myself,' she thought.

She marched up the steps of the town hall. There were no wailing noises, which was unusual, but she knew where the rehearsal rooms were.

'And all my friends will be there.'

She pushed open the door.

'And I guess they'll buy me lots of knick-knacky things.'

She entered the room fully.

'Oh SHIT,' she yelled, as Billy leapt up from the near-prone position where he'd plainly been snogging the dumpy trombonist.

'Fuck! I'm MISERABLE!'

* * *

Julia's hand was sore from knocking on the newly stripped pine bathroom door. She sighed and tugged at her nasty nylon shirt with the pussycat bow rather self-consciously. Ellie was on the other side of the door, and she had locked it and pushed a cupboard in front of it.

'Hedgehog! Please come out! You can't have a tantrum on your birthday!'

From behind the door came muffled noise. Julia leaned in to hear.

'Yes, well, let's just forget ages four, six and eight through eleven for now, shall we?' she said, and sighed again. She gazed through the doorway into the living room. It actually looked pretty ratty, with the basic Ikea covered over in old posters, and two Cabbage Patch dolls posed to look as though they were having sex forming a centrepiece. The Psychedelic Furs were playing.

There were, Julia often reflected, two ways to deal with someone who, on the day in Year One when the photographer comes from the local paper and everyone is scrubbed, brushed, plaited and ironed to the nines, stands next to you and jams their pencil in your thigh so that there are twenty-seven angelic grins in the official 1975 Year One photograph of St Joseph Xaviers, and one agonized grimace. You either never speak to them again and secretly break all their pencils, or you give up and become their best friend, whilst learning to accept a certain amount of unpredictability into your life.

She smoothed down the ridiculous blouse, in which she was actually managing to look quite chic, and knocked again. 'I've fixed Pass the Parcel!' she said. 'Second verse of "Never Ending Story!" Just hang on in there!'

There was silence from beyond the door. The front doorbell rang and Julia stomped off to open it.

'Hello darling,' said Arthur, kissing her on both cheeks and swanning in stylishly as usual. 'You smell nice. I thought I'd come early.'

'God, am I glad you did,' said Julia with clear relief, indicating the bathroom door. Arthur was handsome, charming, kind and everyone was in love with him. He was also so gay you could bounce him like a basketball. He put down a gift and a bottle of champagne and went over to the bathroom.

'No, really?'

Julia nodded. 'Disappeared in there with a bottle of wine to get ready. Two hours ago.'

'Huh, I don't know why she's so bothered. It's only thirty. That's, like, seventy in gay years.'

'Oh, yeah, where is Colin?'

'I left him tied up outside. Come on, darling, what's the matter?' Arthur hollered through the door. 'I don't know what you've got to complain about. I caught Colin eating from the sugar bowl again.'

'I don't know why you don't just get a dog,' said Julia. 'Be a lot easier.'

'But he's so *cute*.'

'Yeah, and wait to see how cute he is with worms.'

'Come on missus!' Arthur banged the door again. 'There's presents out here.'

'Why aren't you dressing up?' said Julia, rummaging in her old make up kit for a blue eyeliner pencil.

'I am,' said Arthur, lifting his Tom Ford shirt to show a quick flash of an old "Frankie Says Relax" t-shirt. 'That's as far as I can go. Anything more eighties brings me out in a rash. I call it Banarama-isus.'

'Ah,' said Julia wisely as, through the open front door, she spotted a couple heading up the pathway of the run-down South London terrace. 'Who's that coming?'

Arthur peered over her shoulder.

'I don't know. Who else has been invited?'

'Not sure. Ellie went through all her old address books and asked everyone she's ever met in an attempt to have a big bouncing birthday party.'

A rather ascetic-looking young man and his even more disinfected-looking girlfriend stood nervously on the doorstep clutching a gift wrapped in a Body Shop bag.

'Hello there!' said Julia brightly. The couple smiled nervously.

'. . . and you are?'

'Ehm, Hi. Yeah. I'm Ellie's chiropodist?' said the awkward looking man. Behind them, alighting stodgily from a taxi, were two more people, who looked middle-aged unless you peered very very closely.

'I can't *believe* she invited George and Annabel,' Arthur whispered to Julia.

'*I* can't believe I gave her free access to her own address book.'

Annabel was truly dressed up for the nineteen eighties only in as far as she hadn't changed her style in her whole life. Her pearls smacked gently off her upturned blue-striped collar as she leaned in to try her hand at the bathroom door of fear.

'Darling, do come out. I've got to tell you the *hilarious* thing George did at the golf club dinner.'

Annabel and George had been together since college and had married immediately after it, which surprised no-one as they'd both looked forty-five on the day they'd turned up for fresher's week. He did the bad dad jokes, she did the baking, and they had been the first to buy a flat, settle down and start complaining about parking in garden centres on Sunday afternoons.

'I brought some home made hors d'oeuvres!'

The chiropodist appeared to be picking up the cheese and sniffing it.

'Where's Billy?' said Arthur, helping himself to a

9

glass of wine, seeing as the party seemed likely to continue hostess-free.

'Aha,' said Julia. 'That kind of explains the bathroom. They've had a little contretemps.'

'Good.' said Arthur. 'Too much saxophone playing. I hope they split up: when you say their names together it sounds like Canterbury Cathedral.'

'No,' said Julia. 'She caught him getting off with a trombonist. Apparently they do amazing things with their lips . . .'

'Oh dear,' said Arthur. 'Things are bad. If this really was the nineteen eighties, we'd have to give her a makeover.'

* * *

Ellie was sitting on the linen basket feeling utterly disconsolate and kicking her white-stockinged toes in the air. The problem about having a huff was it was kind of difficult to know when to stop. She could hear signs of activity outside and knew she ought to go and face them all, but instead she was back looking in the mirror at the amount of polka-dotted lace she'd tied through her curly black hair and thinking, 'thirty!' Okay. Relax. She was fine. She wasn't unhappy. Okay. So she was living with the biggest bastard landlord this side of China. And she had a job which involved a mind boggling amount of paper shifting to no apparent end. And Billy.

She didn't even want to think about him. Okay, so he hadn't been absolutely ideal – he worked all night and slept all day and wasn't even anything cool like a vampire – and, okay, his hair was a bit on the mullety side, but she didn't mind that particularly. But no. He still had to go and bag off with someone who looked like she carried around two ping pong balls in her cheeks. Was this fair? She rubbed roughly at a stubborn tear which had forced its way through several layers of Barry M crème eyeliner.

How on earth could she go out there? Half of her guests she didn't even know. With a wince of embarrassment she remembered that she'd invited the postman. And, yet again, another birthday without a word from her mother, which made sixteen in all. She examined her eyes for wrinkles again and found plenty. 'Not that it matters much from this point on,' she thought gloomily. 'It's all downhill from here, fat arse.'

She touched up her beauty spot. Oh God. Maybe if she stayed in here all night they'd all go away.

'Umm, hi,' came a deep growly voice from the other side of the door. It was Loxy, Julia's super-uxorious boyfriend.

'Julia sent me over to . . . I don't know what really. But here I am. And lots of other people are too. Happy birthday by the way.'

He coughed. Ellie closed her eyes. Loxy was lovely, and so in love with Julia it made Ellie want to puke.

'So . . . Julia's looking good, don't you think? What are you wearing?'

Ellie glanced down at her hybrid 1984 Madonna/ Strawberry Switchblade/Cyndi Lauper outfit and winced a little. Perhaps it was a little bit over the top. She hoped everyone else was dressed up too. (This was to prove a vain hope, although the security guard from her office was wearing differently coloured neon socks, and her hairdresser's assistant had got herself a wet look perm done specially).

* * *

Someone was singing about someone else being their favourite waste of time, and Julia glanced around the room. It had filled up quite nicely, although 'Come Dressed for the Eighties,' seemed to have been literally translated as 'Well, In a Way Gap Did Actually Exist in the Eighties.' There wasn't a boiler suit in sight, despite the pictures of Tony Hadley on the invites.

Siobhan and Patrick were in a mood with each other, not exactly unusual given that they'd been a couple for five years and were both chronic workaholics who'd forgotten how to spend any time together. Patrick was pushing the ironic flying saucer sweets in his mouth with the same relentless mechanical motion he used to sell bonds and, Julia suspected, make love. He was staring straight ahead looking mournful. Siobhan, on the other hand, had turned into a parody of someone trying to pretend she wasn't in a mood with someone; circulating, flirting, laughing loudly. The joys of domesticity. Julia had never lived with anyone, not that Loxy ever stopped dropping hints; in fact, even now as she turned round from pouring wine (Annabel had taken over canapé distribution) he was hovering about worriedly and asking her if she wanted him to break the bathroom door down. Caroline Lafayette was banging on about her gap year in Tibet yet again, despite it being twelve years ago. Colin was hopping from foot to foot, obviously desperate for the toilet. Were all parties always crap, or just Ellie's? Okay, that was it. She marched out to the bathroom.

'Hedgehog!' she yelled. 'I'm bringing out the cake. Everyone is here. We're going to sing happy birthday. You are going to come out and be nice. Or we're going to . . . ehm. We're going to tell your Big Bastard Landlord that you fancy him.'

'How come,' said Ellie through the door, 'when Oscar the Grouch is in a bad mood everyone's really sympathetic, but when it's me I get dire threats?'

'He's cuter than you.'

'He lives in a *bin*!'

'Come on everyone!' said Julia as Loxy came out of the kitchen with the Dangermouse cake. She started singing 'Happy Birthday'.

People started to join in nervously, however just as they were getting going, the front door slammed open. Shadowed in the open doorway against the wet October evening, the light from the streetlamp bouncing off his face, clutching his saxophone and dripping onto the carpet stood Billy. He lifted the saxophone and started to play along. Slowly, very slowly, the handle of the bathroom door started to turn.

* * *

Ellie burst out of the bathroom.

'Hey, sugar,' said Billy, curling his lip at her. Billy was medium height and emaciated and looked, in a bad light, like Rob Lowe's ugly younger brother. After he'd been addicted to crack for fifteen years and had a YTS haircut.

'Sorry,' said Ellie, calmly. 'Did someone say something? Or did I just hear a cat being sick?'

Julia manoeuvred herself to Ellie's side and put her arm round her.

'Why don't you just come over here and we'll cut the cake?'

'It didn't mean anything, sugar.'

'Would you like a canapé?' said Annabel. 'I made them myself.'

Billy ignored her, pulled on his cigarette and dropped his ash on the carpet. Annabel sniffed loudly.

'Babe, I've just composed a little melody for you to show you exactly how much you mean to me.'

'Just as well it's not the other way around,' said Ellie, crossly. 'Otherwise we'd all have to listen to "Agadoo".'

Billy lifted up the saxophone, framing himself artistically in the doorway, winked meaningfully at her and threw back his head to start blowing.

'This isn't the one that sounds like "Baker Street" is it?' said Ellie.

Billy paused and slowly lowered the sax. 'Ehm, yes. Yes it is that one.'

Ellie sighed and slowly began eating a canapé.

'Oh well. Go on then.'

'You've put me off now.'

'Fine.'

Billy looked down at Annabel, who seemed to have accrued a dustbuster from somewhere.

'Excuse me, but I'm trying to make what's known as a gesture?'

'Yes, well, you're actually making what's known as a mess.'

Billy sighed and, very slowly, lowered the saxophone.

'You know darling,' he said to Ellie in a conversational sneer. 'It's not like we were going to get married or anything.'

'*Nobody* gets married,' groaned Ellie.

'. . . it's you that said you didn't want commitment.'

'Yeah, I don't need a lot of commitment to ME.' Ellie found herself yelling. 'But *you* can't make a commitment to a piece of TOAST.'

'Jeez, what happened to everyone being laid back?' said Billy.

'For fuck's sake Billy. Just because I went to Red Wedge doesn't mean that you're allowed to get off with a trombonist, okay?'

He pouted. 'I just don't know why it's such a big deal. It's not like I've bought her her own handset for the playstation.'

'Oh,' said Ellie. 'So she's been round your house.' She stared at him. He was idly brushing back his gelled hair. Fury welled in her.

'It's a studio, not a house, okay babe? Chill! It's ironic really . . . you know . . . being found snogging by someone who says they don't want commitment then them blowing a gasket.'

'For once in your fucking life . . .' she screamed at him. The chiropodist began to edge towards the door.

'Just for once: this is NOT fucking ironic, okay?'

'Not unless he did the same thing on her twentieth birthday in the same clothes,' whispered Arthur to Julia, who nodded.

'For fuck's sake, you prick. You really hurt my feelings. Can't you see that?'

Billy shrugged. 'It's like that movie . . .'

'It's not like ANY movie, Butthead,' shouted Ellie. 'You actually hurt me, and you seem chronically incapable of giving a fuck.'

She burst into tears and retreated into the bathroom.

'Chicks, eh?' said Billy in the bad fake American accent he affected much of the time. He looked closely at the bathroom door. There was no sign of life. He turned and slouched moodily out of the flat.

'And how about another quick "Happy Birthday to You"?' suggested Annabel.

* * *

Six hours later Ellie was still lying across her bed in something approximating despair, although she was coming to the end of the drama queen stage. Mascara was running down her face and she was clinging onto another empty bottle. Julia and Arthur were sitting on the bed, Colin was mooching around petulantly. Loxy was waiting patiently outside.

'Oh God,' she said dramatically. 'That's the worst party I've ever had. Or been to.'

'Nonsense.' said Arthur briskly. 'What about that time at Annabel's when you threw up on her mohair rug?'

'It was round and it was white, okay? Looked like a toilet seat to me. Oh God. I can't believe I'm thirty. I'm thirty and I have absolutely nothing.'

'You have masses of things,' said Arthur, rubbing her back soothingly. 'Friends, and a flat and a job and everything. And your mobile phone is really, really tiny and silver. I mean, what did you think things were going to be like when you got to this stage?'

Ellie's vision clouded over as she thought of what it was going to be like.

'Let me see,' she said, staring into the middle distance. 'I'm wearing a beautiful pink dress.'

'Oh no,' said Julia. 'Not this one again.'

'And I'm in a big pink room with billowing curtains . . . and I'm dancing to Orchestral Manoeuvres in the Dark . . . and my handsome partner leans over and whispers something like . . .'

'Don't worry, I'm sure house prices will keep going up for ever,' said Arthur, squeezing her tightly. 'I can't believe you thought that having an eighties party would make the Brat Pack happen.'

'What are you all talking about?' said Colin, who still lived with his parents.

'God, Colin, what's the first film you ever saw?

Jurassic Park?' said Julia. 'Ellie was talking about a very talented group of young actors in the nineteen eighties . . .'

'. . . who now make furniture sale adverts and appear in films on Channel 5 after midnight on wet Thursdays,' said Arthur.

'And we loved them.'

'Why?' asked Colin.

Everyone looked at each other.

'They had HUGE apartments,' said Ellie. 'Not flats, apartments.'

'And they went to cool dances at school.'

'And they started out unpopular, but then got really popular.'

'And they had makeovers.'

'And they were going to be friends for ever, despite their class and intellectual differences.'

'And they were all going to be famous and successful and live happily ever after for ever!'

Everyone sighed.

'That sounds complete shit,' said Colin.

'As opposed to what?' sniffed Ellie. '*Teenage Mutant Ninja Turtles?*'

'Oh, Hedge,' said Arthur, rubbing her head affectionately. 'I don't think we can get you what you want for your birthday. Although your chiropodist left you some peppermint foot lotion.'

* * *

19

Ellie had been known as Hedgehog since she could talk. Ellie's mum had started calling her it because she was such a prickly little thing, and it had stuck, because the more you called her it, the pricklier she got. After her mother ran away with an chartered accountant called Archie, Ellie got pricklier still.

Whilst Julia was blonde and angelic as a child – she was still blonde now, although it took a little bit more effort, and she was certainly angelic bordering on martyrdom as far as the Hedgehog was concerned – Ellie was wild-eyed and had kinky black hair and sticky pink cheeks and looked as if she'd just run away from the circus. Their teachers in public had called them 'Snow White and Rose Red', in private, 'Good and Evil'.

Ellie's mother had skipped town without warning the year before the girls sat their GCSEs. It shocked their friends and neighbours in the respectable suburb, and no-one ever mentioned it to Ellie ever again, no matter how many tantrums she pulled. Julia, and her parents, had made sure that, when Julia sat down to study for her exams and, eventually, applied to university in Sheffield, Ellie did exactly the same, and they had gone up together. Which usually meant that they just felt like very old best friends, although occasionally it could feel that they were yoked together unto death. Julia looked out for Ellie, and it seemed to Ellie that the trade-off was Julia got to be blonde and gorgeous-looking and pick up the nicest guys.

They'd met Arthur at college. Ellie had marched up to him in the student bar and declared that she fancied him. She'd found as a student that this method worked amazingly well on desperate teenage boys away from home for the first time. She would find in later life that it worked well on some older men too, but that the quality was definitely deteriorating year on year.

'Tough,' Arthur had replied lazily.

'Why? What's wrong with me?'

He looked her up and down.

'One . . . two . . . ehm, three things,' he said. 'Adam's apples I can take or leave.'

'Oh,' said Ellie. 'Ohhhh,' she said again as the ramifications sunk in. 'I've never met anyone gay before.'

'Really?' Arthur had said. 'How is Mars?'

'I'm Ellie,' she had announced sticking out her hand. 'From Esher. Do you have any brothers who look exactly like you?'

'No, Ellie from Esher,' he had said, taking it. 'Do you?'

'Pardon me for asking . . .'

'I'm not sure I like the way this is going.'

'But aren't you supposed to be really stylish and stuff?'

'Clearly,' said Arthur who was wearing satin smoking trousers and had his cigarette in a holder.

'Well then, why do you hang around with Annabel and George?'

He shrugged. 'To be honest, I like to keep a constant reminder around me of what I'll never ever have to be. That and the sponge cake.'

'Really! Me too! That's me exactly! Would you like to be my partner in crime?'

Arthur had considered it for a second.

'Yeah, alright then.'

* * *

'My life,' said Ellie now, sitting up on the bed, 'is like one of those adverts for soup. You know, when someone has a really horrid, cold, rainy, bad day but it's all right because at the end they sink into an armchair with a big cup of soup. WITHOUT THE SOUP.'

'Nonsense,' said Arthur. 'There's nothing wrong with your life that a little scooter wouldn't sort out. Let's go shopping on Sunday.'

'No, it's not that,' said Ellie. 'I mean, just, why do I just feel so *bleargh*? I mean, is all I have to look forward to squeezing massive foreign objects through my own tissues?'

'You know, you really don't have to have a baby if you don't want to,' said Julia.

'We're going to have to go,' said Arthur, looking at Colin who was snoring sweetly in an armchair. 'Come on; why don't we forget tonight and go out tomorrow and drink the cocktail alphabet?'

'Uh huh. Maybe. Okay,' said Ellie. 'You might as well go now. I'm wearing fifteen layers; it's going to take me half an hour to get undressed.'

Julia kissed her on the head. 'Don't worry. There's nothing to be worried about. Not really.'

'Oh, I know,' said Ellie wistfully. 'That's why I'm so worried about why I'm worried.'

'You looked lovely tonight,' said Loxy to Julia as they left.

'Uh huh,' said Julia. They picked their way through the party detritus and the old Classix Nouveaux LPs.

* * *

Ellie didn't sleep. Or she thought she wasn't sleeping, but found out she was when she fell out of bed. Having been dreaming of doing something rather disconcerting with Anthony Michael Hall, she bounced and shuddered awake with a yelp and scuttled about on the carpet, noting as she did so how filthy it was. It was grey outside, inside, on the floor, and especially under the bed.

'Aargh!' she yelped. 'The first yelp of my thirties,' she thought. She paused experimentally, in case the landlord she shared the flat with might get up to make sure she was alright. Her landlord was a bastard and it was a horrible flat, but she'd picked it because it was within walking distance of all her friends.

'Shut up, Hedgehog!' came a sleepy voice from next door. He'd come in late the previous night and eaten the remaining sausage rolls very, very loudly.

'Shut up yourself,' she yelled, snivelling. Unfortunately she wasn't bleeding hard enough to go into his bedroom and do a *Carrie* imitation. She wiped herself with a dirty tissue and crawled back onto the bed, not noticing that the reason she had blood on her head was because she'd knocked the alarm clock off the bedside table. Lying back down, she dropped straight into a coma until the flat farting rev of her flatmate's supposedly trendy scooter underneath her window woke her up at ten to nine.

'Aargh,' she yelped again, and leapt out of bed to look out of the window to try and work out what was going on.

'Late for work again, Hedgehog? Not like you,' shouted her big bastard landlord, a huge rugby player who was so muscular he couldn't cross his own legs. Ellie was looking forward to his thirty-fifth birthday, when he would go to bed a brick shithouse and wake up morbidly obese. His hair was brown and stuck out persistently in different directions, despite his efforts to clamp it down with what Ellie fervently hoped was hair gel and not spit, and his face was permanently red.

She leaned out of the window. 'Give me a lift on your scooter, Big Bastard.'

He snorted. 'No chance. You are at least two hours off being ready and it's morning traffic.'

'*Pleeease*. I'll do your ironing.'

He barked with laughter.

'If I want fewer clothes I'll give them to Oxfam, thanks.'

'I hate you.'

'I know, I've tasted your shepherd's pie.'

'I am thirty years old,' Ellie rifled through her drawers, thinking. 'And yet I do not appear to have a pair of unladdered tights. How can this be?'

'Big Bastard!' she hollered out of the window again. He was slipping his helmet on.

'Ugh?'

'Have you been stealing my tights for hilarious drunken pranks again?'

'Guh . . . Yeah, I think so. We put one on Vince's head for . . . ehm, some reason. Bloody funny though. Oh, and we took a pair of hold ups for Gaz's stag. Oh, and that bet Willis had to put a pair on those monkeys at the safari park. And, ehm, Carmel borrowed a pair one morning. Oh, yeah, and I needed a pair to fix the car.'

Carmel was his dull girlfriend. Her only point of

interest was that, as she was four foot eleven and Big Bastard was six foot four, people were always asking them how on earth they managed to have sex, as casually as if they were asking them if they wanted a cup of tea.

'You are one big bastard,' said Ellie.

'Tough,' he said. 'Oh, and I need your rent and your share of the satellite TV.'

'But I never watch the shagging satellite TV! You only use it for sport and women's bosoms!'

'Just write us a cheque, eh darling?'

'Yeah, minus tight tax. Now I'm going to have to wear my white tights again.'

'Nothing wrong with white tights.'

'Yes, Big Bastard, but you think Jordan's gorgeous. And *please* give me a lift.'

'Phforr . . . Jordan. Sorry, what was that darling? No, I couldn't possibly be seen out with someone in white tights.'

'I hope you get run over by a lorry carrying really stinky chemicals that hurt you really badly and make you stink for the rest of your life. Even more than you do now. And maybe turn you purple.' Ellie petered out, slamming down the window as Big Bastard completely ignored her.

'Aha,' she thought. 'I'm thirty and even the quality of my insults is deteriorating year on year.'

Still, Big Bastard had been right about the ironing.

Prodding desperately at a silk shirt that appeared to have taken on several different shades, Ellie cursed the entire institution. 'In the future,' she growled to herself, 'ironing will be like dunking witches and bloodletting. They won't have a bloody *clue* why anybody bothered.'

She turned the shirt over and groaned at the large water stain that appeared.

'Along with commuting,' she sighed, throwing on a jacket with only one button missing and diving for the door, stopping to scoop up a spoonful of the horrid brown supposedly athletic mush Big Bastard had left behind to cement itself to a bowl. 'And breakfast cereal, probably. They'll discover it on an archaeological dig and say "Well, we've analysed it, and it's not *food*."'

Ellie stormed out of the door, not even stopping to pick up her newly delivered copy of *Smash Hits*.

* * *

'Miss Eversholt! How kind of you to join us.'

Ellie tried to smile without using her teeth. Her boss, Mr Rooney, was of the school headteacher sarcastic variety, but you didn't have the option of sneering back at him or pretending you had your period as compensation. He was pink-eyed, with thinning red hair, and had suspiciously scrofulous looking skin.

'Everyone, we can start now! Miss Eversholt has deigned to grace us with her presence.'

'Sorry Mr Rooney. Sorry everyone.'

As usual, the rest of the surveying team looked at her with complete blankness. They always did this, as if they thought being Assistant Administrative Director of Business Development was in some way odd. Ellie hated her job. Beyond hated it. She'd liked the idea of it, but then her idea of it was kind of sexy architects crossed with sexy builders. This didn't turn out to have a lot to do with what it was, which involved large numbers of protractors and lots of long division. And for some reason the men who worked in it seemed to be required by law to wear loads of pens clipped onto their top pockets, and great big shoes that looked like Cornish pasties.

'Well, you'll be glad to know we've got a new job in, and it's going to be taking up lots of our time. They're turning the old library into . . . anyone? Anyone?'

'Don't tell us, groovy new fake open-plan warehouse flats with fake wooden floors and metal sinks,' Ellie muttered to the person sitting next to her who was wearing a polyester blouse and completely ignored her.

'. . . a revolutionary evolution in inner city migration.'

'Thought so,' said Ellie, slugging back some more revolting polystyrene coffee.

'Miss Eversholt, if you have anything to say, perhaps you'd like to share it with the rest of the group?'

'No Mr Rooney.'

'And are you chewing?'

'No Sir,' she said. That wasn't true. There was an undislodgeable and inedible piece of Brantastic stuck to the roof of her mouth.

'Well, I need a volunteer to dig up the archived Victorian plans . . . anyone? Anyone?'

There was silence.

'Ellie, why don't you take that on?'

This was the filthiest job possible and usually meant several sixteen-hour days in a locked windowless basement, which was good if you were a method actor researching a play about the Beirut hostages, but not particularly useful for anything else.

'Sir, how can I look for things down at the library when you're converting all the libraries?'

'Don't play smart mouth with me young lady. Now, any other business?'

Ellie sighed and ate another fusty custard cream. Rooney & Co. specialized in ripping the guts out of proper, useful buildings and turning them into Lifestyles for young single professionals; identical rough-walled wanker machines that sold for hundreds of thousands of pounds. As well as it being horribly dull, Ellie always had the sneaking feeling that there was something actually totally wrong with what she was doing, but she couldn't quite put her finger on it. Arthur had patiently explained it was post-modern and at least they weren't ripping up the countryside, but the niggling feeling remained, alongside the budding repetitive strain injury.

'What's up?' she remarked to her sullen and uncommunicative temp as she wandered into her cubicle after the meeting.

'Three churches, six cotton warehouses and a shipyard some wanker wants to offload. Did you have a nice birthday?' said the temp without lifting her head from *Take A Break* magazine. What was worse, Ellie wondered: inviting the temp to her birthday party or the temp not turning up?

'Not really,' she said. 'You're not meant to enjoy your own birthdays, are you? Too fraught.'

The temp shrugged.

'Can't remember. I'm always too lashed out of my head.'

'Maybe that was my big mistake,' said Ellie. 'Actually remembering being there.'

What was worse, Ellie wondered: playing patience at work or caring about it enough to change the design on the back of the cards?

* * *

Thank God she had something to look forward to after work. Elms, their Clapham local, looked lit up and busy that evening. There was a band playing in the corner with a saxophonist who fortunately wasn't Billy, friendly waiting staff with aprons, who let you run tabs, and long red-checked-tableclothed tables. Siobhan and Julia were joining them, to see if they could remember what a good night out felt like. As she walked in, Ellie was disappointed at how relieved she was that her friends had found a place to sit and the music wasn't too loud. She plucked off Arthur's red hat and sat down.

'Hey! Where are we up to?'

'B,' said Arthur.

'Perfect. I'll have a Bloody Mary.' The waitress nodded and headed off.

'How are you?' said Julia tentatively.

'Oh, I don't know,' said Ellie. 'I've had the crappiest day in the universe. I just can't . . . God, do you ever feel you're getting into a big fat rut?'

'Aha! The middle class Olympics!' said Arthur.

'*G2* does,' said Siobhan, handing over the newspaper. The headline read, 'Are You and Your Twenty-Something Friends in a Big Fat Rut? Why not Experiment With Scented Candle Sticks, Scatter Cushions and Cocaine, Just Like Everybody Else Is?'

'This is EXACTLY what I mean,' said Ellie. She picked the paper up. 'I don't feel I can have one tiny original thought in my head. And if anything goes wrong I'm just supposed to go and buy something taupe and put it in the right corner of the living room.'

'Thatcherbaby,' said Arthur.

'I know. But I didn't ask to be a Thatcherbaby!'

'Well, you are.'

'I mean, is this it? Is there really nothing more to life than getting your gold card?'

'Oh, I got mine!' said Siobhan.

'Really! Let's see. Ohh. God, I'm so shallow.'

'Of course you are,' said Arthur. 'Your number one fantasy in life is to kiss Andrew McCarthy in a pink dress. Although world peace runs a close second.'

Ellie sipped her newly arrived Bloody Mary. 'I think I'm unhappy. I need an adventure. Maybe I should change jobs. Or career. Or dye my hair?'

'You're affluent, you have no responsibilities, you have plenty of free time . . . you are making up INVISIBLE WESTERN PROBLEMS,' said Arthur. 'Go see a therapist. They love invisible problems.'

'It's just thirtyangst,' said Julia. 'I got that too. Don't worry about it.'

'Easy for you to say,' said Ellie. 'You've got your own flat AND a devoted love slave.'

Loxy smiled and put his arm around Julia. She shrugged him off and raised her eyes to heaven, whereupon his smile faded. Loxy was aware at some level that the more uxoriously he behaved the less attention he received, but was too nervous to put any lovebastard techniques into practice. In short he was universally referred to as Sweet with a capital S, never the epithet of choice for strong-armed love gods, unless your name is Eric Cartman. This often puzzled Loxy, as he was six foot two, built, had a fairly difficult responsible job as a prisoner's advocate and was never normally like this around women. In fact, before he'd met Julia, he'd never done a sappish thing in his life. However he'd never met a woman before who did such a convincing job of combining Felicity Kendal and Ulrika Johnson.

There was no point in envying the fact that Julia got all the great men though, as Siobhan, checking her watch for the hundredth time, was well aware.

'Where the hell is Patrick?' she said. 'He's so unreliable. I wish he wouldn't work so late.'

'Actually, Shiv, Patrick's incredibly reliable,' pointed out Julia. 'He's always working late.'

'Oh yeah,' said Siobhan. 'Christ. He can't even be annoying in an interesting way.'

Siobhan had been Arthur's landlady at college, when they'd taken it in turns to argue about furniture and have immaculacy competitions. No-one liked to go round there too often, particularly not Ellie, who had a bit of a conflict going on between her love for red wine and her red wine's love for other people's carpets.

'What I'd really like,' said Ellie, 'is for something really dramatic to happen. An earthquake or something. Hmm, no, a non fatal earthquake. Oh God, I don't know. Just *something*.'

'How about you fall out with your boyfriend in public at your own birthday party have a yelling match with him then lock yourself in the bathroom?' said Arthur. 'Oh, no, hang on . . .'

Ellie's mobile rang.

'Oh my God,' she said. 'Maybe this is it. Maybe somebody's seen me in the street and wants me to go to Hollywood and become a movie star!'

'I bet that's who it is,' said Siobhan. 'Or maybe it's Prince William telling you he's in love with you.'

'Could be anything,' said Ellie, peering at the phone. 'Oh. It's my dad. Oh no! I take it all back! I don't want anything to happen at all.'

Ellie's dad lived alone. Ever since Ellie's mother had left he drank rather too much whisky and relied on seeing his only child often, otherwise he tended to live in string vests and eat cold beans straight out of the tin.

'Hey?' she said tentatively, then listened patiently as he described his extremely bad heartburn.

'And how many sausages? Uh huh. You know, Dad, I think nine sausages is probably too much for dinner.'

She listened some more. 'Okay, no, they're on the

top shelf of the cabinet. Well, look again. No, I *did* get some. Listen to me . . . Oh, for God's sake.'

She put the phone down. 'Sorry everyone but I think I've got to go and burp my father.'

'But it's C!' said Arthur. 'Your favourite round: Cosmopolitans.'

'I *know*. But I'd better go.'

She shouldered her bag, downed the dregs of her Bloody Mary and headed out of the door, face set against the rain.

'This isn't fair,' she thought to herself, walking down the darkened suburban street in search of a taxi, as the wind blew gusts of rain across her face. Anyone passing her would have thought they were looking at a very upset four-year-old. Her lower lip stuck out tremulously. A bus crashed along the road, spraying her skirt with water, and ploughed on. Ellie stopped in the middle of the street.

'I'm not happy, okay!' she yelled at the open sky. 'I don't know why, but I'm NOT! And I don't know who I'm talking to, because my generation doesn't even believe in GOD anymore!'

* * *

'How are you today, my favourite Hedgepig?'

She gave herself up for a hug inside the gloomy house. An old terrace, it was musty and undecorated, and her father had a thing about putting on

35

the central heating and very rarely did, preferring to stomp about in several layers of faintly grubby pyjamas.

'Hey Dad. Little bit grumpy. What's the matter with you?'

'I think I had a bad sausage.'

'I told you before: you eat too many sausages.' She poked him in the belly. 'Why don't you have something healthy?'

She went into the bathroom and dug out the bottle of milk of magnesia; as predicted it was on the top shelf.

'They make healthy sausages?'

'Not exactly.' Ellie checked the grill was off – he'd already had a minor fire – made him take the medicine and made them both a cup of tea.

'How could you not find this? It was right on the shelf.'

Her dad squirmed and tried to look as if he hadn't done it on purpose so she'd come over and see him. Ellie told him about the party fiasco, and her general sense of being miserable.

'Well, you'd better do something about it then. Haven't you been saying since the day after you got your job that you really want to switch jobs? Why don't you do that?'

'Not this month. Not until they forget about the customer services rep and the bottle of quink.'

'Explain exactly what it is you do again, Hedgepig?'

'Business Development Manager. Oh, never mind. God, they should have a Bring your Parents to Work Day.'

'My theory is, right, if you can't sum it up in a sentence, it's not a proper job. Like, "I nick thieves".'

'Dad, that's a movie pitch, not a career.'

'"I fix hearts" – cardiologist, see?'

'Yeah, yeah, I've cottoned on. Nobody has simple jobs any more.'

'That's true,' mused her dad. 'Nobody does. What is it Julia does again?'

'She's a systems analyst consultant.'

'That's exactly what I mean. That doesn't even make sense.'

'There's too many people in the world. They have to make up stuff for us to do.'

'Ah. That would explain computers.'

Ellie thought for a second.

'God, you know, I think it does.'

'Okay then, if you're looking for something new to do, why don't you paint the front room?'

'Da*ad*! And eat this tomato. It's better than nothing.'

'Shan't. Why don't you . . .'

'. . . get myself a nice young man? Because there are none, Dad.'

'In the whole of London, there isn't one single nice man?'

'Nope.' And I have personally checked most of them, she silently added to herself.

'I know lots of nice coppers I could introduce you to.'

'Yes, but on the whole my motto is the less Freudian the better.'

'Nothing wrong with a nice copper.'

'Nothing wrong with a nice bit of tomato either. Eat!'

He took it reluctantly. This was a constant battle between them. Deep down, he liked his daughter's chiding at him. It showed she cared. In the same way, Ellie liked his bothering her constantly about all the bad aspects of her life. As an only child and an only parent, they'd done the best they could. Which wasn't, Ellie reflected, looking at the congealed-egg washing up, that great when you started to think about it. She squirted the remnants of a dusty bottle of Original Fairy into the sink.

'Dad,' said Ellie, plunging her hands into the lukewarm water. 'Am I a Thatcherbaby?'

He shrugged. 'Well, I suppose so. Do you remember Callaghan?'

'No.'

'That's why people your age are always blaming me for voting in Thatcher.'

'Why did you vote in Thatcher?'

'Well, because it seemed right, you know? At the

time. It seemed the right thing to do: work hard, don't give all your money to the government, get a nice house, get a nice car.'

'And?'

'And then you get comfortable and then you get bored and then your wife runs off to Plockton with an accountant called Archie.'

Her dad shifted in his seat and looked uncomfortable.

'Oh,' said Ellie. They rarely discussed her mother and she hated upsetting him. 'Um. Dad. You really should put these pans into soak.'

'. . . and there are too many cars on the road so you can't get anywhere and everything they're making is absolute crap so you'll buy another one in a month's time and the hole in the ozone layer is about to start poisoning South America but, you know, we're used to it now so we just can't stop.'

'Oh,' said Ellie again. 'Ehm. Bummer.'

He nodded and looked at her. 'Still,' he said, 'Thatcherbaby or not, I still think you're beautiful.'

'How come I can wash all this rotten egg and it didn't make me want to puke, but now you do?'

They smiled at each other.

* * *

Ellie left him to *Match of the Day* and wandered up to her old room, which was exactly as she'd left it eleven years ago for college. She picked up her Strawberry Shortcake doll, inhaled deeply and looked around the room.

It looked pretty much as the flat had done for her party: covered in peeling old thin magazine posters of the Brat Pack: in particular, her favourite, Andrew McCarthy.

'Oh Andrew,' she said, as she had done for so many years in her teens.

'What are we going to do?'

As usual, Andrew stayed entirely schtum. Ellie had never given up, despite the range and variety of questions he'd completely ignored over the last decade-and-a-half, including:

'Should I let Stuart Mannering put his hand up my blouse?'

(The answer should have been no, and she knew that, but she let him do it anyway.)

'Should I finish my homework or go out and hang around the boys doing wheelies on their BMXs at the bottom of the street?'

(Ditto.)

'Will I ever meet a nice boy?'

(Most likely not a pubescent one.)

'Will I ever get over Miles Sampson not being in love with me?

(Yes. Well, pretty much. As long as nobody is playing Lloyd Cole and the Commotions albums.)

'How do I get the substitute Social Studies teacher to notice me?'

(Stop trying; it's working and he might get sent to prison.)

'Am I gay because I really, really like my gym teacher?'

(No, it's a teenage occupational hazard.)

'If I wish really hard, will I grow up to get a huge pink apartment like Demi Moore's in *St Elmo's Fire*?'

(Yes, if you become a coke whore.)

'Now everyone at school has seen *The Breakfast Club* sixty-four times, will school become more like *The Breakfast Club* with everyone breaking down social barriers and revealing their inner selves?'

(Definitely not, although Stuart Mannering will reveal his entire outer self in biology and get two month's detention.)

'Will I get to meet John Cusack on a long trip across America?'

(Perhaps, if you're six foot tall with long shiny blonde hair.)

'Wouldn't it be great if I had a really gorgeous lover who died and then came back and made pottery with me?'

(As yet unexplored.)

'Will you come to rescue me, like you rescued Molly Ringwald?'

(So far, no.)

'Oh Andrew.'

She looked at him again. The poster had worn away around his mouth from chaste kisses.

'Where are you, then? The middle-youth of the world needs you.'

She thought harder.

'Actually, we do bloody need you. Where the hell are you?'

As she stared at the battered magazine-torn image, a thought began to stir within her. I mean, here, surely was a man with a bit of knowledge about growing up and not playing the adolescent for ever. She stared at it a bit more with mounting excitement. 'What,' she wondered, 'is he like now?' She pictured him – a little older, not much. With shock, she realized he was only halfway through his thirties and she gulped internally – not that much older than her. Oh my God. If there was one person in the world who understood what she was going through, she suddenly had the utter conviction that it was him. Why she was feeling so bleargh. And why she felt that something was passing her by, but she didn't know what it was.

Excitedly, she jumped up and took out her mobile.

'Julia? Where's Andrew McCarthy?'

'What?' said Julia. Behind her, someone managed

to drop an entire tray of glasses. The bar crowd appeared to think this worthy of a round of applause.

'Look. I can't really talk. We're up to H, an I . . . an I . . . can't . . . motor functions.'

'Julia!'

She could hear Julia sit up and try and pay attention.

'Is this some guy you picked up on the way over to your dad's house?'

'No, you know, *Andrew*. I mean, what happened to him? He just disappeared. He just stopped being famous and disappeared. Maybe he's dead!'

'Don't be silly . . . he can't be dead . . . you and him have a date . . .'

'Yeah, ha ha ha. This is serious. A movie star has disappeared off the face of the planet.'

'That's not serious. A rainforest tribe disappearing, maybe. But, you know, I just can't see Sting doing the tribute album for the guy who made *Weekend at Bernie's II*.'

'Hmm,' said Ellie.

'What?'

'Nothing.'

'That doesn't sound like nothing.'

'I just might have had an idea, that's all.'

'A grumpy idea or a cheerful one?'

'Hard to say. Depends on whether he's . . . nothing.'

'I don't like the sound of this.'

'Oh, got to go!'

'Go where? You're at your dad's!'

'Yes, and his deep fried lard is burning. Got to go!'

She put down the phone and sat back on the bed, deep in thought. God, she had seen those films so many times. It hadn't been until much later that she'd realized her mother had been desperate to get her out of the house that year, and had let her disappear to the cinema as often as she wanted, so *she* could get on with the business at hand of arguing with Ellie's dad and preparing to move to Plockton.

Ellie looked at the back wall, where her old ice skates were hanging by their grubby white laces. That was what her father had done: every time she wasn't at the cinema, her dad had taken her ice skating. He was mad for it. Of course by the time she'd got to fourteen she'd disdained it utterly and much preferred trying to freeze-frame the video with Julia, to see how far under the duvet they could get in *Class*. And now she was being petulant about doing her dad's washing up. Some things never changed. And what was grown-up anyway? And why did she suddenly have an inexplicable desire to go ice skating?

Absolute Beginners

'Ikea on a Saturday morning,' said Ellie. The rest of the car ignored her. 'Did anyone hear me? I said, IKEA ON A SATURDAY MORNING. ARE WE NUTS??? Why can't we go . . . I don't know . . . ice skating or something?'

Julia turned around from the front seat, where she was trying to navigate her way through Croydon and placate the rest of the car at the same time.

'Loxy needs some shelving, okay?'

'And Patrick needs a new bathroom cabinet – he's been buying a lot of new toiletry products recently,' said Siobhan. 'And he's too busy to make it today, so I said I'd come.'

'Why am *I* here then?'

'You're helping push the trolley,' said Julia. 'And

if you're very lucky, we'll let you choose all the food that you don't know what it is.'

'I can't believe you required a taste arbiter like me to come to Ikea,' said Arthur darkly, buried under *The Times*. 'You're at Ikea; you've already given up and admitted you have none.'

When the gang finally limped in through the underpass towards the familiar blue and yellow factory chimneys, the car park was already overflowing with family-sized monster Range Rovers with special cyclist-killing bull bars on the front.

Ellie pouted as they queued up to get through the open doors. To the left, one hundred and seventy children were trying to stick colourful rubber balls down one another's oesophagi.

'Why are they there?' she said, peering through the glass. 'Contraception?'

The scene opened out slightly to reveal four billion identical couples in casual Gap wear. The girls all had expensively tinted blonde hair cut in Anthea Turner styles, and the men had schoolboy haircuts and emergent paunches.

Arthur and Ellie immediately clutched at their throats and started staggering around with fake choking. 'Argh! Argh!'

'Behave, you two,' said Julia, pushing back her blonde hair.

'She's one of them!' said Arthur pointing. 'Croydon Wife! Croydon Wife!'

'I'll open the book,' said Ellie. 'Up to five quid. Which couple are going to be the first to have a fight.'

'I'll take the couple in the matching Gap separates,' said Arthur.

'Too non-specific.'

A tall, balding man was sighing heavily as a woman castigated him for daring to sit on a sofa.

'Ooh, coming up on the left,' said Ellie.

Arthur, however, was already pointing out a slightly overweight woman with a sensible haircut who was trying to push her way back through the shop, managing to convey how furious she was at the standard lamp in her hand, and deliberately kicking out at trolleys.

'Couples shouldn't really talk about "going to Ikea",' said Arthur. 'They shouldn't even say, "Hey – let's go to Ikea!" They should just say, "Hey – let's have a fight!"'

'Well, I think it's rather sweet,' said Siobhan. 'I used to love it when Patrick and I came here.'

Everyone stood and stared at her. She shrugged. 'You are all just immature.'

* * *

Two hours later in the lighting section, all jollity had gone. One man Ellie could see from her vantage point, hidden behind a desk unit, was actually crying.

Siobhan was marching Arthur round the bathroom cabinets for the fifteenth time.

'For the fifteenth time,' said Arthur, 'it's horrible. It's all horrible, and this is it put up properly. You and Patrick make tons of money between you. Why don't you just use some of the stuff you import?'

'Because it's made out of gold.'

'Anyway, it's only bathrooms,' said Julia.

'Yes, only somewhere where you spend the most intimate times of your life. With this rubbish.'

'Oh, for fuck's sake,' said Siobhan, getting red and hot and agitated. 'Stop being such a poseur. It's only some fucking bathroom shelves.'

'Shit!' said Julia. 'I forgot Loxy's shelving!'

She tried to turn the trolley around. They were completely trapped. Ellie groaned loudly as they backed up four hundred people around the shop; people who showed their horror at this transgression by muttering very loudly and immediately falling out with the person they were with.

'Sorry!' Julia was saying. It was suddenly about 200 degrees in the store.

'Why don't we just cut our losses?' said Arthur. 'Dump the trolley and run like hell.'

'God, this place drives me crazy,' yelled Ellie

suddenly. 'I think it's some sinister rat/maze type experiment. Giant creatures are peering in through the corrugated roof, making notes on us.'

She looked at the crowds, backing up like panic-buyers at a petrol pump.

'There's no way back,' she said suddenly, in horror, staring around her and breathing hard. 'There *is* no way back. Don't you see? Guys, don't you SEE?'

They all looked at her.

'We're on a one way trek through Ikea. This is it. This is our lives. There's no way back.'

'Ehm . . . are you freaking out?' said Arthur, as Julia manoeuvred herself out of position. Ellie was still fixed to the spot and staring straight ahead.

She thought about it. 'Yes. YES I AM.' And she stormed off against the flow of traffic, leaving a chorus of disgruntled middle class tutting in her wake.

* * *

Ellie sat in the car park, thinking furiously. That was it. She was getting off this track right now. The poster in her bedroom came back to her. All those dreams. All those teenage nights. For what? Andrew had disappeared. Emilio; Judd; Anthony. All gone. 'I'm disappearing too,' she thought to herself, sadly. 'I'm getting older, and giving up and fading into the background. And if I don't run away now, then I'll run away to Plockton in twenty years and that really will be a disaster.'

By the time her friends finally emerged ninety minutes later, red-faced and cursing, she had it all figured out.

* * *

'Okay, everyone pay attention to me,' announced Ellie loudly.

'Well, that will be a new experience for us all,' said Siobhan.

It was the following Monday night. Ellie had summoned everyone to a council of war round at her flat, much to Big Bastard's disgust. She had been putting out bowls of crisps when he'd grunted, 'I'm going to the pub. All your friends are morons.'

'Okay, no, hang on, why are my friends morons when your friends moon out of the back of coaches *every week* and think it's *always hilarious*?'

'Because they know how to have fun,' he sniffed, trying to smooth down his unruly hair with his enormous hairy paws. 'Your friends just sit around and talk.'

'Sitting around and talking are what people *do*,' said Ellie. 'Showing off their arses to each other is what monkeys do.' She held up a Pringle and a cashew nut. 'See?' She waved the Pringle. 'People sized brain', then the cashew, 'monkey sized brain. People brain – monkey brain. Ellie brain – Big Bastard brain.'

She ate the cashew nut.

'Big Bastard brain *all gone*.'

'And they're all poofs.'

'How could they all be poofs? Some of them go out with some of the other ones of the opposite sex.'

'That doesn't necessarily mean they're not a poof.'

'Um, yes it does. Oh, Big Bastard, I'm sorry I ate your brain.'

'Well, I'm going to have some of my mates round.'

'What, so that you and all your *non-poof* friends can spend the day showing each other your butts?'

'I might have them round tonight after the pub.'

'You will not!'

'My flat darlin'.'

'Yeah, your flat which will get completely done in when your pissed up friends start picking fights with each other. Or themselves; you all look the fucking same. You'd better take that mirror down, they're like budgies.'

'We do not look the fucking same.'

'Okay, what would you say is the top shirt designer of choice amongst every single one of your friends?'

Big Bastard shrugged. 'Who cares? Clothes are for girls.'

'It wouldn't be Ben Sherman by any chance would it?'

He shrugged again, but his ears went slightly pink. 'So what? 'S comfortable.'

'And what about shoes? A little beige number perhaps? With connotations of being Big Masculine Woodcutters?? Okay, you bring back all your non-gay friends with peanut brains to show each other your arses and worship Johnny Vaughn. We'll see you later.'

'I'm putting your rent up.'

'I'm reporting you to the Inland Revenue for having an undeclared tenant.'

He'd stomped out of the house snarling, although not before Arthur had arrived and maliciously called him duckie.

'I can't believe the way you turn into Graham Norton whenever you see Big Bastard,' Ellie said, straightening out her fishnet tights.

'That's my militant side, sweetheart. It'll do him good in the long run, you'll see. Anyone with that much testosterone can't possibly be straight anyway.'

'Oh, he is. I know, because when he thinks I'm not looking, he touches himself when there are those girls on television who sing pop songs in their school uniform.'

Ellie glanced into the mirror, smoothed down her black curly hair and removed some cashew nut debris from between her teeth. She always felt scruffy next to Arthur, who pretended that his immaculate appearance was a natural gift from God.

'Deviant. Okay, what are we all here for? You never

normally have us round here unless you've broken something.'

'That's not true,' said Ellie. 'What about that time I needed to borrow money?'

Siobhan filed in warily.

'You realize I left work early for this?'

'Siobhan, it's eight-thirty. Was there anyone else in the building?'

'Just some people I know.'

'Okay, how many non-security personnel were there apart from you?'

Siobhan pouted and stretched out on Big Bastard's chair, removing a half-eaten multi-pack of KitKats.

'God, that flatmate of yours eats like a horse.'

'Eats like a horse, farts like a horse and you don't even want to know what it's like when Carmel's round.'

'No I most certainly don't,' said Siobhan. She looked tired and drawn. 'Patrick can't make it. He's working on some buyout. Or it's his evening class. God that's weird; I can't even remember. Christ, I'm so knackered.'

Ellie put a glass of wine in her hand.

'Uh huh. I think I might have something that can cure that.'

'Alcohol! Excellent!'

'I thought you were never drinking again after we reached Kahlua,' said Arthur.

'I don't remember saying that. Although to be fair, I don't remember getting home.'

'No. Not alcohol. It's my fabulous and brilliant plan. But we'll need to wait for everyone to arrive.'

'Ehm, I told Colin he could come,' said Arthur.

'You didn't. He's *so* not in on the big plan.'

'It's alright, I'll make him hand round the nibbles.'

'Yeah, 'cause it's illegal for him to serve spirits.'

'Very funny. I'll have you know that beneath that childish veneer there's a very old soul.'

'Fuck off!'

'True. Well, old soul, good muscle definition – call it what you will.'

'Sorry we're late,' said Loxy apologetically, sticking his head round the door. 'I stopped to get Jules some flowers on the way home from work and missed my train.'

'Bloody idiot,' said Julia over his shoulder, putting down her suede handbag and kissing everyone within reach. 'Hello, hello. Okay, what's going on? And if it's Monopoly, include me out.'

'Okay, everyone,' began Ellie.

'Hang on,' said Siobhan. 'Annabel and George aren't here.'

'They're too old for this plan.'

'That's not very fair. They're the same age as us.'

'I bet you,' said Ellie severely, 'one million squillion

pounds that by the time we do this plan, Annabel will be up the duff anyway. Sproglets leaking from every orifice.'

'What on earth is the plan?'

'Okay,' said Ellie again. She got up and went over to Big Bastard's record player, where he'd filed all his Big Country albums, and put on her specially prepared eighties mix tape. There was a funny little African rhythm, then Pat Benatar began bellowing 'Love is a Battlefield.'

'Come with me,' she started, 'on a mystical journey back into the mists of time.'

'And that's pretty bloody misty,' said Arthur.

'To a time . . . when things were young and fresh.'

'Hey everyone! Booyashaka!'

Colin entered the room wearing sunglasses, despite the September rain outside. And the pitch dark.

'Aha. Speaking of things that are young and fresh . . .'

Colin noisily started to eat the cashew nuts whilst Julia got him some squash.

'When things were harmonious and squabbling was unknown,' Ellie continued.

'We don't *squabble*,' said Arthur. 'Colin, leave some of those cashew nuts for everyone else.'

'But I *like* cashew nuts.'

'Just put them down,' said Loxy, wondering whether a show of supportive strength would impress Julia in any way.

'It's none of your business,' said Julia, nudging him. 'For Christ's sake, shut up Loxy.'

'See!' said Ellie. 'It's Ikea all over again. Exactly what I've been talking about. The really stupid stresses of modern living are all too much. Which is why I propose . . .'

The music had changed to 'Broken Wings' by Mister Mister.

'We all take a trip.'

'What kind of a trip?'

'Please, not like when we all went to Cornwall and got lost and had to sleep in the car even when it was sleeting,' said Arthur.

'Better than that.'

'My verrucca is better than that.'

'My weekends are pretty booked up,' said Siobhan. 'I'm trying to book a slot to see my boyfriend.'

'Oh please, what about that time we hired a canal boat for after finals?' said Julia. 'I'm still under a court order for that.'

'That's because you were the only one mature enough to sign the lease.'

'No, it's because the Hedgehog here was the only one mature enough to see if she could invent a new spin drying method by dragging all our clothes through the engine.'

'That *wasn't* it . . .' started Ellie. 'Okay, look, we're getting off the point. We're older now and if Caroline fucking Lafayette can hike across the Himalayas on a pogo stick, we can bloody well drive a car to California . . .'

There was a silence.

'Do what?' said Arthur.

'Oh, fuck!' said Ellie crossly. 'I've cocked it up now and spoiled my big build-up. I'd drawn graphs and everything.'

'What are you talking about?' said Julia seriously.

'This is my big plan,' said Ellie, looking dejected. 'It's only going to sound stupid now.'

'We were expecting that though,' said Julia kindly.

Ellie pouted a bit more. Then she bucked herself up and smiled.

'Okay. Here's my plan. We all take some time off work.'

'Can't be done,' said Siobhan instantly.

'. . . say, a month.'

'Ha!'

'Then, go to America and hire a car.'

'Why?' asked Julia.

'Okay. Here comes the science bit.'

'Hang on,' said Arthur. He refilled his glass. 'Okay. I'm ready.'

'We go to California and find the Brat Pack. And demand some answers.'

She sat back, legs crossed, waiting for the reaction.

Everyone looked at everyone else to try and gauge the state of play.

'Hedgehog, darling,' said Julia, sitting down on the floor next to her friend.

'You know we love you. But what the hell are you talking about?'

'Look at us! We've already agreed something's going wrong somewhere, haven't we?'

'Err, had we?'

'Yes, we had, Ikea freaks.' Ellie stood up. 'We are going to find those Gods of our youth, and get them to explain a few things. Like – what the hell happened? You guys promised us the world in the 1980s, and you didn't get it and we didn't get it either and now we're all getting fat together and it's WRONG. Your films made growing up look fun. And it's not. It's cynical and stupid and boring. It grinds you down and makes you worry about acronyms you don't understand, like – I don't know; "ISA" and "SERPS". And IKEA. And it rains all the time. And my Visa bill is due. It's time for us to get out for a bit. Because otherwise, we are going to be worrying about fucking PAYE and nothing else for the REST OF OUR LIVES.'

There was a long silence.

Siobhan lightly put her hand on her friend's leg. 'Hedge, I'm not trying to be horrible about your idea or anything, but – all of them? You know, I'm not sure they all live in the same house like Morecambe and Wise.'

'That doesn't matter! Don't you see? Look at what happened. They were told they were going to be the biggest movie stars in the world. Then *they* told *us* everything was going to work out great. Well, it didn't work out great for Robert Downey Junior and it didn't work out great for Charlie Sheen and Emilio Estevez married Paula Abdul, and it's not working out for us either. And I want to know *why*.'

The friends looked around at each other.

'Do you think we'd really find them all in a month?' said Julia. 'It sounds a bit like Pokemon.'

'Well,' Ellie sat back down and got out a sheet of paper, 'I thought we could start with the hardest one. I mean, no point in having a big quest to find Judd Nelson – he's in LA with Brooke Shields looking fat and disappointed. So I thought we'd . . .'

'Hang on,' said Siobhan, putting her hand up. 'Can we just take a quick time out? Julia, why don't you remind everyone what happened when we all tried to go and see *American Psycho* together.'

'Well,' began Julia with a practised air. 'We decided we were going to go two weeks beforehand. Then no-one would take responsibility for booking the tickets, so I had to do it at the last minute, so we could only get the five o'clock showing, so Siobhan wouldn't come because she was working, then they wouldn't believe Colin was eighteen and he didn't get in, then the Hedge phoned me up and told me she was bringing some more people so I booked some more tickets then they got drunk and completely forgot – you still owe me £42 plus booking fee by the way – all about it then I had to take Loxy out halfway through because he was frightened.'

She took a breath.

'And now we're going to plan a month in America?' Siobhan asked.

'Darling, it's a lovely idea, and we definitely need a holiday, and I know we talked about the Brat Pack thing – but a *month*? Haven't you seen *Dead Calm*?'

'But that's how long it will take,' said Ellie stubbornly. 'To find Andrew McCarthy.'

'Aha!' said Julia, scandalized. '*That's* what this is all about.'

'What do you mean?' Ellie tried to look innocent and failed.

'This is what your plan's all about. You just want to meet some childhood fantasy object.'

'No I don't,' said Ellie, unconvincingly.

'What would you do if you actually met Andrew McCarthy? If he walked into this room right now?'

'I'd ask him lots of important questions about life and how the culture of the 1980s changed us all. That's why we're all going. It'll be an educational trip into our past, to help us understand ourselves.'

There was a long silence.

'You're absolutely sure,' said Siobhan finally, 'that you wouldn't try and have sex with him.'

'Yup,' said Ellie.

'Isn't he gay, anyway?' said Arthur.

'He's *so* not,' said Siobhan, Julia and Ellie simultaneously.

'Okay,' said Julia. 'Look me in the eyes and tell me you wouldn't ask him to marry you.'

Ellie sighed and looked at the floor.

'Look. Just because he is not an unattractive man does *not* mean this isn't an important quest for all of us. Come on guys. It would be brilliant. Don't you see? It would just properly close our twenties. Try and move on. And it will be something brilliant we could all do together. All of us, once and for all, before we all settle down and do a George and Annabel.'

'Can I come?' piped up Colin.

'No.'

'So,' said Siobhan slowly. 'Let me just make sure I've got this straight. You want us all to take one month off work and travel thousands of miles on some wild goose chase to try and find a boyfriend for you who was famous fifteen years ago and may well be dead for as much as anyone knows where he is.'

'But he's an eighties God!' said Ellie.

'I'm going to have to get a move on,' said Siobhan heading for the door. 'Got a busy day tomorrow.'

'You've only been here five minutes!'

'I know. Think what a month would be like. If you're looking for a good way to end your twenties, why don't you do the last year of Club 18–30?'

Ellie looked at her. 'But it would be so good for you! Help you work out what to do about, you know, Patrick.'

A silence fell in the living room. They knew Siobhan well and, fussy about almost everything, she didn't ever take kindly to people peering too deeply at her personal things. The Hedgehog had crossed over the line even by referring to the fact that Siobhan's boyfriend had turned invisible.

Siobhan went very white.

'What's wrong with me and Patrick?'

Ellie gulped. 'Well, you just never seem to see him.'

'That's because we're both working hard. Everything's *fine*.'

'I'm sorry,' said Ellie grudgingly.

'I agree with Arthur. You're just making up problems for yourself – and for everyone else.' Siobhan opened the door.

'Maybe next year we should all just go to a restaurant for the Hedgehog's birthday. Goodnight everyone.'

Ellie waited until the door had slammed shut. 'Well, you're not invited.'

* * *

'Don't you think you're getting a bit obsessed by this Brat Pack thing?' Julia said to Ellie gently.

'No! It's not like I'm still wearing the button badges.'

'Hi Fidelity High!' started playing on the stereo. Julia winced slightly.

'If we were in California anyway,' said Arthur carefully, 'we could probably go to San Francisco, couldn't we?'

'What's in San Frass-isco?' said Colin.

'Um . . . lots of trams,' said Arthur.

'Oh, that sounds *great*.'

'Well, you're not coming. Oh God, and I can't really anyway. I'm saving up for an Eames chair.'

'You'd rather have an Eames chair than a big adventure?'

'Mmm,' said Arthur. 'Not sure.'

Arthur was a fabric sourcer for an avant-garde designer who made dresses out of industrial waste. He absolutely loved his job but it paid practically nothing.

'Fine,' said Ellie standing up. 'You're right. Let's keep the status quo completely. Nobody move. Nobody change. See you all at my ninetieth birthday party. I'll still be in the bathroom, because I won't be able to get out of the bath of my own accord.'

'Don't be like this,' said Julia. 'We'll think about it.'

'No, you're right. I should just give up, conform. Maybe if I had a new pair of expensive high heeled shoes my life would be entirely fine again.'

'Come on,' cajoled Julia pouring another glass of wine. 'We could watch a video. Even *Mannequin*, if you like.'

'Ah, no, I say no way,' said Arthur. 'In fact, that would probably be the least persuasive thing you could possibly do.'

* * *

'Looks like you had a brilliant night,' slurred Big Bastard, wandering in later half-cut. Ellie was hunched on the sofa, watching *Mannequin* by herself, the others having made it up until the entrance of Holly Wood, and wondering how many Pringles you could eat before you burst your own colon.

'Shut up Big Bastard.'

'Where are my KitKats then?'

'A big mouse took them and ran away.'

'Uh.' He looked at her squinty-eyed.

'What?' said Ellie. 'Why are you looking at me like that?'

He must have sensed her unhappiness, she thought. God, talk about taking your comfort where you could find it. She prepared to unburden herself to him.

'You know, I feel like I've had a really tough time recently, and I don't quite know why . . .'

'I can't believe we've lived in this flat for a year and never shagged,' said Big Bastard thoughtfully.

Ellie's mouth dropped open.

'That's because I've seen what you let go down the shower plughole,' she said, furious that she had been expecting even an ounce of sympathy from this lout.

'D'ya want to?' he said, sitting down next to her and draping an enormous meaty arm over her shoulders.

'Of course not!' She shook him off. 'And anyway, what about Carmel?'

'Yes, she's a bit skinny, but. Not like you.'

'Oh I see. Excuse me while I go and scrub the toilet bowl with your toothbrush, you big moron.'

'You'll be back,' he sneered. 'Won't be able to resist a bit of big beef loving.'

'Why don't we see how many things I'd rather do than that?' yelled Ellie, heading for the bathroom.

'Number one: cutting off my own fingers.

'Number two: pooing my pants on the tube.

'Number three: watching my dad have sex. With your dad.'

She took his toothbrush and ran it round the toilet rim.

'Number four: moving to Afghanistan.

'Number five: going camping with Anne Widde-combe.'

She dropped the toothbrush in the lavatory, and fished it out distastefully.

'Number six: smuggling heroin through Thailand . . .'

'You'll be back,' yelled Big Bastard. 'You're desperate for it.'

'. . . up my chuff. Number seven: eating an old man's dandruff.'

'You love me really.'

'Number eight: retaking my maths A-level.

'Number nine: being sick and eating it.'

'Oh, I've done that. It's not too bad.'

'Number ten: being eaten by a SHARK.'

'Goodnight Hedgehog.'

'Goodnight Big Bastard.' She set his toothbrush back in the stand. 'And hello amoebic dysentery,' she whispered to herself. 'And don't think I'm going to be here to look after you, because I am going to be far, far away.'

The Breakfast Club

The computers were down again at Julia's office. It was Friday, so she certainly deserved to be kicking back, she thought, kicking back.

'Aren't you even thinking about it?' she said to Arthur, toying with her phone card.

'*God* yeah,' said Arthur. 'I've always wanted to go to San Francisco. I don't feel my cowboy hat has had quite the adventures it deserves.'

'Yeah, right. And also of course you're the most boring monogamous man in the world.'

Arthur liked to think of himself as the dashing gay blade around town as opposed to someone who got endless crushes on people and treated them really, really nicely for ages. Especially Colin, who still lived with his parents.

'I am not!'

'How long have you been seeing the puppy now?'

'Six months. But I don't love him or anything. I'm footloose and fancy free. I'd be *very* fancy free in San Francisco. If I could afford it. But, you know, I've put the deposit on the Eames chair.'

Arthur lived in a minuscule studio filled with beautiful things he saved up for very, very slowly.

'Yeah, right. Coward. I don't really want to go. It's an awful lot of holiday time for one of Ellie's scheme-stroke-nightmare-o-ramas.'

'Oh, come on. You've never been to LA. You must want to at least *see* it?'

'A town entirely devoted to the worship of enormous plastic tits? Not especially. Anyway, it's the most racist country in the world. Loxy probably wouldn't make it past immigration.'

Loxy's family was from Ghana.

'Come without him. We could have a proper girly holiday.'

'Hmm,' said Julia. 'Yeah, you and Hedgehog tart it about and I hold your coats. No thanks.'

'How's the Hedgehog? Still in gloom?'

'She's okay. I suggested she go travelling on her own and she said why didn't I become new best friends with Caroline Snotface Lafayette.'

'Hmm. Well, Siobhan phoned me again and said she would go if we were going for a proper holiday but under no circumstances was she looking for anyone. Except Patrick of course.'

They both sighed.

'I wouldn't mind if it weren't just such a fucking stupid idea,' said Julia.

'I know. George Clooney I could have understood.'

'Ohp, hang on. I've got e-mail. I bet it's from her.'

She clicked.

'Yup, it is. Oh, and it's a circular – you're on the list too. You'd better look and check it out.'

The line went quiet as they read the mail.

From: e.eversholt@rooney&co.co.uk
To: Julia; Arthur; Siobhan

Re: Official 'Let's Go On a Wonderful Trip and Put the Joy Back Into Our Lives,' planning meeting to be held at Elms, 11am Sunday morning.

Dear Guys

Think about it: we're the generation that created Live Aid and now we have to pay Tesco to deliver our marmalade. Get your leave of absence forms today. Can you fucking believe you even have to get a form to have any tiny bit of life whatsoever? One tiny pathetic little month in forty years of grind? Can you believe that someone is actually paid to design those forms? How depressed does that make you about modern life? Remember: everybody wants to rule the world.

ISN'T FUN THE BEST THING TO HAVE?

See you there,

H.xx

For the last three years, Elms on a Sunday morning had been the traditional meeting place for pancakes and hungover gossip.

'She's HIJACKING us!' said Julia.

'At the moment, I could . . .'

'Oh, hang on, I've got a call on the other line. Hi? Yes, we both have. Hang on. Arthur, it's Siobhan. I'll phone you back.'

'You're *call waiting* me? What, you like Siobhan more than me?'

'Good*bye* Arthur.'

'I can't belie . . .'

'She's hijacking us!' barked Siobhan. 'If we all turn up, the next thing you know we'll be on some terrible jumbo jet, then it'll crash and they'll have to identify us by our toes.'

'I know. I know. We could go somewhere else, you know. We could all meet in the Mexican place next door and she could come and join us when she's come to her senses.'

'Tacos at eleven in the morning? That's even grosser than leaving our jobs to spend a month looking for some sad out-of-work actor guy.'

'I like Mexican food. It reminds me of baby food.'

'Yeah, in that it's already been filtered through somebody else.'

'Oh God,' said Julia. 'She'll get out of this, I'm sure. Something will come up to distract her.'

'Can't you wave something shiny in front of her?'

'Maybe she should join S Club 7. They're always up to shit like this. Did you mention it to Patrick?'

'I left a note on the fridge. Same thing.'

'Uh huh.'

'Is Arthur going?'

'He wants to go camping.'

'Whereabouts? The Grand Canyon?'

'Um, not that kind of camping.'

'Oh. Well, good luck to him. If it's the Hedgehog he's going with I'm sure he'll get to meet lots of big beefy policemen. Are you going to sort out Sunday?'

'I suppose,' said Julia, sighing. Siobhan hung up.

'I only stayed on the line so I could hang up as soon as you came back on,' said Arthur. 'Bye.'

Julia came off the phone feeling rather disgruntled with her friends. Not, however, as disgruntled as Ellie was at that precise moment.

* * *

'I will go,' Ellie had told herself, 'and very coolly inform bathead Rooney that I have plans and he'll be fine.'

She scratched at her legs. She'd been reduced to pop socks. This isn't school. Why did everything feel like school?

And now, here she was. Not making a lot of headway with the leave, but en route to getting herself a detention.

'But . . .'

'*I'm* talking, Ms Eversholt. And of *course* there's no question of you taking a month off; that's our budget month.'

'But I'll take it as leave,' Ellie said sullenly.

'Yes, well the only way you could take it as leave is if you worked Christmas days for the rest of your life.'

'I'll do that. I hate Christmas anyway. Me and my dad just get pissed and grumble at the TV, and I have to make brussels sprouts even though neither of us will eat them.'

'Well I'm sorry about your frankly dismal-sounding holiday period, but that doesn't mean I can just let you disappear for a month.' Mr Rooney stood up, to indicate the end of their meeting.

Ellie stood her ground in silence.

'Was that everything?'

'Well, I don't see why I shouldn't be able to take it as unpaid . . .'

'Oh, for goodness' sake. Which particular bit of "no, definitely not, no way, sorry and go away and leave me alone," didn't you understand?'

'Hypothetically speaking,' said Ellie, 'what would happen if someone sorted out cover for all their work and left on unpaid leave for a month?'

'Hypothetically speaking,' said Mr Rooney, 'they wouldn't have a job to come back to.'

'That's hypothetically very interesting.'

'No, that's *actually* very interesting, and I'd recommend it be noted.'

* * *

On Sunday morning, Julia and Loxy strode down Battersea Rise towards Elms carrying their own bodyweight in newsprint.

'This isn't going to be fun,' Julia mused. 'I mean, I'm sorry she had a bad birthday and everything, but I don't think this trip is going to work out and I don't want to have a row.'

'The two of us don't really row, do we?' asked Loxy thoughtfully.

Julia looked at him sideways. 'So . . . ?'

'Nothing.'

'Fine, then.' Julia spotted Arthur coming from the opposite direction and waved him over. Colin trotted on ahead into the bar. He was wearing a baseball jacket and a cap with stars and stripes on it.

'You forgot to lock the gate behind you again, didn't you?'

73

'It's not my fault the paper boy forgot to add in the *Funday Times*.'

'I thought Colin *was* the paper boy.'

'Ha ha.'

'Aha, it's the annoying little brother I never had,' said Ellie as Colin entered. She was leafing through an enormous pile of travel brochures and eating pancakes with one hand.

Ellie didn't mean to be so short with Colin. She realized that in fact, these days, almost anyone younger than her doing anything at all pissed her off. Surely anyone younger than her should still be doing English comprehension tests and appearing on *Young Musician of the Year*, and certainly shouldn't be working for a living or having opinions or driving cars and things. If Ellie was elected as an MP (an unlikely occurrence), she wouldn't even be the youngest MP in the House of Commons. She thought about this a lot.

'Where's Arthur?'

Colin shrugged and twisted.

'He said he was going to see a man about a dog . . . I think he might be buying me a puppy for Christmas.'

'Colin, you live with your parents and their house is really small. Where would the dog live?'

He shrugged. 'In a drawer maybe. Puppies aren't big.'

'Okay, so if under any circumstances you can conceive of Arthur not wanting to buy you a dog, do you have any idea where else he might have gone?'

He shrugged again. 'And I saw Julia up the hill.'

'Oh, right.'

'*Why* can't I come to America?' said Colin crossly.

'Because there'd be too many of us. And you don't understand.'

'I do understand.'

'Okay then, complete this well known phrase . . . "Who you gonna call?"'

Colin shrugged. 'The Samaritans?'

Ellie poked at her pancake. 'Possibly. Look, Colin, you wouldn't like it.'

'I would.'

'You wouldn't. We're not even going to Disney-land.'

Colin sat upright.

'Really?'

'Really we're not.'

'You're *bonkers*.'

Ellie nodded as the others filed in looking reticent.

'Look, guys! I have brochures!'

'Ehm, yeah. Hedgehog.'

Arthur had spoken up first.

'Look, I know you want to do this and you think it would be brilliant and I'm sure it would, but, you know Hedge . . .'

Ellie's face fell. She supposed, on some level, this was inevitable. People never committed to things anymore, even your best friends. Especially not in London. She supposed if she lived in a former coal mining town in the North she'd go everywhere with the same crowd her whole life. And probably have more fun. Down in London if you didn't have fifteen things crossed out every day in your palm pilot there was something wrong with you. Why was that?

She picked up a piece of toast.

'But *guys*.'

'Look, it's just not practical,' said Julia. 'Everyone's so busy, and rushing about so much.'

'And I really can't afford it. I'd have loved to come, really,' said Arthur.

'Oh, shit,' said Ellie with a sigh.

'I'd have liked to have come too,' said Loxy. Julia gave him a look. 'But we decided best not.'

'I wanted to come,' said Colin. 'If we were going to Disneyland.'

'But nothing's going to happen,' said Ellie. 'This isn't how Bob Geldof would have wanted it.'

She stared into space as the others ordered breakfast and coffee. An uncomfortable silence descended, and Arthur started fishing in the papers.

Suddenly, the door to Elms flew open. Standing there was a very pink and white ice-cold, shaking

Siobhan. 'Heh . . . He . . . he . . . hE,' she spluttered. 'He . . . he . . .'

Julia jumped up immediately. 'What is it? Come over, sit down. What's the matter?'

Arthur furnished her with a glass of water until she stopped hyperventilating.

'He . . . he . . .'

'Is it Patrick?' asked Julia. Siobhan nodded vehemently.

'Oh no! Have you split up?'

Siobhan nodded violently and indicated with her hands that there was more to it.

'Oh God! He LEFT you?'

She nodded again and indicated more.

'What a bastard!' said Ellie.

'He left you for someone ELSE?'

More nodding.

'Twat,' said Arthur.

Siobhan was valiantly indicating more.

'He left you for someone . . . he was ALREADY SEEING?'

The nodding became more pronounced.

'Arsehole!' said Loxy. Siobhan began gesticulating wildly at the fourth finger of her left hand.

'He ate all the HULA hoops?' said Colin.

'They're getting *married*?'

Siobhan was practically yelping.

'Cocksucking son of a BITCH,' said Arthur. Siobhan

hadn't finished. She pointed desperately to her stomach.

Julia drew in a breath and went very, very quiet.

'She's . . . pregnant?'

Siobhan burst into enormous sobs.

'CUNT,' said Ellie.

* * *

They clung onto Siobhan as best they could until she could finally talk again, which was a long time, and a couple of emergency rounds of Bloody Marys, and lots of vicious and vengeful plotting and grimly muttered curses later. Eventually Siobhan quietened enough to hold up her hand a second. She fumbled about in her bag.

'I'm going to get him,' she snivelled. 'So many ways. Starting here, with the only fucking thing he cares about.'

Gulping madly she held up Patrick's gold card.

And with her other hand she drew out four return tickets to Los Angeles.

'Oh, crap,' said Colin sulkily, doing a quick head count.

The Sure Thing

'. . . and I thought when we're driving up through the desert we should stop and pick up hitchhikers.'

'Sorry, did you just say hitchhikers or no hitchhikers?' said Arthur, turning his picture of the Grand Canyon upside down.

'Yes hitchhikers. You know – like *Thelma and Louise*.'

'Or *The Hitcher*! I think I'm going to recommend No Hitchhikers.'

'Oh, yeah. Hmm. Also, can we go to San José?'

'*Don't* start,' Arthur grimaced. 'Oh, okay. Are you appraised of the route?'

Ellie giggled.

'I cannot wait till you lot fuckin' disappear,' said Big Bastard. He was slumped in his armchair, blithely chopping between sports channels, watching anything from ping pong to women's gymnastics. Particularly women's gymnastics. Outside it was pissing it down and the pictures of palm trees seemed more alluring than ever.

'Where's Siobhan tonight?' asked Julia, lying on the carpet under Loxy's big arm, licking the top off a French Fancy.

That morning in the restaurant, Siobhan had handed over the tickets then stood up saying, 'I don't care if you use them or not. I don't care if you chuck them in the bin. Just can everyone stop talking about how pettily miserable they are all the time and fucking do something about it? Then those of us who truly *are* miserable can get on with it in peace and quiet.'

Ellie looked up. 'She's keying his Suzuki jeep. In stripes.'

'I still can't believe it,' said Julia. Big Bastard snorted loudly.

'Oh, have you got some useful emotional insight to bring to bear on the situation?' asked Ellie. Big Bastard turned round and opened his enormous meaty paws.

'He's a bloke, right. And this girl comes up to him, right. And she's twenty-one, right. And she's a ballerina, right?'

All these things were, tragically, true. Big Bastard shrugged.

'And?' said Julia.

Big Bastard looked at Loxy. 'Well, d'uh.' Loxy didn't return the look.

'We'll try and bring you back an appropriate present from America,' said Ellie.

'Like a big, pink, glazed American ham, to remind you of your face.'

'Or an American goat, to remind you of how your room smells,' said Arthur. 'Duckie.'

'Actually I'm thinking that I might just rent out your room when you're gone,' said Big Bastard to Ellie.

'Who to? Rentokil?'

'Oh, guys, can we go to Chicago as well?' said Julia, lifting up the map of America for a second.

'What's in Chicago?'

'Well, I reckon if the Hedgehog gets to look for Andrew McCarthy I should get a stab at the cast of ER.'

'Nobody like you. Maybe I'll rent it out to a gorgeous bird with really massive knockers.'

'Don't tell me – who can also do gymnastics?'

'Maybe. It's my flat. I could if I wanted to.'

'Go ahead. Try it. You have my blessing. I only wish I could be there to watch when you're laughed out of the International Homeless Big Titty Gymnast's Convention in Munich.'

Ellie spread out a map on the floor.

'Okay everyone, here are His last known movements,' she announced.

'He's been in a play in New York, a film in Los Angeles and a film in Toronto.'

'Hang on! No-one ever said anything about Toronto,' said Arthur, worriedly. 'November in Toronto – that's not a holiday, that's a Ranulph Fiennes expedition. It's California or nothing.'

'I don't think he's there now. Don't worry. We'll have plenty of time to have fun in the sun and hit the red hot Andrew trail!'

'That red hot fifteen-year-old Andrew trail!'

'Can we . . . are we going to go to Vegas?' asked Loxy suddenly. The others looked at him.

'Not for any reason! I don't know why anyone would want to got there! It was just a random city plucked out of the air! I don't care where we go. Ehm, are we going to . . . Pasadena?'

'Make some more tea will you Loxy?' Julia asked. He did so immediately.

'I think we should definitely go to Vegas,' said Ellie. 'Then maybe as well as getting to meet Andrew McCarthy, Robert Redford might offer me a million pounds to sleep with him. *What* a holiday this is turning out to be.'

* * *

'I'm really looking forward to this aren't you?' tried

Loxy as he and Julia walked home through the pounding rain.

'Uh huh. Well, if it shuts Ellie up for a bit. And Jeez, hot weather in November – I can't wait.'

Suddenly, Loxy turned to her with a strange expression on his face.

'Julia . . . I can't think of a good way to do this, or to be dashingly romantic or anything but . . .'

He knelt down in the road. His right knee went straight into a puddle, but he ignored it. It was pouring.

'I thought that . . . well, what Ellie's been saying has really made me think about life, and where we're all headed and everything, and I wondered if, well, when we got to Vegas . . . that you'd do me the honour of becoming my . . .'

'What?' said Julia, not paying attention. Then:

'Oh MY GOD.' She whirled around. 'WHAT?! WHAT!!? *TELL* me you don't have a ring.'

Loxy rummaged deep into his inside pocket and brought out the small box.

'I bought this after our third date,' he said, quietly. 'I've been carrying it around ever since.'

All Julia could do was stare at him, getting increasingly soaked in the gutter as he gazed up at her imploringly.

'Oh God, Loxy . . . but this is so soon. I mean, it's only been . . .'

'Two years.'

'Really? It's been that long? Christ.'

She walked forward a few steps then turned round looking thoughtful.

'Don't you love me?' said Loxy, his voice quavering.

'Of *course* I do. You know I do, sweetheart. It's just that – God – I mean, getting married . . . that's what grown-ups do.'

'No, I think they let all sorts of people get married . . . especially in Vegas . . .' said Loxy, disappointedly. He looked up at her again with big puppy dog eyes.

'Loxy,' she said, unaccountably angry with him. 'I'm sorry. But I don't know the answer to the question.'

'So that means "no", does it?' he said, slowly.

'No it doesn't mean "no"!' said Julia, stung. 'It means . . . it means, oh my God, it means, you just said the most surprising thing anyone ever said to me and I don't know what the hell to think about it.'

'And you can't think of a good way to let me down gently.'

'*No*, Loxy. For God's sake, it's just a surprise, that's all.'

He stuck his bottom lip out.

'Well, I know how *I* feel.'

'Yes, and you've had two years minus three dates to get used to it! Whereas I've had nineteen seconds! And that's not fair! And, for God's sake, stand up.'

Very slowly, Loxy put the box back in his pocket and stood up.

'I feel stupid,' he said.

'You look stupid,' she said, tenderly. The rain continued to pound down on both of them.

He started to laugh.

'Great. I'm stupid and you're finishing with me.'

'I am not fucking finishing with you! Stop being a baby!'

She stalked ahead of him.

Already drenched, Loxy looked at the ground and started to splosh up and down in the puddles.

'I'm laughing at clouds,' Loxy started singing mournfully to himself.

'You're not listening to me. I just need time to think about this, okay? It's just come out of the blue.'

'. . . so high up above . . .'

'Okay, Lox, I'm going to go home now. We can talk tomorrow.'

'I've sun in my heart . . .' *splish splosh*.

'I'll phone you tomorrow. I'll think about it, I promise.'

She practically ran down the grey and empty street.

'. . . and I'm ready for love . . .' *splish splosh splish splosh*.

* * *

'Wanky doodle *dandy!*' said Ellie.

'Can't you at least try and be constructive?' said Siobhan to her. 'This is exactly the kind of crap you came out with when Patrick . . . went away.'

'Actually, that is kind of how I feel,' said Julia. 'Just a random line of gibberish.'

'But I don't know what to say,' complained Ellie. 'Nobody ever asks *me* anything interesting. I get freaked out if someone asks me if I want large fries. Why don't we all have another Bloody Mary. Then we'll try and talk sense.'

'I think those two things might be mutually exclusive,' said Julia, but made up another batch anyway.

Julia had gone home and sat in the tiny darkened living room of her tiny darkened flat – she'd deliberately bought a small one-bedroom so that Ellie could never conceivably move in with her. She'd always liked the way it was furnished, although these days she was noticing just how much Ikea there actually was – and tried to think long and hard into the night, but she wasn't really of a philosophical turn of mind. So after about fifteen minutes she'd phoned up the cavalry and after mass screaming, they'd marched around with Worcestershire sauce and celery sticks; even Siobhan was temporarily roused from her Medusa-like life-long evil plottings long enough to empathize. Which was pretty good of her, seeing as Julia suddenly had the exact opposite of her own problem. Arthur was excluded – he was going to be furious, as he'd always insisted he'd had just as many childhood wedding dress fantasies as they had, but this was a woman-thing deep down, no doubt about it.

'I thought . . . if, or when it ever happened, it would be, like, just the most exciting moment of my life,' moaned Julia, sucking loudly through a straw.

'That's because the people that made the whole thing up had never had sex,' said Ellie. 'It was a toss-up between getting engaged or dying in the throes of having a bastard in a workhouse.'

'Yes, thank you Catherine Cookson,' said Siobhan. 'Well, I say, if someone asks you, you should just say yes immediately. It's going to fail anyway, and at least this way people buy you stuff and pay you lots of attention.'

'Me and Loxy wouldn't fail! We'd be fine! It's just, I'd kind of hoped for amazing, not *fine*.'

'When you first met Loxy you swore he was the most amazing thing that had ever happened to you.'

'Yes, but that's the same in every new relationship, isn't it? It's new person sex voodoo. I don't think I wore pants for six months, and if I did wear them they were made out of polyurethane and feathers. But now . . . we're just . . .'

'Big pants,' said Ellie suddenly.

'What?'

'You're in the "big pants", stage of your relationship. Okay, what pants are you wearing?'

Julia shrugged.

'I'm wearing La Perla,' said Siobhan.

'Exactly,' said Ellie. 'You're suddenly single, and you never know whether or not you'll bump into John Cusack on the way home. I'm wearing special Marks and Sparks green pants, because if I buy white, black, pink or red, Big Bastard steals them off the washing line. Jules?'

Julia sighed. 'Well, okay.' She reluctantly tugged them over the waistband of her trousers.

'Yeuch,' said the other two simultaneously.

'They are clean, thank you.'

But it was true that the outwardly fastidious Julia had a pair of massive saggy washed out grey knickers with a hole in them.

'You're just too comfortable. Your relationship has become a takeaway,' Ellie said.

'What?'

'You remember when you started going out together? You used to lay the table? Light candles? Cook for him so you could pretend to be his mum and play house together? And now it's just, sod it, let's get a takeaway and eat it watching the TV and not talking to each other . . .'

'I miss it *so* much,' said Siobhan sadly.

'. . . and that's why I never have relationships. I really can't stand takeaway food.'

'And absolutely nothing to do with deep-seated psychological trauma.'

'Siobhan, I order you to shut it. Anyway, that's the takeaway relationship – lukewarm, stirred over, made up of lots of different kinds of crap. And yet everyone seems to want one. God, I'm good tonight.'

'Have you heard from Billy?' asked Siobhan suddenly.

'I have actually. He said if I came back he'd hand over my Terence Trent D'Arby album. I'm standing my ground.'

'Ignore her, Julia,' said Siobhan decisively. 'You and Loxy are great together. You're relaxed and comfortable enough with each other not to have to worry about your underwear or nutritional intake. He's a lovely guy. We like parties. Get married.'

'Oh God,' said Julia.

* * *

'You're late.' Mr Rooney was patrolling the corridor outside Ellie's office.

'I was helping a friend in crisis, Sir.'

'Don't tell me – she wanted to take four weeks leave to do something stupid?'

'Oh no sir – when *she* asked for leave she got it straight away.'

'You're trying my patience, Miss Eversholt.'

'You're ruining my life, Mr Rooney.'

'You'll thank me in the long run, Miss Eversholt.'

'This is the long run, Mr Rooney.'

* * *

Ellie hummed and hawed, stomped around the office, made coffee, went to the loo, played about with her e-mail and finally flicked around the large scruffy piles of paper on her desk. This wasn't looking good. Her plan couldn't possibly come together without her. This stupid fucking job.

'Oh God. Can you think of anything interesting to do?' she called to the temp.

'Well, there's fifty voicemail messages piled up from over the weekend if you're interested,' said the temp in a bored voice. Ellie stood up and marched over to the doorway.

'Why didn't you tell me before, when I walked in?'

'Because I hate this job and everyone here.'

'Can you take the messages down for me?'

'No. I'm only supposed to do word processing this week.'

'But there's no word processing to do.'

'But I don't care.'

Ellie sighed. Five of the messages were from one potential client with an old tile making factory who was deliberately trying to push Ellie to see how nice she could be to him. Ellie was getting increasingly tetchy. Now he wanted to be taken to a horse race then a car rally in return for possibly sending them a small bit of business that would involve ripping out a century and a half's worth of hand fired tiled walls to provide extra metal bathrooms.

Six were messages from another firm to whom Ellie had lied about some paperwork she had been supposed to send to them, which she had no intention of ever sorting out before the world's end; seven were from different people she had been trying to arrange a meeting between, none of whom appeared to have a simultaneous opening until 2020. Eight were about the buildings insurance which would require her to meet with the fire officer, who had only a moustache differentiating him from a toad who could stand up, nine were from the finance office – no problem, she had her phone on automatic delete for those, and ten were from Billy, starting off apologetic and finishing actively offensive.

'And a Partridge in a Pear Tree,' said Ellie crossly. 'Oh God. This is all unbelievably shit.'

The phone rang. She picked it up.

'Sugarcakes,' said the voice. 'You know, there's no trombonist like you.'

'Well, thank fuck for that,' said Ellie conversationally. 'Now fuck off please.'

'Hang on, baby.'

Then came the sound of someone trying to lift a phone and a saxophone at the same time, followed by the sound of a saxophone crashing to the floor and taking a phone with it and, possibly, a vase, followed by extended cursing on both ends of the line as Ellie put the phone down.

She started shouting at the temp again.

'This is all crap. Cancel it all, chuck it in the bin, and if anyone asks, tell them the phone system's down but I'm working on it. Oh, and I have a tropical disease.'

'Really,' said Mr Rooney, walking into her office. 'You won't be wanting to go away anywhere then.'

Ellie jumped up and just stared at him, mouth wide open in shock.

'Do you know,' he said, plonking his gingery-haired arms on her desk and trying to look caring and concerned, 'why I came down here?'

She swallowed heavily.

'Ehm, you'd heard what a joker I was?' she started nervously. 'And you wanted to hear if you could catch me in the middle of any hilarious pranks making up phone messages with the temp.'

'No,' said Mr Rooney. 'Actually, I came down here to say that if this trip away was so important to you

92

and all your work was squared away, I was going to let you go. Hmm, perhaps an unfortunate turn of phrase . . .'

Ellie started turning very red.

'. . . I was going to allow you to take the leave of absence. However, it appears that your ideas of finishing work and mine are rather different.'

'*Please* Sir . . .' muttered Ellie, wretchedly.

He snapped upright.

'Any leave at all you've got booked is cancelled until further notice and you can report to personnel to pick up your written warning.'

She watched him turn around and walk out, absolutely dying inside.

* * *

'Why the *fuck* didn't you tell me he was on his way in?' she asked the Temp.

'I was bored and wanted to see what would happen.'

Ellie idly started throwing pieces of paper around her desk.

'Oh God, oh God, what am I going to do?' She bit back tears. 'This is going to fuck up everything.'

'If you walked out I'd get a half-day,' said the temp.

'Oh, well, I'm hardly about to . . .'

She thought for a second. Then she sat down, picked up the phone and dialled nine.

'Arthur, have you ever walked out of a job?'

'Oh, so you're phoning me up for career advice but when it comes to the *really* important things in life I'm chopped liver am I?'

'You're what? Art, I've got a bit of a crisis on here.'

'Never mind. Siobhan phoned me. We've only got a wedding in our midst and nobody bothered to inform me.'

'Except for Siobhan obviously. Look, do you think . . .'

'So is Julia getting married or not?'

'She doesn't know. She wanted our opinion. Our opinions were divided. Happy now? Okay, I want to . . .'

'Well, I think she should. I don't think they get any nicer than Loxy, and he has a tush to die for.'

'Good for you. Now PLEASE help me.'

'Oh well, seeing as you're begging.'

'Arthur, my boss just caught me misbehaving and he won't let me go away.'

'Oh no!' Arthur was sympathetic, with a touch of natural fascination. 'What did you do? Were you getting it on with the stockboy in the stationery cupboard?'

'No, Arthur, that was you.'

'Oh, so it was. Oh well. I hated that job.'

Actually, Arthur had a tendency to make up

encounters like this, otherwise the others teased him for being a married man.

'I hate this job,' said Ellie defeatedly, kicking the toe of her shoe against the rubbish bin. There was a silence.

'You know,' said Arthur, 'you were going on and on about trying to get out of your rut.'

'Yes, but I wasn't planning to go directly from the rut to "do you want fries with that?"'

'Well,' said Arthur. 'You could just take off. You'd be able to get another job somewhere, they're all over the place. If all else fails you can always raise some capital and become Ellie.com . . .'

'Uh huh . . .' said Ellie uncertainly, although inside she was starting to feel very excited.

'Why don't you tell them to take their big fat job and shove it up their big fat asses?'

'And I'd get a half-day,' shouted the temp who was listening on speakerphone.

'Okay, can we just put aside how much fun this would be for everyone else for just a tiny second?' said Ellie, but her brain was working overtime. 'I've never done anything like this before.'

'What about that time with the Copydex?'

'That was completely different. The guy was losing his hair anyhow.'

'Hmm.'

'Oh God. I don't want to be skint again.'

'You could move back in with your dad.'

'Do you know what? I'm already skint. Oh my God!'

'What?'

'I've just had a horrible thought. Do you think Visa and Mastercard are run by all the companies in the world to stop their employees getting up and walking out *en masse*?'

'It would explain a lot. Why don't you phone the girls?'

'Because I know what they'd say. "Don't rush into anything, Hedgehog. You're always full of wild schemes that don't work out, Hedgehog. Remember when you left your architecture degree and thought you were doing the right thing, yada yada yada . . ." oof, hang on. I've got a call on the other line.'

'Excuse me? Do NOT do this to me . . .'

'Hello?'

'Hey, yeah, hi . . . is that the lovely Ellie Eversholt?'

'No, this is the stroppy Ellie Eversholt.'

'Ha ah! *So* funny. This is Edgar Wilkins from AZP&P.'

The tile factory. Ellie held up the receiver and made V signs at it.

'So nice to catch you! Anyway, I was thinking, remember we talked about maybe having a little day out to sort out some business? Ho ho!'

'Two point five billion men in the world,' thought

Ellie. 'They can't all be like this, can they? *Can* they?'

'Well, don't you think we could go on a little adventure, make it fun? Silverstone's coming up, or Goodwood . . . just you and me? Little bit of . . . *after hours?* Ho ho!'

* * *

'I love him,' thought Julia mournfully, staring at her computer screen. 'I do. But . . . is this it? *Is* it?'

Her mother was all in favour of the idea, but then her mother would seemingly have been quite happy to see her married off to any one of the assorted lowlifes she'd dragged back over the years, as long as there was the promise of grandchildren and some sort of joint mortgage paraphernalia.

'But what was it that did it; what really made you think about dad, this is it, this is the one I want to get married to?' she'd asked her mother once.

'Because we wanted to have sex, stupid.'

Everyone seemed to be treating Loxy's proposal like it was absolutely not a big deal, and why the hell shouldn't she? She put it down to a conspiracy of silence from her married friends, and the enticing prospect of a free piss-up from her singletons. No-one seemed to be sitting her down and telling her what to do. Which, of course, was fair enough, but still.

'I love him,' she thought. 'He loves me. We have

97

a good life together. He loves kids. He's got a good job.'

'It's just sometimes,' she thought, 'he really fucking irritates me.'

She phoned Annabel, who at least had some experience in the matter.

'Annie – does George ever really, really annoy you?'

Annabel sounded slightly exasperated.

'How could George ever possibly annoy me? He works until 8.30 every night and plays golf all winter and cricket all summer. And of course he never goes in the kitchen, so he can't possibly pester me while I'm doing the washing up or the laundry or the cooking or unpacking the shopping and of course, I'm a woman, so I love doing all the shopping anyway and I do actually understand that using an iron and having a penis are mutually untenable.'

'Righty ho,' said Julia. 'Um, Annie, Loxy's asked me to marry him.'

'Really? Oh, that's *wonderful!* That's really brilliant! I'm so pleased for you both.'

'Um, I haven't given him an answer yet.'

'Oh, don't worry, you'll have such a lovely party. Ooh, can I help choose your frock?'

Julia widened her eyes.

'Ehm . . . can I get back to you on that?'

* * *

98

Ellie sat in her cubicle and pondered for a long time. Which was worse, she thought. Having a job she hated or having nothing at all but enjoying a little bit of a shout and a little bit of drama *and* getting to go to America? Her heart in her mouth, she made up her mind and headed out towards the conference suite, trying to keep her chin up like Michael J. Fox in *The Secret of My Success*.

'Mr Rooney?'

He looked up.

'Miss Everhart, I really don't have time for this.'

The conference room was full and smelled of burnt coffee and low level anxiety. Rooney was standing beside an overhead projector, pointing out seemingly meaningless graphs. Ellie stood in the doorway, white and nervous, but determined.

'Hmm. Not even if I tell you to stick it up your BIG FAT ASS YOU BIG FAT BASTARD?'

The entire room turned round as one, exactly the effect Ellie had intended. Mr Rooney opened his pink eyes wide and pointed his laser stick at her.

'What? Can anyone here tell me what you just meant by that? Anyone? Anyone?'

The general plethora of ill-nourished surveyors gazed fiercely at their Cornish pastie sandals. Mr Rooney slowly lowered his laser stick.

'Written warning not go too well then?'

'I don't know,' said Ellie. 'Because those big fat

personnel bitches CAN STICK IT UP THEIR BIG FAT ASSES.'

'Oh yes,' said Mr Rooney gently. 'I see; it's a kind of general invitation.'

'Yes it is,' said Ellie. There was a silence. This wasn't going quite as she'd planned. She'd expected everyone to quiver with rage and Mr Rooney to get absolutely apoplectic, before bursting into tears and having her frog-marched from the building in a moment of high drama that she could replay down the pub in a deeply wronged tone. Instead he was looking at her concernedly.

'Oh well, dreadfully sorry. Um. Have you got those figures we asked for?'

'No! I stuck them up the accountancy department's BIG FAT . . .'

'Yes, yes, I'm beginning to spot a pattern! No matter.'

He smiled benevolently and leaned over, resting his arm on the projector.

'Are you leaving us, Ms Eversholt?'

'You can take your job and shove it up . . .'

'That's a shame.'

He stared philosophically into the middle distance.

'Ms Eversholt. Did it never occur to you to come to me and tell me you were unhappy before you started shoving things up other people's . . . things?'

Ellie shrugged and suddenly felt eleven years old. She stared hard at the floor.

'Just because I can't let you go swanning off for months at a time doesn't mean I can't listen you know.'

'. . . *big fat asses*,' whispered Ellie mournfully to herself.

'Or', he tapped the overhead, 'you could even have come and seen me about voluntary redundancy. We haven't had the figures on time for so long, it's got to the point where we need to make quite drastic savings.'

Ellie's head shot up.

'Oh well,' he said, 'I suppose you would only have taken the redundancy money and shoved it up somebody's ass.'

'Not . . . necessarily,' said Ellie in a very small voice.

'Oh really?' he said. 'Well, maybe you might want to stop by my office on your way home . . . if, that is,' he chuckled in his unhumorous schoolmastery way, 'you think that you, me and my ass can all fit in there at the same time.'

The surveyors laughed like sycophantic drains.

* * *

'I have to see you tonight,' hissed Julia.

'But I have to see you too!' hissed back Ellie, mindful of the temp.

'I have news!'

'And I have news too!'

'Well . . . okay then!'

'Okay then!'

'Bye!'

'Bye!'

'Are you leaving?' asked the temp, 'Only, if you are, would you mind signing my timesheet for double overtime?'

* * *

Mr Rooney and the woman from personnel sat her down and made her promise to stay for a couple of weeks to try and sort out the mess, and got her to sign lots of papers. Then they countersigned a cheque. Ellie, too mortally embarrassed to say anything, sat in the chair, trying to make herself as small as possible. She muttered appreciatively from time to time.

After the clearly disapproving personnel woman had gone, she finally felt able to offer some thanks.

'Call me Craig,' said Mr Rooney, leaning back, taking off his glasses and rubbing his eyes. Ellie prayed to any Gods that might exist that this didn't mean he was about to ask for a grateful blow job. He leafed casually through her personal file and glanced up at her.

'How old were you when your mother left, Ellie?' he asked suddenly.

No-one had called her Ellie in so long it took her a second or two to respond.

'Fourteen,' she said diffidently, and stared at the floor. 'It's in the file, *Craig*.'

'I was twelve,' he said, and stared out the window. 'So, you know, I suppose I win on points.'

Ellie didn't say anything, because she knew what she could say that would be helpful: absolutely nothing. Craig continued to stare out of the window.

'Wouldn't recommend working your way out of it,' he went on. 'Doesn't work, not in the long run, the old "desk cure".'

He nodded to himself.

'A little bit of travelling, mind you – probably couldn't hurt.'

'Prob'ly not.'

He nodded again.

'Hmm. No, I don't think it could hurt at all.'

He handed her the cheque, patted her once on the shoulder, shrugged on his overcoat and stepped out into the already darkening evening.

* * *

Ellie couldn't sit down once she got home and it was driving Big Bastard crazy.

'What the fuck's the matter with you? Have you got piles?'

'I know, Big Bastard, that it is very difficult to think of anything other than piles in your delicate condition but actually no. Something wonderful has happened, and I'm excited, thank you.'

'What's that then – don't tell me. The European Union has announced that all women on the blob get a week off work.'

Big Bastard had strong and regularly expressed views on the European Union.

'No. But did you hear they're going to make all the rugby balls square to fit in with common agricultural policy and stacking regulations?'

His beefy face went puce. 'Those bastards. We'll show them. Two world wars and one World Cup.'

Julia came rushing up to the door with Arthur in tow.

'What's your news??' she asked, pulling off her coat.

'I'm here under duress,' said Arthur. 'Do you know, I spent six hours on your call waiting.'

'Tough. Okay, here's my news . . .' said Ellie, mixing Cosmopolitans with one hand.

Julia's face fell. Ellie stopped stirring.

'. . . or we could have yours first . . .'

Julia beamed, sat down and composed herself on the sofa.

'Do you want a Cosmopolitan, Big Bastard?' said Ellie, pouring the mixture into tall glasses.

'What, poof juice? Sorry Arthur mate, no offence.'

'None taken, duckie. All the more for us.'

'I didn't say I didn't want one.'

'Here you go then. One glass of Fairy Fruit cocktail.'

Big Bastard grimaced and gulped it back.

'Okay. Final scene,' said Julia. '*Pretty in Pink*. Well, near enough final scene.'

'Do you know,' said Ellie, 'I think that dress really *was* hideous. Even then. Do you remember? It was actively unpleasant. Really unflattering. And pink with red hair. I still don't think that's right.'

'I agree,' said Arthur. 'Even by the standards of the day. And the standards of the day were *vomitous*.'

'Shut up a second, okay? Just cast your minds back.'

'Okay.'

'What does Andrew say to Molly right at the end?'

Ellie squinted, trying to remember.

'Does he say "I'm really not sure that pink dress goes with your red hair"?' hazarded Arthur.

'No! He says, "I believed in you – I just didn't believe in myself."'

'Jules, that's the cheesiest line of all time.'

'No, you don't see. I think . . . that's exactly what I need to do. Or at least, find out if I do.'

'What?' Ellie leaned forward.

'About Loxy, stupid. I mean, I know he's fine. He's great. It's me that's the problem. So . . .'

'Uh huh?'

'So, you know. Going to find Andrew McCarthy. I'm with you, all the way. I want to know what the hell he meant by that. I want to know if he did find love, just by being,' she coloured, 'the loveliest man in the world. And I'm going to find out if I – ahem – believe in myself enough to go through with it and, well, maybe get married, maybe not.'

'Oh my God! That's brill!' said Ellie.

'Don't! Don't congratulate me. I've had enough of people congratulating me. Everyone seems to assume that no-one else could possibly want me and just because I've been asked I'm automatically going to say yes, like some dried up old tart. Which I'm *not*,' she added, when it became clear that nobody else was going to.

'You getting married Jules?' said Big Bastard. 'Congratulations. That Loxy's not bad for one of our . . . foreign brothers.'

The others swapped a characteristic look.

'It's alright,' whispered Ellie, 'I save my toenail clippings and leave them in his sock drawer.'

'I heard that,' said Big Bastard.

'So Loxy's not coming?' asked Arthur.

Julia shook her head. 'Loxy isn't even answering the phone at the moment,' she said shamefacedly.

'I think this is a trip I have to make myself.' She stared into the middle distance. 'God, Hedge, what's your news?'

'You'll never guess,' said Ellie.

'You're up the duff,' said Big Bastard. 'Neh. Who'd do you?'

Ellie turned round.

'Excuse me, but precisely two weeks ago, you were desperate to "do" me.'

'Yes, but I was fucking pissed, weren't I? I'd drunk myself blind.'

'I've left my job.'

'You've *what*?' screamed Julia, then saw Arthur's face.

'You *knew* about this?'

'Hey, you were the one that was going to get married and not tell me.'

'I hardly think . . .'

'It's okay! They've given me redundancy money,' said Ellie.

'And how long is that going to last? How could you do this, Hedgehog, with nothing to go to?'

'I have *everything* to go to,' said Ellie stubbornly. 'California for starters.'

'But what about after we get back? Are you going to blow it all on this trip?'

'Things will be different after we get back. That's the point of going away. Don't you see? This is about radical change. This is about shaking things up. I have already officially begun shaking things up. So have you.'

Julia shrugged slightly. 'Well, I suppose.'

'. . . and anyway, Andrew will tell me what to do.'

'No he won't! All he knows about is acting. And perhaps a little bit about waitering.'

'Well, you're going to ask him whether you should get *married*.'

'Girls, calm down.'

'Well I was pleased for *her*,' grumbled Ellie.

'I'm sorry,' said Julia. 'I know you hated that job.'

'I bloody did!'

'You were very brave.'

'I bloody was.'

'It's just . . . it was a good job, and have you ever liked a job?'

'Yes! I *loved* being a majorette.'

'Hedgehog, that wasn't a job! That was meant to be fun!'

'Oh. Well, it was. *Bloody* good fun. I thought it was kind of like being in the Territorial Army.'

'No, it was for the girls who were too ungainly for ballet.'

She saw Ellie's face,

'. . . and had special gifts all of their own.'

'Well, it's too late anyway,' said Ellie. 'I've signed the paperwork. In two weeks' time, I'll be a free woman.'

'Hang on!' said Big Bastard. 'Where the hell is my rent going to come from?'

'Oh, I know someone who's looking for a place to stay,' said Arthur suddenly. 'Just for a bit, maybe while the Hedgehog's away.'

'Who?' said Ellie, instantly suspicious.

'He's living with his parents,' went on Arthur, 'and he just needs a little bit of space.'

'No!' said Ellie. 'I absolutely forbid it.'

'Can he pay?' said Big Bastard.

'Oh yes, no problem. He's in telecommunications.'

'He fixes telephone kiosks!' said Ellie. 'No no absolutely not. Big Bastard, I don't think you want to live with Colin. You're really prejudiced and he's really gay. It would be like a terrible premise for a sitcom.'

'But he can pay your rent,' said Big Bastard thoughtfully.

'What is your rent?' asked Arthur. Ellie told him a figure almost double what she was currently paying.

'He can give me the cheque and I'll carry on paying Big Bastard.'

Big Bastard screwed up his face and tried to do the sums.

'I guess that sounds okay,' he said finally.

'Great!' said Arthur. 'Now I get to have sex on weekdays.'

'It would almost be worth not going to see this,' said Ellie. 'I might set up a video camera.'

'We've got one,' said Arthur.

* * *

The next two weeks passed so quickly they were packing before they knew it. Or almost; on the day before departure, Julia's immaculately packed bag was sitting neatly in her flat. Ellie was throwing her possessions at random into a rucksack.

'Torch!'

'Check! No, hang on Hedge, why the hell do we need a torch?'

'Haven't you seen *The Goonies*? Dry matches!'

'Check.'

'Now have you got this?' said Arthur. He was watching them get ready. In the end, because Arthur's work for the next season started directly after the Spring collections in October, he'd only been able to get two weeks, so they'd decided that Ellie and Julia would spend some time in Los Angeles tracking down the Brat Packers, then pick up Arthur and his cowboy hat for a couple of weeks bumming around San Francisco. Loxy had the fourth ticket, but no-one was talking about this to Julia, even as it became more and more obvious that he wasn't coming.

'You get in a taxi at LAX. You tell the driver the address of the hotel. This address, here. Go find your wee man from the 1980s. Then three days later you pick up the hire car. Drive drive drive along this line *here*.'

'Like the roadrunner cartoons,' said Ellie.

'With less fatal results if possible. And you are picking me up in San Francisco, *here*, the following day. After that you'll be in capable hands.'

'*Very* capable,' said Colin.

'And *you*,' said Ellie, 'are moving in your own bed linen. Do I make myself clear?'

Siobhan let out a dramatic sigh.

'And don't forget: you're sending the anonymous death threats from every small town you stop at.'

'Oh for God's sake, Shiv. Why don't you just beg a week off and come out with us? It'll be just what you need,' said Julia.

'And you could take the ticket from Lo—' Arthur grabbed Ellie from behind and clapped his hand over her mouth.

'What a fantastic travelling companion I would be,' said Siobhan. 'Nope. Sorry. I'm going to stay here and plot my deadly revenge.'

'But think of all those gorgeous tall white-teethed corn-fed American men! I don't know how you can

111

afford to pass this up!' argued Ellie. 'Look, if you like we could take a detour to Alaska. There's forty men for every woman up there.'

'I insist we take that detour,' said Arthur.

'Or we could go to Seattle – bag yourself a dot.com billionaire.'

'So it's between a woodcutter and a nerd? Or of course one of the 45% who are clinically obese. Plus the subset of bastards, which is all of them.'

'Hawaii?' asked Ellie.

'Hedge, you do know America is bigger than Britain don't you?' asked Julia a tad worriedly.

'Yeah, but not much bigger, surely. Anyway, once we've found Andrew McCarthy we'll have plenty of time to pootle around. He'll probably insist his chauffeur takes us anyway. Ooh – I wonder if he's got a helicopter?'

Arthur and Julia exchanged a look.

Loxy knocked and entered the flat warily. He and Julia were tentatively on speaking terms. Julia had attempted to explain her decision to go and try and ascertain her true feelings. Loxy suspected that this was just a long-winded way of dumping him and going on holiday at the same time. When she got back she'd probably change her telephone number and walk past him on the street.

Everyone greeted him with a bit too much enthusiasm. He walked up to Julia.

'So, Lox,' said Siobhan, falsely. 'Aren't you going to take advantage of Patrick's largesse then?'

Loxy shrugged and stared at the floor. Julia tried to take his hand. He let her, but just let his hand hang there, to show he wasn't enjoying it.

'Thought I'd better come and . . . say goodbye,' he said gruffly.

'We're not going until tomorrow.'

He shrugged.

Julia looked around. The others quickly took the hint and disappeared.

'Darling,' she said, touching his face. 'I think this will be good for us, you know. A little bit of time apart so I can think about it.'

'Yeah, right,' he said. 'And have sex with cowboys.'

'I'm not planning on having any sex with cowboys!' said Julia, shocked.

'No, that's me,' whispered Arthur from their vantage point hidden behind the kitchen door.

'Well, go *find* yourself or whatever it is you're so desperate to do so you don't have to spend any time with me.'

'For God's sake, Loxy! Can't you listen to me at all? Why does this all have to be about what *you* want?'

'Yeah, right, that's so selfish of me: to want us to be together.'

They weren't holding hands any more; they were several feet apart, glaring at each other.

113

'Well, I'm not going to marry someone just because they're in a massive strop with me, okay?'

He stared at her for a long time, then made a sighing sound.

'Have a good time,' he said shortly, turning on his heel.

'I bloody will!' shouted Julia as he left the flat. Then she sat down and had a snivel. The others re-emerged immediately and put various arms about her.

'Oh God! He's being so weird about it! He thinks I want to chase other men!'

Ellie and Arthur raised their eyebrows at each other.

'Really, he should be chasing me out to the airplane or something and then I'd know and change my mind and we'd all live happily ever after!' She sniffed a little more.

'That's what Ferris Bueller would do,' said Ellie, nodding in agreement.

'Oh for fuck's sake,' said Siobhan. 'You have not the slightest inkling of how fucking lucky you are. I'd have him.'

* * *

'I wish I were going,' said Ellie's dad dreamily, switching on the grill.

'I know. It's going to be quite something.'

'I was out there in '68 with your mother, before

she decided she preferred cavity wall insulation to us.'

Ellie's dad had a very precise set of ideas about what her mother's new life was like, based on absolutely no information whatsoever. Ellie flashed back a second to a picture of her father, sitting with his back to her when she got home from school with a note in his hand and a half-empty bottle of whisky by his elbow.

'Dad?'

He had turned round then, looking heavy and crumpled.

'What are you doing?'

'It's your mother,' he had said. Horrified, she had watched him try not to cry. Her parents never cried. 'She's gone to Plockton. With an accountant called Archie.'

'How long for?' said Ellie.

'Forever, I think, love,' said her dad, swallowing painfully. 'Come here then.'

And he put his arms around her, and, as Ellie realized what had happened, all she could do was stare into space, her eyes wide open.

This wasn't the worst of it though. Mums and dads were splitting up all the time, everyone's parents were at it. Mostly, though, they were fighting about custody and the kids were complaining about how often they had to go to the zoo at the weekends. From Plockton, however, emanated a deathly silence.

At first her father tried to make a joke of it. 'It's the post you see,' he'd say. 'Hasn't quite reached Plockton. No electricity either. She's trying to write by candle light.'

But as this became more and more obviously not true, he stopped mentioning it at all.

'Are you sure,' Ellie had asked timidly when she was about sixteen, 'that she didn't just die and you don't want to tell me about it?'

Her father's eyes had misted over. 'Neh, she's in Plockton with an accountant. Believe me, it's a fate worse than death.'

* * *

'Wow, what was it like?' Ellie asked now.

'It was great. We came into New York harbour by boat as dawn broke, right past the Statue of Liberty.'

'God, that must have been amazing,' said Ellie. 'Kind of like the Titanic, but, um, afloat.'

'Your mother got in a right strop with me because I wanted to send postcards and held her up.'

'No, not much of a writer,' said Ellie quietly.

'And always in a hurry,' said her dad. 'Just like you.'

'Oh, great,' said Ellie crossly. 'I'll just nip down the clinic and get sterilized, shall I?'

'Sorry Hedgehog.' Her father put his arm around

her and gave her a squeeze. 'You'll come back to me, won't you?'

'Of course I will, Dad.'

He hugged her briefly then moved away, both of them mildly embarrassed by the display of emotion.

'. . . and anyway they served us the best breakfast I've ever had in my life. Did you know they put maple syrup on bacon?'

'Bleagh.' Ellie pottered about, her aim now to try and work out a way her father wouldn't accidentally turn off the freezer and starve to death for the weeks she'd be away.

'Okay. Here's your list of instructions.' She handed him a note in large type. He looked at it for a long time.

'I'm not sure about the egg quota,' he said finally.

'It's still a lot of eggs,' said Ellie. 'I just like to be here when you eat them, just in case.'

He shrugged. 'And you better make sure to bring me back some duty-free.'

'Sure – what do you want? An enormous bar of Toblerone, or a little bear with goggles on?'

He gave her a hug.

'Look after yourself, Hedgehog. Lots of bad people in America.'

'I know. Well, the president for starters. Don't worry, I'll be careful. I'll just pop by a supermarket and buy an assault rifle.'

'Hedge. I'm not joking. Look, I know you're thirty . . .'

'Da-*ad.*'

'Sweetheart, you know you're all I've got. And you're still my little girl.'

'I know.' Ellie pulled herself away.

'Don't worry. If I learn to live like an American, by the time I get back I'll be your quite remarkably big girl.'

* * *

Colin looked tiny with his bags around him.

'I've never lived away from home before.'

Big Bastard was hovering nervously in the background.

'You'll be fine,' said Ellie encouragingly. 'Just remember; in other people's houses, you pee *in* the pan.'

Arthur hoisted the last of Colin's stuff up the steps.

'Here you are, chicken,' he said. 'Your *Sweet Valley High* books.'

'Now remember,' said Ellie. 'If you're cooking, Big Bastard only eats food beginning with B.'

From the hall, Big Bastard grunted.

'Baked beans, biryani, beer and Big Macs. Okay?'

Colin nodded solemnly.

'But don't let him have any chocolate buttons. His fingers are too stubby to get in the packet, and he gets all frustrated.'

'Tell him I eat Bird's Eye stuff too,' said Big Bastard anxiously.

'Oh yes. Fish fingers are fine. But brown sauce, not ketchup.'

'Okay,' said Colin, looking down.

'And bed by ten,' said Ellie.

'Hedge!' complained Arthur.

'Oh, you know I can't help it,' said Ellie. The taxi started honking outside.

Arthur slung an arm around her.

'Where are we meeting again?'

'Um . . . San Diego?'

'*Where* are we meeting again?'

'Um . . . San Taclaus?'

'You're very funny.'

He fished out her diary and opened it up. On every page it said, 'San Francisco minus-eight days, seven days,' etc.

'I'll see you there. In TEN DAYS.'

Ellie nodded feverishly.

'Honk honk,' said the taxi.

'Hooray! I'm off!' she said.

'Thanks for the room and everything,' said Colin shyly.

'Not at all. I'm just glad you remembered your Action Man pyjamas.'

'Thank fuck for a bit of peace and quiet,' said Big Bastard. 'Now I can watch porn in peace, without certain people talking deliberately loudly over it all the time.'

'It was only that one time,' said Ellie. 'Anyway, it wasn't me who invited your parents over in the first place.'

The cab honked again.

'Please go,' said Arthur. 'Partings make me teary, and if you miss this cab, you'll never fit that rucksack on Big Bastard's scooter.'

'And you won't get the chance to try, neither,' said Big Bastard. 'Come on Colin, let's watch the football. You'll like it. It's like ballet, right, only it's for blokes.'

'I am going to miss you all so much,' sighed Ellie, hoisting her ratty old pink and grey Bunac rucksack onto her back. She looked back at the shabby room, the worn curtains and the view of the bins with a fat arsed tabby sitting on the top.

'When I get back,' she vowed to herself, seeing the P60 sitting lonesomely on the sideboard, 'everything is going to be better than this.'

'And I'll show you how to make a Bovril. The spoon just stands up in the jar, then you never have to wash it.'

'*Everything* is going to be better than this.'

* * *

Julia sat alone in her small, immaculate flat, waiting

for Ellie and the taxi and staring at her ring finger. Loxy wasn't returning her calls. Part of her knew that all she had to do to stop this, to make everything better, was to call him up and say . . . what, exactly? Let's get married because one in two marriages fail, and that's across the general population including arranged marriages and strict Catholics, and in fact amongst late marrying metropolitan middle class spoilt independent thirty-year-olds it's probably two out of three and if you add in that mixed race marriages also have a high failure rate, they probably had a five out of four chance of getting divorced and when her parents had got divorced she'd fallen in love with a pony and tried to run away from home to live in a field?

Or that the thought of never seeing him again felt like the onset of a convulsive illness?

For the billionth time she cursed him for putting her in such an all or nothing state of affairs and throwing her calm, well organized life so entirely out of whack.

She looked at the phone, which declined to ring. She stared at her neatly arranged suitcase and wondered whether to add a packet of three.

Footloose

'Any chance of getting upgraded?'

The stewardess stared straight through them, as if nothing had been said. Julia punched Ellie on the arm.

'Did you pack these bags yourself?'

'Excuse me,' said Ellie, again. 'But we're on our way to America to . . . uhm . . . get married . . .'

'Umm . . . or *not*,' muttered Julia,

'. . . and we wondered if there was any possibility of an upgr . . .'

'No,' said the stewardess. 'I didn't answer you earlier because I thought it would be less embarrassing for you that way.'

Ellie took stock of the situation.

'Okay then,' she said. 'New lives here we come! Cattlestyle!'

'It's gate 354. The final call just rang so I'd get along now, little dogies.'

'No, it's okay, we want to hang around and see if they call our names out.'

Julia pulled desperately at Ellie's rucksack. 'Come *onnn* . . .'

'They won't, necessarily,' said the stewardess, smiling sweetly. 'It's up to me, you see.'

'Bye!' yelled Ellie as the two girls took off at full speed for departures.

'We won't be able to go to duty free now,' grumbled Julia as they ran from one end of the concourse to the other, desperately searching for the fifteen-foot sign that announced 'International Departures'.

'So what? So you can carry around a big sticky clanking bottle of Baileys for three thousand miles? Anyway, we're going to the land of the cheap EVERY-THING. God, I think I'm going to start smoking. And using petrol.'

'I just can't believe we're so late.' They thudded down the heavy metal corridors, running like the Bionic Man along the moving walkways and trying not to knock down more old ladies than strictly necessary.

'I just can't believe Big Bastard wouldn't give us a lift.'

Julia hit her with her prepacked bag of magazines.

'Have you never heard of the repetitive banality of evil?'

They could see a huge queue at passport control, and the TV screens were flashing 'final call'. Ellie fumbled for her ticket. Julia flapped frantically.

'Come on! Come on!'

'Okay, okay. Don't worry. It'll be fine. Andrew will be waiting.'

'They won't hold the plane for us, you know,' said Julia. 'They'll chuck the bags out on the tarmac.'

'For God's sake will you stop panicking? Okay, here it is. RUN!'

'Shit! Shit, hang on!' screamed Julia, stopping suddenly.

* * *

'Hold on! Stop!' Julia shouted again. She dropped her hand luggage and spun around.

'I cannot believe this,' said Ellie, unfurling herself. 'Are we late or not? Do they change the time zone as soon as we get in the airport?'

'Shut up. And look!'

Hanging over the departures barrier, waving desperately, was Loxy.

'Would the last remaining passengers *for* flight BA1273 to Los Angeles please go to Departures immediately. This flight is closing. The last remaining passengers *for* this flight please go to Gate 354 immediately. Thank you.'

'Oh my God, he did it!' said Ellie, her panic

momentarily lifted by the sheer movie emotion of the moment. 'He did a Ferris!'

'Lox!' squealed Julia, racing over and hugging him over the barrier. Some elderly people looked on, smiling and nodding encouragingly.

'I didn't say goodbye properly,' said Loxy, breathing in her hair. 'I'm really sorry.'

'I'm sorry too!' said Julia. They clutched one another.

'Would passengers Eversholt and Denford *please* go to Gate 354 immediately where this plane is ready *to* depart.'

Ellie looked round for everyone applauding. Nobody was.

'Just . . .' He pulled her tighter. 'I love you. You love me. Come on. Let's just go get married. Let's get a plane somewhere else. There's a chapel here. Let's just get married RIGHT NOW on the CONCOURSE.'

As he yelled this, people were gradually starting to clear a space around them. A couple of Americans whooped and cheered.

'I'm not going to let her go!' shouted Loxy, galvanized by the scene. 'We're getting MARRIED.'

People started to clap and sigh.

'Ah,' said Julia.

'Passengers Eversholt and Denford – your luggage will be removed from this flight if you don't present yourselves *at* Gate 354 immediately . . .'

Julia shot a desperate look at Ellie, who flagged down one of the small carts.

'Well?' said Ellie. 'Are you coming or not?'

'Loxy,' said Julia. 'I already told you. I just . . . I just *don't know*.'

His face turned to stone. The cart came over and Ellie jumped on it. Loxy lowered his arms very, very slowly.

The crowd started to boo.

'What!' yelled Julia crossly. 'This is the noughties, for fuck's sake. A woman has the right to . . . oh, fuck it.'

'Miss, you're going to have to go NOW,' said the man on the cart.

'Passengers Eversholt and Denford . . .' said the speaker.

'JULIA!' said Ellie and Loxy, in simultaneous anguish. Julia looked desperately from one to the other. Then, suddenly she jumped onto the cart.

'Okay, okay. GO!'

The cart started to move off at top speed – i.e. about five miles an hour – leaving Loxy standing desolate in its wake, holding the ring box and being patted on the back by bystanders.

About a hundred feet on, however, Ellie had the misfortune to take a glance back, and spied a familiar figure barrelling its way through the crowd behind them.

'Jesus,' she said.

'Hedgehog!' the voice cried.

'Aw, Jesus,' said Ellie again.

And then, drowning out the tannoy and the hub-bub of the entire airport, from a figure standing outlined against the departure lounge, came a very bad, very out-of-tune version of something that might have been, but wasn't quite 'Baker Street' played by a skinny man with a mullet.

* * *

Filing onto a plane late, Ellie reflected, couldn't be entirely unlike filing into a dock when everyone knows you've done it. In fact, judging from some of the looks they were getting, people would be happier if she'd chopped up her father with an axe and eaten the bits, rather than be making BA flight 1273 miss its time slot from terminal four and have to join the very long queue for naughty jumbo jets.

'Can I have a gin and tonic?'

'No,' said the tight faced stewardess. 'Not until we leave the ground. If that ever happens.'

'No,' Ellie repeated sarkily to herself when the stewardess has gone, 'Not until you get promoted from your job as Wobbly Waitress – if that ever happens.'

Ellie studied the film menu. 'Oh look,' she said, pointing it out to Julia. 'They've got *Runaway Bride*.'

'Ha ha ha. You're very funny.' Julia took the menu off her. 'Oh God! Look at them all! They've got *Love Story, The English Patient, Titanic* and *Terms of Endearment.* Don't they have any films called *The Two People Who Had Doubts About Getting Married But Then Everything Worked Out Just Fine?*'

'It's in the Science Fiction and Fantasy section,' said Ellie.

Julia tried to stare out of the window, but it was miles away. All there was to stare at was a small child trying to catch her attention by kicking the side of her chair. He seemed to be conserving quite a lot of energy in his kicks, though, and looked like he was heading for a long distance endurance record.

'I think these people hate us,' said Ellie, watching a grim stewardess performing a safety demonstration.

'Look at the expression on her face. I think she wants us all to die.'

'What do you expect during the safety demonstration – a cabaret? I just want her to get it over with, so we can get on with the true fun of air travel – being allowed to drink at absurd times of the day. And I really think I need one NOW.'

Julia had already reset her watch.

'It's four o'clock in the morning in Los Angeles,' she said. 'That seems to me a perfectly reasonable time to be out drinking.'

'Absolutely,' said Ellie.

They eventually managed to clink the first of their plastic glasses of double gin and tonic together.

'We're on holiday!'

'To holidays!'

'To Andrew!'

'To finding . . . things . . .'

'Do you think I'll get back that twenty-inch waist I had at sixteen?' said Ellie.

'Only if you start wearing braces again. It's a mysterious power trade-off.'

'Huh, you can talk, Mrs Pimple Head.'

'You were always one for the snappy nicknames, weren't you?'

'Snappy nicknames, snappy knicker-elastic,' said Ellie. 'Can't beat either of them.'

* * *

'I hope they caught that flight,' said Siobhan, moodily sipping her Cosmopolitan at Elms that evening. 'Although Patrick paying for tickets that nobody used would also have its appeal.'

Loxy winced and explained what had happened at the airport.

'I'm sorry,' said Siobhan, patting him.

Loxy shrugged. 'Forget it. How have you been today?'

Siobhan shrugged in return. 'I think I've come through the white hot revenge mode, unfortunately.

I'm kind of getting into the hours of insane crying. They BETTER have a good time, that's all I can say.'

'Hmm,' said Loxy, staring into space. 'Not *too* good.'

'Well, obviously,' said Siobhan. Then she tapped Loxy on the arm. 'Don't worry about Julia. You know she'll be incredibly sensible.'

* * *

'Wha' time is it?' slurred Julia fifteen hours later, staggering across the concourse.

'Dunno. You've got . . . bags . . .'

'Lossa bags. An . . . still gaw this.'

Julia held up two full plastic miniatures of gin.

Ellie rubbed her gritty eyes and clumsily reached for one. Julia punched her on the shoulder.

'You shouldn't; you *shouldn't* have said communist, to nice man, no, shouldn't.'

'People should . . . take . . . a bloody joke . . .'

'Look! Nother man!'

A gigantic guy wearing a yellow jacket was ushering people into cabs. They staggered up to him and he bundled them into one speedily.

'Where you goin', pliz?' said the cab driver without looking at them.

Ellie looked at Julia, whose head had flopped to one side. With effort, she straightened up again.

'79a Balham Park Road,' said Julia in her best posh voice, enunciating every syllable.

'Huh?' said the driver, turning round.

'No!' said Ellie. 'No! Los Angeles!'

'Yes pliz. Where in Los Angeles, pliz?'

Julia took one look out of the window, her head flopped again and she fell asleep instantly, and all Ellie's shunting, or the frantic honking of the cabs behind them, couldn't wake her.

Ellie fumbled through her handbag, but couldn't see anything that looked like a hotel address, even with one hand held over her eye. And she knew, even in her fuddled state, that the chances of getting into Julia's password-protected Palm Pilot were infinitesimal.

She sat up and stared at the lights in the distance for a second trying to think of somewhere she knew in Los Angeles.

'Take me back to the Hotel California,' she said woozily.

'I'm afraid I don't know that address, ma'am.'

Ellie blinked heavily and forced herself to try and think of a hotel.

'The Ritz, please,' she said finally, and sank back into unconsciousness.

* * *

Pitch dark it may have been, but Ellie awoke anyway

132

on the stroke of 6am, staring at the ceiling and trying to identify where the hell in the universe she was and what on earth she might have been doing. Perhaps, she speculated, she'd been in a car accident and was now in hospital. That would explain the headache and exonerate her from having done anything embarrassing. Still, she was fully clothed at least. With intense effort she stretched out her arm and managed to turn on the bedside light.

'Fuck!'

The ornate and overdone surroundings gradually filtered into view under the warm lighting. On another double bed, Julia was snoring soundly, tucked up in crisp white sheets. Their bags were very carefully lined up against the wall.

'Arse!' said Ellie, and decided to wish for death. In a hideous flashback sequence reminiscent of *Altered States*, she recalled various choice scenes from the night before, which included somebody falling up some steps (the presence of a rather large bloodied scab on her knee seemed to indicate that it might have been her), the desperate waving of a credit card; some overtly solicitous room staff. And, oh God, oh God, she was wearing a crisp pair of cotton pyjamas. Ellie had never owned a crisp pair of cotton pyjamas in her entire life. Either these were magic pyjamas, or the alternative didn't bear thinking about.

She pondered whether to wake Julia or not. Get the

agony over with quickly, or give her a happy hour or two more of oblivion. The problem was solved by a desperate need to go to the bathroom and the rather sudden rediscovery of the scarred knee and what felt suspiciously like a twisted ankle.

'Christicles!' she shrieked, on attempting to stand up.

Julia's eyes blinked open immediately in alarm

'What? What is it? Ohmigod. Chuffing hell.'

She clasped her head tightly.

'What the Jesus fuck is going on?'

'I don't exactly know,' said Ellie, hopping about on one leg and yelping, 'but I'm hoping they've got plenty of Red Bull in the minibar.'

Julia shook her aching head.

'Oh, Jesus Christ. Where are we?'

'We're in America.'

'Yes, thank you, I remember that much. Ouch.'

Ellie put the kettle on, and examined the china cups tentatively.

'We're in LA . . .'

'God, I must have fallen asleep in the cab. Jet lag.'

Ellie snorted loudly.

'Jesus. And what the hell am I wearing?'

'Magic pyjamas,' said Ellie quickly.

'Did you get me changed?'

'Umm, yes, that would have been more logical.'

'Into pyjamas that say . . .'

Julia gradually took in her surroundings.

'This is a bit bloody nice for a Holiday Inn,' she said slowly.

'I didn't realize it was such a different chain over here.'

'Ah,' said Ellie.

She winched back the curtains a little and, sure enough, the sun was starting to come up. Over the ocean. The famous view of endless palm trees stared back at them through the sunny windows of the thirty-fifth floor.

'Well . . . welcome to America.'

* * *

Julia was staring miserably into space. Ellie would have been staring miserably into space had she not just been distracted by the largest plate of pancakes she'd ever seen in her life being set down in front of her.

'So you're telling me,' said Julia slowly, pulling on her fourth orange juice, 'that we just spent half our allocated holiday budget on the best hotel in the world and we don't remember a thing about it?'

'I think,' said Ellie carefully, licking maple syrup off her fingers, 'that that shows a certain amount of style.'

'I think,' said Julia, 'that that shows we have just burnt hundreds and hundreds of dollars.'

'Well, it's not like it's real money,' said Ellie. 'That's probably only about a fiver.'

'It is a *bit* more than a fiver, Hedgehog! Jesus. Why the hell couldn't you have learned the name of the hotel we were supposed to be staying at? Why couldn't you just have barked out "Holiday Inn"? That would have been at least *logical*.'

'I don't know. Why couldn't you have kept yourself from passing out in the gutter, like the first time we ever got into Fat Sam's and you discovered Cinzano and lemonade and thought you were being chatted up by one of A Flock of Seagulls?'

They had found a diner across the road, after realizing that having breakfast at the Ritz would cost the same as their car hire. They had, however, had to hail a taxi to get them across the road. The suited bellboys had given them knowing looks as they stumped in crushed combats through the sumptuous lobby.

'Oh my God,' whispered Ellie. 'Do you think they took photographs?'

'I know they *took* photographs,' Julia whispered back, 'what's worrying me is, do they *sell* photographs?'

Colour mounting, they walked through the held-open doors into warm sunshine and waving palm trees. Beautiful blonde people were rollerblading down towards the sand. The sky was a hazy blue.

'Ow,' said Ellie. 'The sun's hurting my eyes.'

'And I wish all these people would get the fuck out of our way,' said Julia.

Now they were sitting sulkily in the little diner, trying to see at what point the waitress's indefatigable good will would be tested beyond endurance with their endless free coffee refills.

'This your first time in LA?' she had asked when they came in. They had nodded, trying not to disturb their hangovers too much.

'This the first time you've tasted a cup of cwaffee?' she asked now, testily, after being summoned to refill Ellie's mug for the seventh time.

'What are those funny stars up there that look like tiny suns and yet shine in the day?' asked Ellie, pointing to the overhead lights. Julia kicked her hard on her sore ankle and smiled winningly at the waitress.

'Are you an actress?' she asked, interested. The woman looked like the type who goes out with footballers and sells their stories to the tabloids. Her fingernails were frightening and her hair a candyfloss-textured blonde. Every time she leaned over to refill their coffee cups, her breasts stayed where they were.

'No, I really am your waitress. Years of college. It's a wonderful job.'

'I thought Americans weren't supposed to have a sense of irony,' said Ellie.

'You're using irony in the wrong sense. Ironic, isn't it? And that's your last cup of coffee,' said the waitress. 'Now, excuse me. I've just got to go and schmooze those disgusting middle-aged men over there, because yup, lucky me, I am indeed an actress.'

The table-full of overweight guys in sunglasses grinned and waved, pointing out the waitress's breasts to each other.

'Whatever happened to dumb blondes?' said Ellie.

'They just write the parts that way,' said the waitress. 'Coming, sweeties!' she cooed to the men's table.

'Well, well,' said Ellie. 'We're learning already.'

'We have to check out of that hotel,' said Julia. 'We're going to be here a long time. Our credit cards might not hold out.'

'I think mine is looking a bit wobbly already.'

'Well you shouldn't have bought all that stupid shit on the plane then. You don't even wear perfume. And you don't need two watches.'

'Course I do. London time and LA time. I'm *international*.'

'And what about the aeroplane-shaped pencil case . . .'

'Okay, okay.'

'And we'd better pick up a car. I have a funny

feeling their underground system might not be up to much.'

'Then we can start our quest!' said Ellie excitedly.

'Or go lie on the beach . . .' said Julia.

'Quest! Quest! Quest!'

'Oh, well, okay. We should get hold of a phone book.'

'A *phone* book?'

'Yes. How else are we going to find him?'

'A *phone* book?! That's . . . the least romantic thing I've ever heard. Anyway, I don't think big movie stars are in the phone book.'

'No, big movie stars aren't. He probably is though.'

'Don't be mean. I think we should go to somewhere cool, where the stars hang out. We've got to let this happen naturally. Ehm, excuse me?' Ellie beckoned the waitress over.

'No,' said the waitress. 'That much caffeine can't possibly be good for you.'

'Not that,' said Ellie. 'Although, now you mention it . . .'

The waitress sighed. 'Well, it's your coffee breath . . .' she said. 'I wouldn't want to be kissing you. Unless you're a producer . . . ?'

Ellie shook her head.

'No, I didn't think so. You said "excuse me".'

'Um,' said Julia, self-consciously. 'Where do the movie stars hang out?'

139

The waitress barked with laughter. 'Planet Hollywood, where d'ya think? Or at my place, of course. Why, who are you after?'

They explained.

'That's the dumbest idea I ever heard.'

'Yeah? You're the one who took a job as a waitress,' said Ellie.

'Have you thought about trying the phone book?'

'Yes, yes we have.'

'Okay. Well, you could try The Sky Bar I suppose. On Sunset. Although I'm telling you, you're going to need to wear a bit less clothing than that to have a hope of getting in.'

'How much less?'

'I'd say eighty, eighty-five percent.'

'That only leaves my swimming costume,' said Ellie.

'You haven't got a bikini?'

'Ever seen a sand dune collapse? That's what I look like in a bikini.'

'Better make it the bathing suit. And put some make-up on. You both look like ghosts.'

'Don't they go for "pale and interesting", out here?'

'No, they go for "slutty and obvious".'

'Interesting,' said Ellie. 'Let's phone up Caroline "Snotface" Lafayette.'

'Thanks for your help,' said Julia.

'Not at all,' said the waitress. 'If you were looking for Rob Lowe I'd come with you.'

'*See?*' said Julia to Ellie. '*Everyone* says that.'

'Yes, well, if that's what we were doing it would just turn into a sad little fan hunt,' said Ellie. There was a silence.

'Well, have a good day y'all!' said the waitress.

* * *

The hotel receptionist looked at them sniffily, even though Ellie was loudly declaiming their plan to 'just drop by the SKY BAR'.

'I'm sure he's really nice inside, like in *Pretty Woman*,' she whispered to Julia, who was trying to quietly check them out without drawing any attention to themselves.

'I must ask that *if* you come here again you book in advance,' said the receptionist.

'. . . or Norman Bates, perhaps.'

Julia had on her best 'I check out of five-star hotel receptions all the time' face on as she handed over her credit card, crossing her fingers tightly behind her back.

'Thank you ma'am.' Relieved, they headed for the waiting cab.

'Oh, and ma'am . . . you left these.'

And he held up the two half-empty gin miniatures.

* * *

'Well, this is nice,' said Julia, looking around their new tiny dark hotel room tentatively. They'd already seen one gigantic cockroach skitter across the floor.

'Jules, I can hear gunfire.'

'That's not gunfire, it's . . . well, I'm sure it's fine. Let's just get changed and go . . .'

But Ellie was passed out on the bed, snoring rather more like a warthog than a Hedgehog.

Pretty in Pink

They stood outside the roped-back entrance feeling entirely stupid. After waking up at stupid o'clock again that morning, starving hungry, they had wandered out of the grotty hotel and finally made it to the car hire centre after waiting two hours for a cab.

'They have cab companies here?' the reception guy had said.

'I thought you were meant to be the most advanced nation on earth,' sneered Ellie.

'We are, ma'am. That's why we all drive our own cars.'

Then they'd picked up their little Toyota, which looked like somebody had taken a real car and chipped out the inside. They both immediately got in the wrong side. They did this every time they got in a car for the entire trip.

'Okay,' said Julia, once they'd swapped over, examining the layout. 'At least it's got gears.'

'Those are gears? They look more like lollipops.'

'Shoosh. I need to concentrate.'

Outside the dusty, hot car hire place were ten lanes of freeway steaming from somewhere they didn't know to somewhere they didn't know either. And Julia had forgotten to buy a map, and Ellie was continuing to have a mental block about the name of their hotel. The sticky plastic seating was already adhering itself to the backs of their thighs and secretly they both wished they were back at home.

'Well, faint heart never won fair movie star,' said Ellie finally, and shook the keys gently in Julia's face.

'Okay, okay,' said Julia, her face grim. She fired up the puttering little engine and gradually shifted the car away from the door. The owner watched them with marked trepidation.

'How far is it to San Francisco again?'

'Oh, about half an hour I think,' said Ellie. 'It's in the same state.'

'Well, let's just take a pootle around town, get acquainted. We're not going out till tonight.'

Almost instantly, a truck as big as the side of a house came tearing down the freeway, almost landing on top of them. Next, an actual *house* came tearing down, white, wood framed, securely fastened to a flatbed truck.

'SHIT!' screamed the two girls, Julia clenching the wheel.

'Oh my God,' said Ellie as the danger passed. 'Maybe we should have planned this trip on bicycles.'

'Yes, bicycles would be a *lot* safer on this road,' said Julia, still white and breathing hard. 'It's okay. We're okay. We're sitting in a tin can balanced on a hairdryer built by people who've never had the slightest reason to like Americans. We're going to be fine.'

She turned on the radio. Thankfully, out came some familiar 80s chords. Ellie turned it up.

'Now THIS,' she said, 'is beginning to sound like Los Angeles.' And a lost Los Angeles band blared back,

'TAKE YOUR BABY BY THE HAND. AND DO THE NEXT THING THAT YOU PLANNED . . .'

Ellie turned down the windows, so they could let their hair flow out of the gaps and, loudly and happily, they puttered West, into the heart of Los Angeles.

* * *

Unfortunately, as they started to discover an hour later, Los Angeles doesn't have a heart, physically or metaphorically.

'How on earth can this still be the same street?' said Ellie. The radio was now playing 'Don't Stop

145

Thinking About Tomorrow'. Julia hadn't relaxed her grip any, and they still didn't have a map.

'It's not a street, it's a boulevard,' said Julia grimly. 'With, so far, 11,000 houses on it.'

'Wow. That must be crap if you get off at the wrong end. And what about the postman . . . I'll shut up now.'

The sun squinted through the window.

'Is that the sea?' said Ellie finally, pointing to a shining line, 'Or am I going blind?'

'It is! It's the sea!' shouted Julia excitedly.

'Woo hoo! We're . . . actually getting somewhere!'

'Woo hoo! God, I suppose we are still in LA, aren't we? What if the whole of the West Coast is actually really built up and we've just driven to Seattle?'

'No, look, there's a sign. This is Venice beach!'

'I didn't think we'd made it as far as Venice . . . oh my God!'

They drew up on the seafront. Stretched out for miles in front of them were endless acres of golden sand, blue sea, and hordes of utterly fabulous-looking women and utterly ridiculous-looking men. And some you couldn't tell which were which.

'Look at all that *muscle*,' breathed Julia.

'They're all so *shiny*,' said Ellie, stepping out of the car.

She caught sight of her own reflection in the car window and looked at the shimmering tanned dancing

146

girls on the beach; playing volleyball, rollerblading, wandering around slowly in bikinis and tossing their hair a lot, or simply lying on the sand, revelling in their own bronzed, toned fabulousness.

'Jules, am I fat?' yelled Ellie.

Julia locked up the car.

'Of course not.' Then she took in the whole scene. 'Oh. Well, compared to what?'

'I *am*. I'm locally fat,' said Ellie, glumly, a cheerfully British mismatched uppy/downy person on the whole. 'Oh no. Do you think they'll throw things at me?'

'Do you throw things at people you think are fat?'

'No . . . well, there was that early morning DJ . . .'

'Come on,' said Julia. 'Let's get changed. FINALLY I feel like we're on holiday, and not trapped in some screaming nightmare.'

* * *

'If you scream one more time I will just walk out of here and drive away,' Julia was saying threateningly, four hours later.

'But it's so *sooorrre.*'

They were back in the hotel room. Julia was helplessly trying to apply E45 to Ellie's third-degree burns.

'How many times did I tell you to get out of the sun?'

147

'But I can stay out longer than you – you're a blonde!'

'You've known me twenty years, and you know my hair colour isn't really blonde, Hedge.'

'OUCH! Oh, yeah. I wasn't sure how that worked.' Ellie writhed in pain. 'Could you just fill the entire bath with cream and I'll just go lie in it?'

Julia tried to smear the cream as gently as she could.

'God, Hedge, what were you *thinking*?'

Ellie screwed up her eyes.

'Umm . . . I was thinking, "every year I burn myself really badly so I must remember to get out of the sun in time *this* year."'

'*And* . . . ?'

'No, that was genuinely what I was thinking. Then suddenly it was too late. Argh.'

'But you have *two watches*!'

'I've got an entire sense of touch, and if that can't save me, nothing can. Ooh!'

'Do you really still want to go to this Sky Bar place tonight? I'm worried you might get a little feverish. Plus, you screamed all the way back in the car.'

'That car is holding onto several layers of my skin, I'll have you know. We're not exactly friends.'

'Well, do you want to just stay in tonight, and we'll go tomorrow night?'

'No,' groaned Ellie, standing up. 'What am I going

to do in this shit hole, play stomp the cockroach? I think I feel better now. As long as I don't come into physical contact with anything.'

'Well, given that we have to wear the skimpiest clothes we have, that's going to work out just fine.'

Ellie, with much wincing, slipped into a red shift dress she'd brought from French Connection before they left.

'That . . . doesn't look too bad,' said Julia, as they peered into the dark mirror. In fact, Ellie was the same colour as a big lobster, and the dress made her look as if she was on fire.

Ellie gazed at her reflection in the mirror.

'Oh my God,' she said. 'You know who I look like here?'

'Somebody who's very, *very* embarrassed?' said Julia.

'No, *look!* I'm Molly in reverse!'

'Molly in reverse,' said Julia. 'Now, why wouldn't I have known that?'

'Pink skin, red dress instead of pink dress and red hair! It's fate I tell you.'

'Fate for *what*?'

'If I wear this dress tonight, I'll meet Andrew. Don't you see? It's too coincidental.'

'We're definitely not going now,' said Julia. 'You're delirious.'

'It's a sign.'

'What if you meet Andrew in reverse? He'll have

a really wide chin and narrow forehead and you wouldn't like him at *all*.'

* * *

Julia had eventually managed to coax Ellie out of the red dress and into something which made her look less like a volcanic pustule, and now they were hanging behind the ropes at the Sky Bar on Sunset Boulevard, glancing at each other nervously.

'You on the guest list?' asked one of the alarmingly attractive bouncers.

'No, but I love you both,' whispered Ellie to Julia.

'No,' said Julia. 'We've just arrived from London for a couple of days and we were really hoping we could go and, you know, take a look around.'

The bouncers looked at each other and shrugged. It helped that Julia stood almost entirely shielding Ellie with her body. Julia's blonde hair and long legs did the trick and one of the bouncers pulled back the rope, then did a huge double-take when he saw Ellie.

'This your first day in LA?' he said, looking aghast at her flayed legs and arms.

'No, I've been here ten years. I like to do this every day.'

Inside a woman surely too beautiful to be doing this for a living, asked to check their ID.

'They think I'm under eighteen?' said Ellie in disbelief.

'It's twenty-one here ma'am,' explained the attendant.

'You think I'm under twenty-one? Fantastic.'

'No ma'am, we have to check everyone who looks under thirty.'

'You think I'm under *thirty*?' She dragged out her passport. 'Well, better than nothing I suppose.'

'She's not,' said Julia helpfully.

'Yes, thank you, lifelong friend.' They bounced up the circular staircase, and outside into the bar beyond. There they stopped and gaped.

'Christ,' said Ellie. 'This is one up on the Dog and Duck.'

In front of them was a large terrace, shrouded by trees which were dotted with fairy lights. The end of the terrace had huge pillars framing a vast view of Los Angeles, the lights endless. In the middle was a cool-watered marbled swimming pool. Beautiful people were being brought sticky coloured drinks by other beautiful people. It was a perfect fantasy of a Hollywood bar.

The girls both gasped then attempted to look nonchalant.

'Are you sure we haven't stumbled onto an advertising set,' whispered Julia. 'For one of those products for people who are better than you are?'

'I'm not sure . . . God, isn't that xxx over there?' said Ellie, naming a famous television star.

'It can't possibly be,' said Julia dismissively. 'He's got his tongue down the throat of another bloke.'

'Huh,' said Ellie. 'A gay actor. That could never happen.'

'I still prefer to think of him as an army vet who solves crimes in his spare time, if that's okay with you.'

'Oh God. Look, that fifty-year-old guy's snogging a teenager!'

'Should we tell someone?'

'I don't know. I suspect that's okay here.'

'Yeah . . . who was it Catherine Zeta-Jones married again? Was it Michael Douglas or his dad?'

They sat down – Ellie extremely gingerly – and were too relieved to be served Cosmopolitans to do the necessary currency conversion. If they had, they would have realized that there might be another downgrade in hotelling necessary.

'It's like the UN of beautiful women,' said Ellie, in awe, looking at the multicultural perfection surrounding them. 'Even if they don't know what UN stands for.'

'Is one of my breasts larger than the other?' asked Julia, looking at her reflection in the water.

'I think, while we're here,' said Ellie, 'we should just get off this perfection kick. Just accept that in this currency we're a couple of trolls and everyone else here can ignore us. And remember, anyway, if someone starts chatting you up it's because they want to put you in a porn film.'

'Thanks for that little vote of confidence,' said Julia, slurping her drink.

'That's okay, troll-face.'

* * *

Two Cosmopolitans later, they were experimenting with their new found invisibility. People's eyes passed over them as they would over dog shit on the pavement. Ellie had already flashed both breasts (one at a time) and was trying to get Julia to pick her nose when a short, chunky guy came up to them. He had fine features and an all-American corn-fed glow, getting slightly older, on him. They'd noticed him before, being hailed by various groups of girls, but ignoring them and moving on.

'Hey . . . you two new in town?' he said, looking at Julia.

'No,' said Ellie immediately. 'And we don't want to make any porn, thank you.'

'If that's okay,' added Julia, in case they sounded impolite.

'Hey, *I'm* not in porn!' he said, throwing his arms wide and giving a big laugh. He held the position for several seconds then gradually brought his arms down.

The girls stared at him.

'Jeez, if anyone in here is old enough to recognize me it ought to be you two.'

'Hey! I'm practically under eighteen,' said Ellie.

'It's the colour,' said the guy sorrowfully, shaking his head. 'Oh God, I'm so depressed.'

'What's the matter?' said Julia kindly.

'Don't you know who I am? From the movies?'

They looked at him.

'You were once inside a wookie suit?' asked Ellie.

'You were somebody's best friend at college who treated women really badly but got his comeuppance at the end?' guessed Julia.

The man sat down beside them.

'*Soul Man?*' he said.

'Oh my God!' said Ellie. 'You're . . . you're . . .'

'C. Thomas Howell!' said Julia, exultantly. 'Our first real life movie star!'

'It's Thom now actually.' He took a reflective draw on his beer. '*Newsweek*'s "New Star" of 1986.'

'Oh my God! Do you want to come and join us?'

'Yeah, whatever . . .' he said, glancing around the bar. 'You just arrived?' he asked, looking pointedly at Ellie's puce legs.

'No, I was trying to change my skin colour to get into an elite college,' said Ellie.

'God, that movie was fun wasn't it?' Thom said this and shrugged casually, as though of course it was

154

no big deal really, he almost couldn't be bothered bringing it up.

The girls made encouraging noises. Ellie's left leg was twitching uncontrollably in excitement. Score! This wouldn't have happened if she was still at Rooney & Co! Although they sold Rodney Bewes an apartment once.

'So, what are you up to these days?' asked Julia encouragingly.

'Made three straight-to-video movies this year,' he said, ordering them all beers.

'Oh, that's fantastic! They're the *best* kind!' said Ellie. 'Do you do any where beautiful prostitutes get murdered?'

'You're still a movie star!' said Julia, and he grinned very nicely, so they told him about their quest.

'Yep,' he said. 'Actors know everything alright.'

'Why is that?' asked Ellie. 'Pop stars are always being asked things too.'

'Search me,' he said. 'You know, in the eighties they used to ask me about things like Star Wars.'

'You were never in *Star Wars*,' said Julia.

'I mean the defence programme.'

'No,' said Ellie.

'Absolutely. All the major political events of the day. It's important to have input from celebrities don't you think? In fact, why the heck doncha do your quest with me?'

'But then we'd have to go home tomorrow,' said Ellie.

'Do you really think you could help?' asked Julia tentatively.

'Shit, I know nothing. But could be worth a shot.'

Ellie looked at Julia suspiciously, who shrugged back.

'Okay,' said Ellie.

'Okay,' said Thom. 'My yoga teacher taught me this.' He sat back and crossed his legs.

'Crossing your legs. You're practically a guru,' said Ellie. 'Okay, here's what we want to know. Is it just us or, after all the promises we got during the 1980s, is grown-up modern life disappointingly hollow?'

Thom pulled on his beer and looked thoughtful. 'Hmm. Interesting. I don't know. Might be just you. Do you have a lot of personality flaws?'

'Aha!' said Ellie. 'But perhaps I'm only responding to my disappointing environment!'

'Neh,' said Thom. 'You're just older, aren't you. You just get older and you get cynical.'

'Is that true?' said Julia. 'Seems to me these days *everyone* is cynical.'

Thomas thought about this for a while.

'Hmm,' he said. 'Well, you know. Why wouldn't you be? I don't know about Great Britain, but you know, we all grew up with Reagan as a president and he told us things were just going to be bully brilliant for ever.'

'And they weren't?' guessed Ellie.

'Well, look at it this way for starters. How many black Brat Pack stars were there?'

They looked at him for a second.

'Just me,' he said.

'And you're not . . .' Julia decided not to state the obvious.

'Why was that?'

'Didn't want to mess up our nice little middle class America with any actual facts, did they?'

'Hang on,' said Ellie. 'Please be very careful with my belief that Brat Pack movies are documentaries.'

Thom laughed and slapped her on the back. Ellie bit her lip and managed not to scream.

'Okay. Just pointing it out. It's just, Hollywood only really likes poverty gaps when they look like Molly Ringwald. Or, I guess, me for a bit. They don't really care much any more.'

'Hmm.' Ellie was intrigued. 'But you're doing okay?'

'Sure,' he said. 'I'm still working. And I got out of the Brat Pack alive. And I'm not one of the billions of let down wage slaves who saw the jobs come and saw the jobs go and don't trust any-one.'

'Oh, we're them,' said Julia.

'Huh,' he said. 'Yeah, my wife works in market-ing. Well, until the next reorganization, which will probably be in about a month's time. But for me, you know, I'm pretty good. That's my best attempt to stifle my cynicism.'

'Do you know?' said Ellie. 'You're not a bad guru.'

'Thank you,' he said solemnly. 'And it's good practice for me – in my next role I'm playing a psy-chiatrist tracking a serial killer who attacks beautiful prostitutes.'

'You're doing great,' said Ellie. 'And anyway, you're famous. Society has pre-conditioned us to find you cool. And, um, do you know how we could get in touch with Andrew McCarthy?'

'Oh, God, Andy.' He shrugged. 'I haven't seen him for years. He's not a mad party-scene person.'

'No, he wouldn't be,' said Ellie dreamily.

'Have you thought about trying the phone book?'

'Yes thank you.'

'Alright. Well, hey, great to meet you.'

'And you,' said Julia. 'No-one at home will believe us when we tell them.'

'Especially since when we tell them you'll be John Cusack,' said Ellie.

Over by the pool there was a cacophony of over-excited screaming as various nubile teenagers were thrown into the pool, the girls often without tops on.

Thom looked over with an expression of distaste.

'The bikinis are back,' he said. 'The cocaine's back.'
He sighed. 'Here we go again . . .'

And he kissed them politely and disappeared back
into the crowd.

* * *

'Well,' Ellie was saying, back in their tiny, non air-
conditioned bedroom. 'I say that's not a bad start.'

Julia nodded wearily.

'Are you sure you don't think he was trying to chat
me up?'

'For the four thousandth time,' said Julia. 'He
accidentally touched you on the leg when he was
walking off and you screamed the place down.'

'Our making friends with movie stars skills are
clearly second to none,' said Ellie, ignoring her.

'Yes, although I think that was probably a kinder-
garten class . . .'

'But a good one. Out of interest, does Loxy like
Brat Pack movies?'

'Hmm,' said Julia thoughtfully. 'No, he can't stand
them. I just assumed he thought they were for girls.'

'It hurts to lie down on these sheets, I'll never sleep,'
said Ellie. 'Snort. Zzzz.'

'Tomorrow,' said Julia to herself, 'we are definitely
trying the phone book.'

* * *

Siobhan stepped out of her car into the November drizzle and sighed. Suddenly she could do with a bit of sunshine in her days. And she was getting tired of having to referee the boys all by herself, especially on chilli night.

'Hey!' she shouted, feeling her way through Big Bastard's dark and cluttered hall. The bulb had gone and there was obviously a Mexican stand-off going on in the building as to who was going to change it.

'Hey! Anyone there!'

Big Bastard grunted.

'Don't just grunt! You could come and . . . welcome me in or something.'

'Hello sweetheart! We've all been here for hours,' said Arthur, coming out of the kitchen. 'We waited for you and tidied up the kitchen cupboards. I didn't even think they *made* Crispy Pancakes anymore. Beef flavour. YUG.'

'Well, you knew I'd be late,' said Siobhan. 'I've got a big job on . . .'

'A big bathroom job,' said Colin, sniggering.

'Hello Colin,' said Siobhan indulgently. 'Taking a break from your Tonka trucks?'

'What are Tonka trucks?' said Colin. 'Are they like Transformers? I've been helping Arthur clean out the cupboards and cook dinner.'

Siobhan looked mischievously at Arthur.

'Did you let him lick the spoon?'

160

Arthur made a face at her and ushered her into the living room.

'Loxy's here. Go cheer him up.'

'Ah yes. I am so good at cheering up boys. I give them the necessary moral fibre to go out and find somebody better than me. Let me at him.'

Loxy and Big Bastard were slouched in opposite easy chairs. They didn't look up when she walked in.

'Hi guys!' said Siobhan heartily. 'How's it going?'

Loxy lifted his heavy-lidded eyes. 'Have you heard from . . .'

Siobhan shook her head. Loxy sighed.

'Which means they're probably having a great time,' said Siobhan. 'If they're dead, I'm sure we'd have heard. Or, you know, if they get arrested they're allowed one phone call . . .' her voice trailed away. 'How've you been?'

'Fine,' shrugged Loxy. 'Apart from the non-sleeping, non-eating bits.'

'What about your non-shagging bits?' said Big Bastard suddenly, and choked with laughter.

'Ellie was right,' said Siobhan, 'when she wondered what the point of you was.'

'Merely adding to the gaiety of nations,' said Big Bastard. 'Oh no – that's those two in there.'

'Hasn't she left a number telling you where she is?' Siobhan asked Loxy softly.

'No,' Loxy shrugged. 'At this point I don't even know if she's ever talking to me again. I can't believe I went to the airport.'

'It was a lovely thing to do,' said Siobhan, sincerely. 'Really romantic and honest. There's not enough people around like you. Most of them are shits.'

'You should take it as time off, mate,' said Big Bastard. 'Go out and get shagging. There's some right tasty dark birds out there . . . I'd do that Naomi Campbell. Do you know her? Oww! Owwwww! What the fuck did I say?'

'Now, unless you want the other stiletto, you shit,' said Siobhan, 'and reporting to the Equal Opportunities Commission, I'd recommend you get the fuck out of your own sitting room.'

'Christ,' said Big Bastard. 'I think some people round here need an Equal Opportunities Shagging Commission, so they've got a chance of getting themselves fucked out of their DEMENTED MOOD-SWINGS. I'm going off to see what the fairy blossoms have gotten up to.' He raised himself up heavily and lumbered off to the kitchen. 'Hey . . . don't throw those fucking crispy pancakes away . . .'

'I brought a bottle of wine,' said Siobhan, slumping onto the floor. 'Want a glass?'

Loxy nodded disconsolately.

'You know, I don't think I understand women,' he said as she poured.

'That's because men's brains are wired to their bollocks,' said Siobhan. 'The circulation doesn't work right. Don't worry. You're doing okay. In fact, I wish I had someone . . .' She tailed off.

'What?'

'Nothing. She's lucky. At least you're trying.' They each took a sip and stared into space.

'Chilli's up!' Arthur, Colin and Big Bastard came into the room, carrying a steaming pot and a motley selection of cutlery, chipped plates, and bread of varying textures and ages.

'Wine for me,' said Arthur. 'Beer for Big Bastard. Shandy for the boy.'

'I am old enough to drink, you know,' said Colin crossly. 'Ooh – did you make jigsaw toast?'

* * *

'Can we borrow a phone book?'

'Hey!' said the waitress. 'You still staying at that fancy place across the street?'

'Nope,' said Julia. 'But you're the only person in Los Angeles we know well enough to borrow a phone book from.'

'Apart from C. Thomas Howell. We know him. In fact we had drinks with him only last night,' said Ellie importantly.

'Well, shaft me sideways with a saveloy,' said the waitress.

163

'Sorry,' said Ellie, 'we only speak English.'

The waitress wobbled off in shoes that surely weren't in the health and safety regulations for food preparation.

'Excuse me.'

Ellie turned to see the most achingly beautiful young man she had ever laid eyes on sitting next to her. He was regarding her with a look of puppyish devotion, resembling nothing more than Emilio Estevez sighting Andie McDowell.

'Oh no,' she thought. 'Here I am, ten thousand miles from home, and this poor boy has just fallen hopelessly in love with me. But it can never be.'

'Hello,' she said kindly, giving him her best eyes wide open smile.

'Hey,' he said, with a melting smile. 'Look, do you think you could introduce me to that waitress? You look like you know her.'

'Jeez, I cannot cut a break,' thought Ellie.

'I don't know,' she said. 'She'll only talk to you if you're in movies.'

'Hey, wow, are *you* in movies?' he said, his wide eyes opening even wider. 'Only, because, well . . . I'm an actor.'

'No shit. Well, maybe I could get you into *Animal Hospital*, chipmunk-face,' said Ellie in a growling voice.

'Yeah?'

'Ellie, pay attention,' ordered Julia. 'Okay, there are six Andrew McCarthys and another five A. McCarthys.'

'That could be if he's trying to hide his identity,' observed the waitress over her shoulder.

'In the phone book. Under his own surname,' said Ellie.

'Hey! You want my help or doncha?'

'Did we ask for help?' said Ellie to Julia.

'I'd recommend you don't play smartass with the person you're relying on to bring you foodstuffs.'

Ellie hung her head. 'Sorry.'

'Alrighty then. Are you going to phone them all?'

'No, just the real one,' said Ellie. 'We're psychic.'

'You can't help yourself, can you?'

'No. Please don't spit in my pancake mix.'

'Makes 'em better for you. Well, don't phone that one,' said the waitress, pointing out the second name. 'That neighbourhood, I'm surprised he's even got a phone.'

'Handy,' said Julia, scribbling it out with a pen. Unable to get a grip, she tore the entire page out of the book.

'Hey,' said the waitress. 'We might need that page!'

'Oh yeah?' said Ellie, holding up the book. 'You already let somebody take the "Lowe" page. Oh, and look, the "Clooney" page.'

'For Rosemary, would you believe. You all done?' said the waitress, retreating to the kitchen.

165

'Can we change some quarters?' asked Julia.

'Sure.'

'Umm . . . excuse me.'

The young man waylaid the waitress as she went past his table.

'Ehm . . . can I . . . look, do you want to have dinner some time, or something?' he asked.

'Are you in movies?' asked the waitress, waving her coffee pot alarmingly.

'Well, I've got the possibility of a part coming up on *Animal Hospital* . . .'

'Yeah?'

'To the batphone,' whispered Ellie, and Julia nodded as they crept out, leaving a massive tip.

* * *

With five handfuls of change, procured from a man entirely covered in tattoos, they found a relatively quiet telephone box by the beach.

'Here goes,' said Ellie.

'Please deposit one dollar seventy,' said a mechanized voice on the phone.

'Weird,' said Ellie. 'What if we just ran away?'

'Doesn't your mobile work?' said Julia.

'I had to hand it back to work. Actually,' Ellie thought about it for a second, 'nothing has rung at me for three days. God, that's magnificent.'

She enjoyed the thought for a moment.

'Okay, get on with it!' said Julia, 'What are you going to say if he answers?'

'Ooh!' said Ellie. 'I hadn't really thought about that.'

'Hedge, this is the point of the whole trip.'

'Yeh, I know but . . . Oh, I know. I'll ask him if he can still get into that ladies bra he wears in *Class*.'

'. . . or anything on earth other than that,' said Julia.

'Um . . . maybe we should pretend to be film directors.'

'Let's keep the whole disaster-inviting pretending stuff to a minimum shall we? You've seen *Weekend at Bernie's*. Just say hi.'

'Okay.' Ellie took a deep breath. 'First number please.'

'310-555 . . . 1796.'

The phone clicked to itself at the other end and rang.

'Hi!'

'Hi!' said Ellie excitedly.

'Andy and Maggie can't come to the phone right now . . . you know what to do!'

'I cannot believe I fall for that every fucking time,' said Ellie. 'I'm like Charlie Brown and the football. What possible reason could people have for trying to make you look stupid when they're not even there to enjoy it?'

'Was it him?'

'Nope, definitely not. Far too jolly and upbeat. Anyway, he's not an "Andy". That's a puppy's name.'

'Okay . . .'

'Do you want to do the next one?'

'No, this is your thing. Anyway, it's not like you're trying to sell them life insurance.'

Ellie sighed and dialled the next number.

'This is Captain Jean-Luc Picard of the Starship *Enterprise*. If you wish to leave a message for my loyal lieutenant Andrew, make it so after the tone.'

Ellie hung up, shaking her head fiercely.

'Well, if that was him, *this* quest is over.'

'Hello, this is Andrew's microwave. His answering machine just eloped with his tape deck, so I'm stuck with taking his calls. Say, if you want anything cooked while you leave your message, just hold it up to the phone.'

'Jesus, what is WITH the people in this town?'

'They're just trying to get noticed,' said Julia.

'As MORONS?'

'Now I lay me down to sleep; leave a message at the beep. If I die before I wake, remember to erase the tape.'

'Christ, that's it,' said Ellie, slamming down the phone. 'Let's just assume he's not in the phone book.'

'There's one Andrew left here on this list,' said Julia. 'You might as well give it a shot.'

Ellie raised her eyes. The phone rang for a long time, then was sharply picked up.

'Yeah?'

Ellie froze and shook her hands desperately at Julia, who shrugged emphatically.

'Hi . . . hi, is that Andrew?'

'Who's this?'

Ellie shook the phone in excitement.

'Andrew McCarthy?'

'Do I know you?'

'No, well, not exactly, but . . .'

'Aw, Christ, not this again. Don't tell me, you want to know if I still have the bra and panties from *Class* . . .'

Ellie's mouth dropped to the floor.

'Is it him???' whispered Julia frantically.

Ellie tried to mime 'maybe', whilst speaking calmly into the phone.

'No, no, but, I'm a big fan and . . .'

'Just fucking grow up, okay?'

'Click.' The phone went dead.

'Oh my God,' said Ellie. 'OH MY GOD!!!'

'Was that him????'

'I think so! He was really pissed off at being disturbed and being asked questions about his movies . . . oh God, it must have been!'

'Seems like maybe he shouldn't put himself in the phone book,' mused Julia.

'Oh my God . . . it sounded like him. Well, it was male, and American . . . Oh, and he was at home during the day! It is him!

'Do you want to phone him again?'

'No, he obviously doesn't like it . . . and we don't have to now, do we? We've got his home address!'

Say Anything

'Hey!' yelled Siobhan, fumbling with her car keys, house keys, three bags of shopping and an umbrella. 'Where are you off to?'

Loxy turned round halfway down Lavender Hill, padding home to his flat at the bottom. 'Oh, hi there Siobhan,' he said. He looked uncomfortable.

'Shitty day!'

'Yes, yes it is. I was just out for a walk.'

'Loxy, it's pissing down.'

'Sometimes I like that though.'

'You're laughing at clouds,' said Siobhan, opening her front door. Loxy stopped short and turned around.

'Ehm. Yes. I suppose . . . yes I am . . .'

'Do you want a cup of tea?'

'Alright.'

* * *

'Is it just me?' said Julia, 'or is this car filling up with dead skin?'

'I'm *scratchy*,' said Ellie. 'That is not a crime.'

'It should be. This isn't *Zombienation*.' Julia squinted at the map again, and compared it to the page ripped out of the telephone directory. They were high in the Hollywood Hills, trying to navigate off a 'Homes of the Stars' map. Andrew wasn't on it, but as Ellie had pointed out, it covered the right area.

'Okay. I think we're just about there . . .'

'Oh God,' said Ellie nervously. 'I think that bacon quadruple cheeseburger I had for lunch might be making a reappearance.'

'Well, if you will immerse yourself in local customs and traditions . . .'

'Are we really here?'

They were facing a low whitewashed villa, behind a low fence. Pink bougainvillaea flourished in the garden and there was an expensive German car in the driveway.

'1134. That's what it says,' said Julia, backing up the car nervously.

'Oh my God,' said Ellie. 'Are we really just going to march up to his door and demand . . .'

'. . . satisfaction? Your call, sweetie.'

'He's going to think we're weird.'

'We are weird. Well, you are, Cornflake Girl.'

'Aaah,' said Ellie. 'I'm really nervous.'

'We don't have to, you know,' said Julia. 'We could just go to Disneyworld or something.'

'No,' said Ellie. 'No no no. How would we ever explain it to Colin? I'm going to do something positive, goddamit, and ring that doorbell.'

She looked in the sunvisor mirror. 'I look like the Singing Detective.'

'I know, but we've already agreed you're not going to try and have sex with him, so it doesn't matter. Now, get out the car.'

Ellie emerged into the bright sunlight, took a deep breath and moved towards the door. Just before she got there, it was pulled open abruptly.

'What? What do you want?'

Momentarily blinded, it took her a second to focus on the tall blond character in the doorway.

'Um . . . hello. Yeh, um,' she scratched nervously, 'I'm looking for Andrew?'

'Yeah? What do you want?'

'Um . . . well, is Andrew in?'

'I'm Andrew. What is this?'

Julia stepped up and out of the car.

'Jeez, what are you two – Interpol?'

Ellie stood frozen to the spot and just stared at him.

'Oh God . . . I'm . . . I'm sorry,' she eventually choked.

'You're that girl that phoned me yesterday aren't you?'

'No.'

'Yeah, right, tons of British girls phone me every day.'

He smiled and relaxed a little and slowly shook his head. He looked like a surfer.

'Did you have your autograph book and camera all ready?'

Ellie nodded mutely. He smiled.

'It's only the seven billionth time I've been mistaken for him in Los Angeles. Although it's been pretty quiet lately. Sorry I sounded pissed yesterday, but really, why do people think celebrities would put themselves in the phone book? Hi there,' he said to Julia, who'd wandered over to join them.

'We're so sorry to bother you.'

'Not at all,' he said. 'Usually it's hysterical Japanese girls who turn up at 2am then just giggle at me. What were you two doing?'

'Oh, nothing much,' said Ellie, twisting her hands.

'Well, you've interrupted my work now,' he said, looking at Julia. 'Do you want an iced tea or something?'

'No we don't want to make any porn thank you,' said Ellie quickly.

'Oh, no, we wouldn't want to intrude . . .' said Julia.

'Don't worry – come out back and sit by the pool. Your friend looks a bit – what is it you Brits say? – hot and bothered?'

'I am not,' said Ellie crossly.

'Darling, you're a hot cross bun,' said Julia decisively. 'Okay. Thanks. We'd like to. I'm Julia.'

'Andrew,' he said, putting out his hand.

'Yes, we knew that,' said Julia, shaking it.

* * *

Andrew McCarthy II had a luxuriant back lawn with a small swimming pool and smart garden furniture, and, at the moment, Ellie sitting under a black umbrella wearing a deerstalker.

'It's all I had I'm afraid,' he said apologetically, bringing out three very welcome cold drinks.

'That's okay!' squeaked Ellie, fully aware of being red-faced, peeling and dressed ridiculously in front of someone who was clearly a bit of a blond, floppy-haired hunk.

'So what do you do, gets you a place like this?' asked Julia.

'I write straplines,' said Andrew. Then, when their faces failed to register, 'the bit that goes on the bottom of a movie poster to get you to watch it. Like "This Time, It's Personal".'

'What was that?'

'That was *Jaws III*,' said Andrew. 'I didn't write it. But that's the kind of thing I do.'

'How personal can a shark be?' wondered Ellie aloud from the sunbed, wondering if constantly talking would render her worth investigating beyond just the skin deep. Well, several layers of skin deep. She sighed. 'What does he do, make remarks about your weight before he chomps you in half?'

'Shh,' said Julia. 'I think that's a really interesting job.' And she smiled winningly.

Ellie looked at Andrew's muscled forearms and reflected that he was the most interesting job around here.

'Thanks,' he said, looking at them both. 'But I do a lot of straight to video stuff too. They like it pretty basic. Ooh, that'll work – "They Like It Pretty Basic". That should do for *Basic Desires*. It's a movie about a guy who has sex with prostitutes then . . .'

'Kills them, yes. Is C. Thomas Howell in it?'

'Thom Howell? No, not this one. Do you know him?'

'Yes, quite well actually,' said Ellie.

'Cool. Nice guy. So, what brings you to LA? Apart from pestering minor celebrities of course.'

'No, that was pretty much it,' said Julia.

'You're kidding.'

'Nope. Ask the Hedgehog.'

'Oh yeah, make out like it was all my idea,' said Ellie, who was getting hot and sticky underneath the hat.

'Hedgehog. It was all your idea,' said Julia, and Andrew laughed. Ellie did not like the way this was going at all.

'So are you working on any other emotional animal movies?' she asked.

'Just one. It's about a man and a cat who get together and solve crimes.'

'"The Purrfect Combination"!' said Julia.

'Hey – yeah! You'd be good at this.'

'But that's shit!' said Ellie. 'Sorry Julia. But it is though.'

They both looked at her.

'The film's shit too though,' said Andrew. 'So, it's kind of the point. You write the strapline so you know what kind of film to expect.'

'Anyway, do you think you could do better?' said Julia with a sniff.

'"Claws of Steel",' said Ellie petulantly. There was a silence. Andrew and Julia looked at each other indulgently.

'That's very good,' said Andrew.

'Thank you. Oh, how about . . . "you can only stop a crime wave by raining cats and dogs" . . .'

'There aren't any dogs in it.'

'It's metaphorical. Or you could get them to put some dogs in it. And maybe a rain sequence.'

'Uh huh.'

'"Pussy Power".'

'Ehm, I know! Why don't I go and get some more drinks,' said Andrew suddenly, jumping up. 'Julia?'

'Ooh, yes please, I'd love another iced tea,' Julia said, handing him her glass. He took it and smiled at her, then walked into the house.

'You TART!' whispered Ellie, grinning, as soon as he'd gone.

'What? What are you talking about?'

'Look at you! You're all over him like a rash.'

'I am *not*. He's just being polite.'

'Oh, and you are just inviting him into your pants.'

'Don't be silly. Anyway, I've got a boyfriend.'

'I don't believe it,' said Ellie. 'I'm the sad single person. I ought to get first crack at him. He's completely gorgeous. But what do you do? You put me in a ridiculous hat and make me sit under an umbrella while you go, "*ooh yes, I'd love another iced tea. And some sex please!*"'

'I was not!'

'You *so* were. "*Andrew, I'd like an iced tea and all the sex please.*"'

'I never did!'

'"*You know, I think I'll just have my iced tea naked!*"'

'Do you want me to hit you on your sunburn or not?'

'Whatever gets you going, seeing as you're obviously *so turned on*.'

'Do you two squabble a lot?' said Andrew looking amused, as he came back out with three iced teas. Julia shot Ellie a dirty look. 'Have I always been this jealous of Julia?' Ellie thought to herself ruefully.

'No. The Hedgehog was just saying how much she loved your hat and how she wished she could keep it on all the time.'

'Oh, that old thing. You can have it – I picked it up on a set somewhere, but it's really too hot to wear it here. But I'm glad you like it though.'

'No shit,' said Ellie grumpily, pulling the flaps down over her eyes. She pretended to go to sleep as Julia filled Andrew II in on what they were doing in LA. Listening to Julia tell it made it sound even stupider than it normally did, particularly with Julia omitting all the Loxy bits and making it sound as if she was humouring someone on the brink of insanity. 'Yes, I have always been jealous,' Ellie realized. 'Completely and utterly.'

Andrew II listened patiently to Julia. 'Hmm,' he said, when she had finished.

'Yes, hmm exactly,' said Julia conspiratorially. Ellie made Evil Eyes of Death under the flap of the deerstalker.

'What makes you think he lives in LA?'

'Because it's where movie stars live?'

'You know, being a movie star isn't exactly like being President. They can live anywhere.'

'What do you mean?' said Ellie, sitting upright.

'Well, I don't want to rain on your parade or anything . . . but, in the late 1980s I got fed up of having teenage girls hanging around my house all day . . .'

'*Really?*'

'Yes, I've had all the jokes, thank you . . . anyway, I hate to tell you this, but I did a bit of research, and I'm afraid your guru lives in New York.'

* * *

There was a silence on the end of the phone.

'No way,' said Arthur.

'It's just a teensy TEENSY tiny little change,' said Ellie.

'Hedge, have you *any* idea how much my Prada swimming trunks cost?'

'But you'll *love* New York. Think: ice skating in Central Park!'

'Exactly! It'll be below zero! That's no good for swimming trunks! Oh, for fuck's sake, Hedge, why couldn't you have sorted this out properly?'

'What do you mean, *sort this out properly*? This is

not the kind of thing you can plan. If it was, you'd be able to visit him on package tours.'

'Well, why didn't you look up where he was on the Internet or something?'

'Because the Internet is the most vile thing I've ever seen in my life and I won't go near it.'

'That's just because you're using Big Bastard's computer. It's different on every computer you know.'

'Is it?'

'Of course. Did you really think everyone has goat/women sex as their home page?'

'I wasn't sure, and I was too frightened to check. Anyway, that's fucked now, plus we've spent most of the money on the Ritz, so we're going to have to drive. We can borrow somebody's car and drive it across the country for them and it hardly costs anything. Why don't you come and meet us halfway?'

'So I can sit in somebody else's car in the freezing cold instead of dancing around San Francisco in my Prada pants,' said Arthur thoughtfully. 'I've got a better idea – why don't I just smash a bottle over my head for fun and take up mini-cabbing for the experience?'

'Don't be like this. It will be fun. I promise. We're having fun. Well, Julia is.'

Julia shot Ellie a warning glance across the room.

'Ooh, gossip? Immediately please,' said Arthur.

'Nothing,' said Ellie, in a tone of voice which

clearly meant 'loads'. 'Can't talk now. But if we meet you about halfway across . . .'

'Oh for fuck's sake,' said Arthur. 'Where's halfway across? I'll tell you where it isn't: it isn't on a beach which requires the wearing of Prada swimming trunks.'

Ellie cringed. She wasn't looking forward to this bit. 'I think . . . Kansas City.'

'Kansas City?'

'Uh huh. Andrew reckons we could make it in four days.'

'Who?'

Julia picked up a bottle of deodorant in a vaguely threatening fashion.

'Umm, nobody. This, err, woman we met called Andrew. You know people have the craziest names out here.'

'What the hell am I going to do in Kansas City?' howled Arthur.

'Well, you could drive us the next three thousand miles.'

'Christ.'

There was a bumping noise in the background.

'Okay, you two, stop it.'

'What's going on?'

'Nothing. Colin and Big Bastard are having a little . . . contretemps.'

'Give me that you little fucker,' could be heard

in the background, along with some high pitched yelping.

'Colin borrowed one of Big Bastard's Pringles and wore it. So now Big Bastard won't wear it ever again and he's currently trying to stop Colin getting into his room . . . put the wardrobe down, Big Bastard!'

'How's Loxy?' Julia gesticulated wildly from the bed.

'Arthur, how's the Loxster?' asked Ellie.

'Colin, vests are for wearing, not for slapping. Huh?'

'Julia wants to know how the Loxster is.'

'Um . . . fine, I think . . . Jesus! Look, I'm going to have to go. They've started to throw shoes. Look, I'm not sure . . . You're going to have to phone again . . . For fuck's sake, Big Bastard, call that a shoe? That's not a shoe, it's a fucking boat!'

'Bye,' said Ellie, a little sadly, putting the phone down.

'How are they?' asked Julia anxiously, getting up and going into the tiny bathroom.

'Fine. Well, murdering each other obviously. Ehm, Arthur is dead set against this.'

'I'm not surprised. How's Loxy?'

'He didn't really say. Okay, I think.'

'Hmm. That doesn't give a lot away. Do you think I should phone him?'

'Are you thinking of committing adultery?'

Andrew II was taking them out to dinner.

'No!'

'Are you sure? Why else are you phoning home then?'

Julia ignored her. 'Is Arthur serious about not wanting to come?'

'I'm sure there's lots he can get up to in New York. He's just going to take a bit of persuading, that's all. Anyway, if he doesn't come, we can still have fun, can't we?'

'Oh yes,' said Julia, artfully plucking out one of her near-invisible eyebrows.

'Okay, I'm going to phone my dad.'

'Okay!'

'Hello my favourite Hedgepig.'

'Hello Dad.'

Her father sounded sleepy. Well, it was late at home.

'What are you up to?'

'Hey, don't talk about me: sheesh, I'm trying to stay awake through *Newsnight*. Hasn't got much more exciting than that all day. Tell me everything you've been doing.'

Ellie told him some of things she'd been doing, omitting anything embarrassing to herself or potentially dangerous that might worry her father, e.g. having iced tea with a stranger, driving through unknown territory, harassing people over the phone, getting drunk on the plane . . . so, mostly, it boiled down to pancakes.

'Hey, didn't I tell you the food would be great over there?'

'Yup,' said Ellie. 'And you were right. Dad, are you eating okay?'

'Yes, yes,' said her dad. 'Don't worry about me sweetheart. Just you have a good time.'

'Are you eating the stuff I left you in the freezer?'

'Yup. Mostly in conjunction with meat pies.'

'Da-ad.'

'I said don't worry, love. You just have a wonderful time.' He sounded sad.

'I'll try.'

'But not too wonderful, eh? I want you home again. You might be a royal pain in the you know what, but you're still my little Hedgepig, okay?'

'Yes,' said Ellie uncertainly, suddenly, against her wishes, feeling very far from home. 'I miss you Dad.'

'Well, I miss you too sweetheart. Give Hollywood one for me. Tell them they should make a film about a retired cop.'

'Who eats pies.'

'Yeah.'

'And who actually worked in back office logistics.'

'I'll be world famous.'

'And I'll be a baboon's waistcoat.'

'Oh God. That's Plockton language darling, not worthy of you.'

'No,' said Ellie, suddenly sad.

'Make the most of it, eh, sweetheart?'

Then he put the phone down right away. Ellie hung up and sat on the bed, swinging her heels and trying to work out what he meant, until she heard Julia start to sing 'Saving All My Love For You' in the bathroom. Chuckling, she launched herself up and headed for the door. 'Are you shaving your legs in there?'

'They're prickly!'

'They're horny!'

Julia poked her head out of the bathroom door.

'You're going to have to stop this or I'm not taking you tonight.'

'He invited both of us, so there.'

'Yes, but I have the car keys, SO THERE. Also, you'd better wear that deerstalker. He gave it to you as a present – he'll be expecting it.'

'Chuff off,' said Ellie sullenly.

'Heh heh heh,' said Julia.

'Are you really going to cheat on Lox?' said Ellie suddenly.

Julia came out of the bathroom entirely.

'Look. This is the whole point of this trip. To discover things about myself. How much I fancy other people. How much I miss Loxy when he's not here. If it doesn't work out, I'm going to call it quits when I get home, which means anything that goes on here doesn't count.'

Julia started combing out her long blonde hair.

'Hmm. So basically it's an excuse to behave like a complete bike,' said Ellie reflectively.

Julia threw the hairbrush at her.

'Hey! Leave me alone.'

'Well,' said Julia. 'Where is he on the scale, after all?'

Ellie shrugged. 'If Jono Coleman is a one . . .'

The scale started from people who had fights with themselves in public and went on up to someone with whom it would be considered a crime against the universe not to sleep.

'. . . I'd say he's a James Spader.'

'He is *so* not a James Spader. You're trying to mark him down so I'll lose interest and you can have him.'

'Okay. He's a Lloyd Cole.'

'He's a Judd, and don't forget it.'

'He is *not* a Judd.'

'He is.'

'Fine. Sleep with him then. See if I care,' said Ellie.

Julia disappeared once more into the bathroom.

'Actually, I care a lot,' said Ellie loudly.

'I know. But it's my marriage on the line!'

'Does that line get you out of parking tickets as

well?' grumbled Ellie, tying a red-speckled headband through her unruly curls.

* * *

The restaurant was set high on a shady terrace covered in palm trees, looking over the ridiculously ugly mixed-origin houses that made up posh Los Angeles.

'I didn't know the Tudors needed half-timbered four-car garages,' Ellie said. 'But I guess it makes sense.'

Julia was wearing a pretty white linen dress and sipping a mineral water next to the hibiscus. The evening was positively balmy, and across the sky the jet streaks of a hundred planes could be seen.

Ellie had removed the deerstalker and was actually looking simply ruddy, rather than like the unfortunate survivor of a burning oil spill. They were feeling warm and happy and very pleased to be looking out onto a sweet scented pink evening and not, say, a fat tabby and a wet dustbin.

Andrew II entered just after 7.30pm. He was wearing khakis and a shirt with tiny flowers on it, and his blond hair was freshly washed and flopped over one eye.

'Cor,' said Ellie and Julia simultaneously, then looked at each other.

'You know, technically speaking, I saw him first,' hissed Julia.

'I rang his fucking doorbell!' said Ellie. 'If that's not seeing him first then I'm a badger's auntie.'

'You said it, you are it,' said Julia.

'Right! That's it,' Ellie hit her on the hand with a bread stick.

'Hi, you two,' said Andrew II suavely, coming up to their table. 'Everything okay?'

'*Hi Andrew*,' they both said immediately in twinkling tones.

'Look, I hope you don't mind, but I brought a friend . . . he's just out in front sorting out the car.'

Ellie and Julia both looked politely interested, each desperately hoping the friend wasn't for them – Ellie with rather less confidence, which turned out to be well placed, as a slouchy-looking guy wearing an enormous Jamiroquai hat walked in.

'Um, Ellie, Julia, this is Chip, but we call him Hatsie.'

Hatsie grunted and sat down. A bread roll disappeared under his hat and didn't come out again.

'Ho ho!' said Julia jovially, leaning over to shake his paw. 'God, you and Ellie are going to have *so* much in common, I can just tell. I'll bet your shared love of hats is just the beginning.'

'You know it's amazing!' said Ellie to Andrew. 'Julia hasn't been able to stop talking all afternoon! We think she might have Tourette's.'

Andrew smiled at them both a tad awkwardly.

'Right. Ehm, can I get you both a drink?'

'What would you recommend?' they both said simultaneously, leaning in towards him and, consciously or otherwise, pushing out their breasts just a little.

'Uhm,' he suddenly looked frightened. 'Why don't we all just start with mineral water and see how it goes.'

'Oh, that sounds *great*,' said Julia, shaking her shiny blonde hair out of her eyes.

Ellie sat back half-smiling. Oh well. You don't mess with the experts.

She turned to Andrew's companion. 'Well then, hello there Hatsie!'

'Hgnfu,' said Hatsie. Another bread roll vanished.

'Sorry?'

'Hgn-FU!'

'Oh. Oh, yes,' said Ellie, picking up one corner of the tablecloth and fiddling with it.

'Hgn-fu corh*ayy*.'

'Good one!' said Andrew, overhearing and laughing.

'*What?*' said Ellie.

'Ha ha!' laughed Julia.

'Hatsie knows everyone in LA, don't you Hatsie?' said Andrew encouragingly, 'in fact, that's how we got a table here tonight.'

Julia patted him coyly on the arm.

As if to prove this, an impossibly stupid-looking/beautiful (delete according to gender preference) blonde woman with massive rigid breasts walked past and stopped at the table.

'Hatsie!' she squealed. 'So great to see you! How was Malibu?'

'Gnrgch,' said Hatsie.

'Oh, you are wicked. I'm sure Puffy doesn't think so.'

'Kfnia.'

Ellie beckoned the waiter over. 'Can I have another basket of bread rolls please? And a triple Bacardi.'

* * *

Halfway through the meal, Ellie gestured Julia angrily to the bathroom. Julia had been hogging Andrew entirely with such inclusive topics as how to keep your natural blonde hair out of the sun and just how difficult it was to keep your Italian linen uncreased.

'Julia,' said Ellie sternly, running her hands under the tap. 'You're hogging.'

'Oh, don't be silly,' said Julia. She had had a couple of glasses of wine and her eyes were sparkling. 'I'm on holiday. I'm not being old Julia anymore. I'm having fun, okay? And anyway, I'm only flirting.'

'Julia, the only thing you're flirting with is what

191

kind of breakfast you're going to let him make you after he gives you a jolly good . . .'

'That's *not* true,' said Julia, blushing. Then she looked up. 'If I did . . .'

'Let's just assume it's going to be you shall we?'

'If I *did* . . . you wouldn't tell, would you?'

'Of course I would!' said Ellie. 'What, you shagging some other bloke? Not only that, a bloke who's like a photographic negative of Loxy! You and Andrew are like the Nazi Twins!'

'Yeah? So why do *you* keep pouting in his direction?'

'Yes, but it's okay for me – I'm single. I deserve him. Also I've been sat talking to a drain all night whilst you try and break the world giggling record.'

'So you'd ruin it – you're jealous.'

'So what if I am? Not that I am. Dammit, I said those in the wrong order.'

'Oh, go on Hedgehog. Please.'

Ellie wiped some mascara from under her eyes.

'As you're driving, I don't exactly think I have much choice, do you? You might sever my arms in a freak window winding up "accident".'

'Thanks,' said Julia, touching up her blusher. 'Oh God. I'm sure I won't get off with him really.'

'Can't we just leave this at how good I'm being about it?'

'Yes. Sorry.'

'And you *have* to talk to me more. I've been saddled with someone without physical characteristics. I keep expecting him to pull the hat off and shout "I am a human being!"'

'Maybe it's a zombie,' said Julia.

'Maybe it's the black face of death,' agreed Ellie. 'Nobody order the fish. You'll start choking, and he'll just stand up and pull the hat off . . . and there'll be NOTHING THERE.'

'Okay, you're scaring yourself now,' said Julia. 'Let's just go in and have a nice dinner.'

'Yeah, well you have a nice dinner – I'll throw Hatsie bread rolls like a seal.'

'Well, you know what they say . . . big hat . . .'

'. . . complete inability to talk, I know . . .'

Julia wiped a smudge of rose-coloured lipstick over her lips.

'Okay. Let's go.'

'So we're agreed,' said Ellie. 'You're going to have to tell me all the sexy details so that I can revel in them and hold them over you as blackmail for the rest of your life if you marry Loxy. Practically, it'll make you my slave.'

'We didn't agree that!'

'Oh yes we did . . .'

* * *

'So, yes, they're always bickering . . .' Andrew was

saying as they came out. 'Oh, hello you two! Have you decided what you want to eat? I hear the seafood here is great.'

'No fish,' said Ellie sternly.

'You choose,' said Julia, in a giggly way.

Andrew suavely ordered huge plates of salad, grilled chicken and the fish, which Ellie studiously avoided. Everything was delicious.

'So, Hatsie, what do you do?'

Hatsie looked up from his plate from which he was transferring food under his hat at an astonishing rate.

'Hatsie! Hatsie does everything, don't you Hats! Knows everyone, does everything,' said Andrew jovially.

'Except talk and . . . things,' Ellie's voice petered out.

'Snghfrh,' said Hatsie.

'Ha! Yes, I know exactly what you mean,' said Andrew.

'Ha ha ha,' giggled Julia again, along with him. Ellie gave her a resigned look and went back to fiercely crunching the croutons out of her Caesar salad.

Two enormous mafioso-type guys stopped by the table and laid their beefy hands firmly on Hatsie's shoulders and started having an intense conversation with him.

'So have you decided what you're going to do?' asked Andrew II.

'Uh huh,' Julia nodded. 'We're definitely heading East. We're going to drive somebody else's car across the States for them. That way it doesn't cost us any money.'

'Courier cars! Great! I hope you get something cool – an open-topped Jag or something.'

'Or a '59 Chevy,' said Ellie. 'I have no idea what one of those is, but it sounds about right.'

'It's a bit like a buffalo with wheels,' said Andrew. 'Not necessarily recommended. Ehm, listen, where is it you're picking up your friend again?'

'Kansas City,' said Julia.

'It's about sixteen cheeseburgers away from here,' added Ellie. 'We're meeting Arthur there.'

'He's gay,' added Julia quickly.

'Oh – is he chasing after your movie star too?'

'Oh no, that's just Hedge . . . Ellie.'

Ellie's mouth fell open with the injustice of it all.

'And you!' she yelped. 'You're going to ask him . . .'

Julia made judicious use of a fork.

'I really like British girls,' said Andrew, leaning back. 'You're feisty.'

Ellie and Julia glared at each other. There was a bit of a silence. Then Julia turned round with her smile back on.

'So – what's it like living in LA?'

'So, Hatsie. What's your favourite kind of hat?' asked Ellie, a tad sullenly.

'Oh it's great, really shallow,' Andrew said. 'Actually, it's weird. It's like living in one of those factory communities. Everyone knows everything about everyone else and basically works at the same place.'

'Plus, they all look like big genetic weirdo science experiments,' added Ellie, licking her spoon.

Andrew laughed as another young woman, skinny to the point of anorexia but with two grapefruit stapled to her spine, flounced past on shoes made out of matchsticks.

'Yes, you do get a bit of that. It tends to be a bit homogenized.'

'Like milk.'

'Some people like milk.'

'Yeah, really boring people. I like Bloody Marys,' said Ellie.

'So do I.'

He grinned at her, and suddenly Ellie found herself holding his gaze.

Julia coughed none too subtly.

'Need the loo again, Ellie?'

Ellie grudgingly obeyed the rules and got up. 'Sorry,' she said apologetically to Andrew.

'That's okay, people go to the bathroom all the time in LA. Which is it: powdering your nose or making yourself vomit?'

'Neither!' said Ellie, shocked. 'Actually, we're going to talk about y . . . owww.'

Julia put her emergency fork back in her handbag.

* * *

'I reckon he wants both of us,' said Ellie, punchily. 'Three in a bed. What do you say?'

'I say that is crap and also you never would.'

'I would!'

'You would not. You think you're really cool and hip when it comes to sex, but what about that time Billy tried to put his finger up your bottom?'

'Thanks for that. I can't pee now.'

'Look. I'm sorry. I don't like us muscling each other. But you have your whole life to find a boyfriend and I have three weeks, okay?'

* * *

'Kansas City,' said Andrew. 'You know, I have a bit of business that's going to take me up that way.'

Julia's face lit up.

'What do you mean?' said Ellie scornfully. 'I thought you wrote tag lines. How much research do six words need?'

'I am writing,' said Andrew, 'the tag line for next year's big film, *actually*. It's about space aliens who bomb a city with earthquakes and meteors. Then it turns out that the space aliens are actually mutated dinosaurs and that's how the dinosaurs disappeared – by going into space.'

'Do any beautiful prostitutes get murdered?' asked Julia.

'Not murdered as such. But the explosions tend to make their clothes fall off. AND it's set in Kansas City. So I have to go there to get a feel for it before I can write my tagline.'

Ellie pretended to sneeze and actually said 'bullshit!' into her napkin. Andrew noticed this and smiled to himself. The mafioso-type guys, after much patting on shoulders and congratulations and a couple of kisses had gone on their way. However, now the chef had come out of the kitchen and was anxiously eliciting Hatsie's opinion of the food. Hatsie was snurkling at him.

'I mean, when I wrote that one about the big lizards coming up through the sewers of Washington DC and having their brains modified by toilet cleaners to make them super-intelligent hunters . . . that was "It's a Capitol Offence – Murder in the First Flush". And, you know, I had to go to DC to get that inspiration.'

'You did?' said Ellie.

'Oh, sure. And do you know what? That film did $22 million in its first weekend.'

'Is that good or bad?'

'It means I earn my gigantic salary, okay? And that research is important.'

'But what's in Kansas City?'

'Well, you two for starters.'

Ellie was going to stick two fingers down her throat when she remembered that that was socially acceptable behaviour here. She stuck them up her nose instead.

'Are you okay?' asked Andrew II.

'Fine thanks.'

'Okay! Well, if you're looking for hat tips, you should take your special cowboy hat . . . It's like, "Go West young man."'

'Except we're not men.'

'Or going West.'

'We're very young though.'

'*Extremely*,' said Ellie. She turned to look at Hatsie. 'Shall we get the bill?'

Hatsie indicated with a snorch and a wave of his hand that the bill had been taken care of and they wandered out into the scent of oleander and car fumes.

'Can I drop you two?' said Andrew II. Julia was standing close to him.

'No!' said Ellie. 'We've got an early start tomorrow. Off to . . . Kansas and all that.'

'That sounds lovely,' said Julia at exactly the same moment.

Andrew looked from one to the other. 'Well?'

There was a long pause. Hatsie was snuffling around next to Ellie's shoulder. Suddenly, on a whim out of nowhere, she leaned over and snatched his enormous Jamiroquai hat and ran halfway across the darkened car park.

Hatsie let out a loud screech, and Julia jumped away from Andrew's side.

Standing on the restaurant forecourt was, now, a shortish bald man who looked a lot like Duncan Norvelle.

'CHASE ME!' shrieked Ellie.

'Christ,' said Andrew, wincing.

'SORRY! COMPLETE ACCIDENT!'

'Snffghhg!' Hatsie implored Andrew desperately.

'Yes, yes of course,' said Andrew. Then, across the car park, 'Look, I'm sorry . . . Ellie can you bring back the hat, please?'

'Why?' said Ellie. 'Is this a medical emergency? Do we need to call 999? No, hang on, it would take them too long to get here from Britain – call 911.'

Hatsie was whimpering. Ellie turned around and wandered back.

'No problem,' she said, walking up to him insouciantly. Hatsie tugged on Andrew's arm anxiously.

'Oh, look . . . I think we'd better be going,' said Andrew.

'Hfn,' said Hatsie, nodding his head vehemently. As soon as Ellie got close enough he grabbed the hat back and forced it down onto his head.

'I'm sorry . . . Hatsie can't stand people touching his hat,' said Andrew apologetically, jumping into his car. 'It's like . . . the Fonz's leather jacket.'

'*Ohh*, that makes it even cooler,' said Ellie. 'Come on Julia.'

Julia looked imploringly at Andrew.

'Bye then.'

He leaned out the car window. Hatsie had ducked down where he couldn't be seen.

'Have a good trip,' Andrew said, looking at them both. Ellie couldn't quite tell, but he looked like he was trying to hide his amusement.

They watched the car dip below the crest of the hill.

* * *

'Well, thank you very much,' said Julia, as they puttered to the less nice end of LA.

'I'm sorry,' said Ellie. 'I don't know what came over me. But I know what didn't come over you.'

'Yeauch,' said Julia. 'And that makes it an act of sabotage.'

Ellie leaned her head against the window of the car, watching the lights fall away behind her.

'I'm sorry, I just suddenly thought . . .'

'Look, let me make the moral decisions around here, okay?'

'Yes. Yeah, alright.'

* * *

'It's a shame you can't come with us, make pancakes for us on the road,' said Ellie hungrily the next morning. Julia wasn't eating.

'Well, like I told y'all . . . if you'd stuck to Rob Lowe.'

'I know.'

Julia sat and sipped her coffee in silence.

Ellie turned back to the waitress. 'Do you really like Los Angeles? Living here, I mean?'

The waitress stared straight ahead, as if she'd never really thought about it.

'Well, yeah . . . I mean, I guess so . . . I mean, there's the ocean out there, and, I tell you what, if you've not got too much money . . . best to live somewhere hot.'

Ellie nodded. 'What if you never make it as an actress?'

'Sweetheart, hardly any of us are going to make it. We hang out. We support each other. It's cool. And think of all the millionaires here. Hell, if we're having a pretty day, who knows what can happen.'

She jutted her hip out in the direction of an old, slavering guy.

'It's cool. Plus, Christ, you should have seen where I grew up.'

'Where's that?' asked Ellie, with a sudden leaden sense of oncoming doom.

'Kansas City.'

* * *

'I can't believe it.'

Ellie stood staring at their transport car.

'We don't have any money left,' said Julia patiently. 'We might have done, if you hadn't insisted giving all that cash to the waitress.'

'Which *should* have come back to us as fantastic karma. But LOOK at this.'

They were standing in the forecourt staring at an even older and tinnier model of Toyota than the one they were currently driving.

'This just isn't fair.'

'At least it's not covered in your dead skin.'

'Who on earth would care enough about this to transport it from one side of the country to the other? Why not just cut your losses and replace it with an electric toothbrush? All the power at a fraction of the cost.'

Julia got in the car to forestall further argument.

'Oh well. At least it's not going to work as a massive pick-up man magnet. Keep you out of further trouble,' said Ellie.

'I heard that!'

Ellie sighed.

'Just get in.'

'Okay,' said Ellie, slinging her bag in the back. 'Here we are. The low-rent Thelma and Louise. Tracy and Denise.'

Julia pulled out of the lot onto the left slipway, reversed and managed to make it onto the intersection on the right side of the road, heading in the direction of the rising sun.

Planes, Trains and Automobiles

Arthur gazed into the dark night and gave a melodramatic sigh. 'Is it *ever* going to stop raining?'

'Huh?' said Big Bastard. He was utterly engrossed in Colin's video of *The Sound of Music*.

'Are you enjoying the film?' asked Colin from Arthur's lap.

'No, it's shit. Now, shut up,' said Big Bastard, not moving his eyes from the screen. 'Oh God! Don't marry that bitch!'

'Hi everyone,' said Loxy, sidling in. Colin couldn't be trusted with keys, so the door was permanently on the latch.

'Hey, Loxy, what's up?'

Loxy shrugged.

'Oh, nothing. Oh no, hang on, my girlfriend's on

the other side of the world chasing some other guy she's never met.'

'I didn't want to say anything before,' said Colin. 'But that's getting really boring.'

Big Bastard and Arthur nodded vehemently.

'Fine,' said Loxy, sitting down heavily and pulling out some tins of beer. 'I'll do the traditional British thing and swallow all my emotions. Maybe it will turn into cancer.'

'Actually, if your balls fell off that would solve all your problems, mate.' Big Bastard threw a practised hand round the back of the chair and picked up a can of beer without looking.

'Lox, would you shag Julie Andrews?'

'Depends if I've got any balls left after all the cancer.'

'I can't decide either. I mean, do you think she'd like it? She looks so clean.'

'Hey!' shouted Arthur. 'If you want to keep watching this film, I'd recommend you show a little bit more respect.'

Big Bastard shrugged. 'I couldn't possibly care less. Pff, but she's not going to like being back at the convent, I can guarantee you that.'

'Oh God!' The front door slammed open, and Siobhan ran in, sat down in the middle of the floor and burst into tears.

'Jesus!' said Big Bastard. 'If you're going to have

a major dose of the waterworks, can't you do it somewhere else?'

'I'm not crying,' snarled Siobhan. 'This is what a woman having an orgasm looks like. You just don't recognize it.'

'What's the matter, sweetheart?' said Arthur, getting up and pushing Colin off his lap.

'I just saw Patrick and that ballet *bint*,' she sniffed. 'Out choosing fucking DINNER PATTERNS together!'

'Ohhh.' Arthur put his arm around her.

'I couldn't get that man to come with me to buy his own fucking *underpants*. His own, fucking skiddy *underpants*.'

'Do they do those with the skids already in them?' asked Big Bastard.

'Oh God. I'm just so . . . I'm never going to meet anyone again, *ever*. I had one chance and I picked a complete cunt and I've just blown it and I'm never going to have a baby . . . Arthur, please will you be the father of my baby, like in that Madonna film?'

'No,' said Arthur, 'but I'll let you play with Colin on the weekends.'

Siobhan's sobs were growing quieter. Loxy reflected that he would get lots more attention if he burst into tears too but wisely refrained from attempting it as a practical experiment.

'Plates are so out this year anyway,' Arthur went

on. 'Everyone who's anyone is getting Bento Boxes. And not from Habitat either.'

'How did you know I saw them in Habitat?'

'Because Patrick is the most boring imagination-free turgid lout I ever met in my life, and they don't let ballerinas walk further than their own postcode or they start fainting all over the place.'

Siobhan managed a wan grin.

'Were they stupidly enormous plates like nothing you'd ever use for real food?'

'Huge.'

'There you go then. The man can't even buy crockery that isn't a penis extension. Their emotional lives are a nightmare just waiting to happen. Those plates will be smashed to fuck all over their stainless steel kitchen by Christmas.'

Siobhan sniffed loudly again.

'Can I have a beer?'

'You can have anything you like,' said Arthur. 'Except my sperm.'

'I can give you a lift home later if you like,' said Loxy. 'We can drive past his house and throw things. Or maybe if you're not feeling brave you could just make a few rude gestures.'

'Thanks.'

'Don't do it Rolf!' shouted Big Bastard in anguish.

* * *

Ellie leaned her head against the window, staring out at the endless desert ahead. The radio had started up with 'de der der . . . de der der' and the familiar refrain of 'The Boys of Summer' was coasting through her head. She felt an odd misty longing.

'Julia?'

'Mmm?'

'Do you ever feel . . . that you really want something, you just don't know what it is?'

'No,' said Julia. 'You're implying I don't know the difference between a chocolate cake and a handbag.'

'You never just feel . . . there must be something more, I just don't know what it is?'

'No,' said Julia. 'I'm on holiday. You're the one with the yawning existential angst. Why that makes it me that has to do all the driving I have no idea.'

Ellie slumped back and looked at the huge horizon and wondered, yet again, what she was doing.

'What do you think it's like being famous?' she asked, idly.

'Oh, I don't know,' said Julia. 'Probably you get to lie back in cars and be driven about.'

Ellie ignored this.

'Remind me again why it is you never learned to drive?'

'Because of the stag,' said Ellie.

'Oh, yes. That wasn't a stag, was it, Hedgehog?'

'A stag, gracefully leaping out of the bushes . . .'

'It was a cat, wasn't it Hedgehog?'

'Prancing gracefully through the early morning mists on its way to a meeting of other great forest creatures . . .'

'A big fat tabby who'd just fallen off a dustbin . . .'

'. . . or possibly a tiger. Anyway, I didn't like my driving instructor. On my first day he said to me, "There are two things in this life that women can't do. One is drive and the other is . . ."'

'. . . scratch their balls? Ejaculate semen?'

'No, although actually now I come to think of it, perhaps he should have revised up his estimate. No, the other one was make compilation tapes.'

They drove on in silence for a hundred miles.

'Actually, I make terrible compilation tapes,' confessed Julia. 'I can never work out when to press the pause button, and it always runs over and . . .'

'. . . exactly,' said Ellie. 'He'd already got it so right that I didn't see much point in continuing, really.'

'Okay, well you control the radio then.' Don Henley had finished. Ellie fidgeted for a second.

'Do you want country country or Christian country?'

'Hmm,' Julia looked at the dial. 'Don't they do that one – "Drop-kick me Jesus Through the Goal Posts of Life"?'

'They surely does. But if you stick to country country you get "I've Never Been to Bed With an Ugly Woman But I've Sure Woken Up With a Few".'

'Hmm.'

'Okay, hang on,' Ellie twiddled the radio some more. Suddenly, the booming power chords of Glenn Frey's 'The Heat Is On' came booming out.

'Now THIS is more like it,' said Julia, and they turned it up ear-splittingly loud and yelled along.

* * *

Ellie remembered how excited she'd been about driving. Her mother had never driven, so this was going to be her and her dad's big project together, without her; something she would never even know about.

'They don't have cars in Plockton,' her dad had said. 'Just big horses that shit everywhere.' She had giggled and then jerked the car off down the road. Two screaming hours of pain and terror later they had resolved never to sit in a car together again. When you only have one person in the whole world, don't try and teach them to drive.

* * *

'Oh my God, a man in a cowboy hat!' shouted Ellie, pointing and gathering astonished stares from the other punters in the dusty and over-heavily air conditioned diner at the side of the road.

'Oh,' she said, coming into the room fully and realizing it was in fact packed with massive men in cowboy hats.

'How y'all doing?' said a short, friendly-looking man, coming over with two menus.

'Oh my *Go* –'

Julia clapped her hand over her friend's mouth.

'Two please. Non-smoking.'

'As opposed to what?' he said, without comprehension.

Julia led a stuttering Ellie to the seat.

'But he's a . . . he's a . . .'

'Native American, yes. Good God, Ellie, when you were a kid did you used to point out Down's Syndrome kids on the street and old ladies with wigs on?'

'No! Just that old lady with Down's Syndrome *and* a wig . . .'

'That'd better not be true.'

'But he's . . . !'

The man came back up with glasses of icy water. The girls were in South East Nevada and were just coming down from an enormous fight about the two potential two-hundred-mile detours possible at this point – one to Vegas, one to the Grand Canyon. No prizes for guessing who was arguing which case, but it had come down to some very frosty exchanges focusing on the amount of watches worn by one of the occupants of the car and the moral standards, or otherwise, of the other. The result was that they had bypassed both places and gone straight on up route 15, ploughing on and on through the dust, and Julia was now eyeing up any coffee-related products with a ravenous half-open eye.

'So where are you guys from? Poland?' asked the waiter chummily.

'England,' said Ellie eagerly, looking at his fine forehead and large brown eyes.

'England, yeah? So, that's like, near Britain?'

'It's in Britain,' said Ellie, less eagerly. 'It's kind of the biggest part of Britain.'

'You're shitting me! I thought that was London.'

'Well, we're from London.'

He looked confused.

'Okay. So – where you headed? The Grand Canyon or Vegas?'

'Neither,' said Julia. 'We're going to Kansas City. Can I have some Jolt cola please? And a double expresso?'

'Gee, you foreigners sure are weird,' he said, shaking his head.

'So you are really a Red Indian?' asked Ellie through a mouthful of bacon and sunny side up eggs. Julia tutted loudly.

'Yes ma'am. I'm a Havasupai.'

'I've never met a real . . . umm, Native American before.'

'Well, I've never met a real London person before.'

'Really? There's tons of us.'

'There's a few of us too.'

'God, isn't travelling weird?' said Ellie to Julia. Julia raised her eyes to the ceiling and downed another black coffee.

'We came from Los Angeles,' added Ellie.

'Really? I used to live there. In the eighties.'

That caught Ellie's attention. 'Yeah? Oh my God, what did you do?'

'I ran a restaurant there too. Course, this was in the days when restaurants weren't much about food.'

'Yeah?' The girls were agog.

'Aw, jeez, Jimmy, are you startin,' wit that Hollywood shit again?' said the man in the next booth, good-naturedly.

'Yeh, you shut your mouth,' said Jimmy, waving the water jug alarmingly.

He schooshed them over and sat down. Ellie put her chin on her hands, all ready to listen.

'It was just off Rodeo, real nice spot. We used to get everyone in there.'

'What was it called?' said Julia.

'"Flash". We got it all done out in pink neon and black leather and served portions that wouldn't feed a rat. It was pretty cool.'

'Sounds it,' said Ellie. 'Come on! Who used to come in?'

'We had to widen the doors to let the shoulderpads

through. On a good night you could choke on the hairspray and Giorgio perfume. And great big cell phones like bricks.' His voice went misty.

'Did the Brat Pack come in?' said Ellie anxiously, unable to hold back for another second.

'Oh yes,' he said.

Ellie's face lit up. She imagined them, at their peak, in their glitter, laughing and chatting and raising glasses to their youth and success and joy. She imagined walking through the widened doors; sitting down at the black leather banquette; sweeping up her (now miraculously straight) hair.

'More bitching bunch of ingrates I never met in my whole life.'

'Do you mean "bitching" in the good sense?' asked Julia, shocked. Ellie was suddenly rigid.

'Maybe you just caught them on a bad night,' she said desperately.

'Neh, they were in there all the time. Getting drunk. Falling over. Complaining about Tom Cruise getting all the good roles.'

'Well, they were right there,' said Julia. Ellie was still looking deeply unhappy.

'Was . . . was Andrew McCarthy there?'

'Who?' He thought for a second and scratched his head. 'No, he really didn't hang out with those guys. Not really a party animal.'

Ellie's grin was back instantly. 'So. Not him then.'

He shook his head.

'Have you any idea where he might hang out now?' asked Julia.

'Just not in restaurants, I guess.'

'Hmm.'

'Oh, but they were great days,' he went on. 'The tips. I can't even explain it to you. Thousands of dollars, flying all over the place.'

'What happened?' asked Julia. Then, gathering herself, 'Not that this place isn't really nice and everything.'

The man grinned at her and nodded over at the swing doors into the kitchen. A beautiful and filthy little boy was sticking fries in his ears.

'Oh, you know . . .' he shrugged. 'Times changed. Fashions changed. People started turning up in jeans and mucky old Nirvana t-shirts and asking for mineral water. It wasn't as fun any more. The glitter starts to fade, you know.'

Julia nodded.

A woman scooped up the child and came in from the back of the restaurant. She had long dark hair and large dark eyes, and had obviously once been extremely attractive, but was now insanely over-weight.

'And this is my wife, Sharalees.'

The woman smiled a warm smile. Ellie gave the child a piece of toast to stick in his ear.

'I just been talkin' to these fine young ladies from Iyerland . . .'

'Hi there y'all. Has he been boring you with his old war stories again?'

'He certainly has Sharalees,' said the man in the cowboy hat.

'It sounds great,' said Ellie.

'It was horrible, actually.'

'Sharalees was going to be an actress,' said the restaurant owner. 'She was in an erotic thriller with Mark Hamill.'

'Wow, that's amazing.'

'Yeah, but mostly I was his favourite waitress.'

'Yes you were,' said the man.

'And let me tell you, it was pretty horrible in there. Lots of shouting nobodies who are all now either miserable or dead. Tips were good though.'

'Uh huh,' said Ellie.

'Well, lovely to meet y'all. And can I just say your English is really good.'

'We better be getting on,' said Julia, regretfully. 'We have to be in a motel before it gets dark, so Ellie can see to stomp the roaches.'

'You don't want to hear about the night Dudley Moore and Robert Downey Junior . . .'

'*I* do,' said Ellie.

'Sorry,' said Julia, 'but if I have to drive all day, she has to stomp roaches.'

'Oh, well, you make sure you look us up next time you're coming through, okay?'

'Absolutely. And the next time you're in Europe, come and check us out.'

'Yeah, we'll do that. It's Ellie and Julia, right?'

'Yup.'

'Great. Shouldn't be a problem in your little bitty country.'

* * *

The next morning started nice and clear and Julia dragged Ellie away from the Eat All The Bacon You Want table as quickly as she could.

'Let's get a move on!'

'Okay! He'll wait for us in Kansas City you know.'

'Who?' said Julia. 'Andrew II? I wasn't even thinking about him.' She fingered his cellphone number in her trouser pocket.

Ellie jumped in the tiny car. 'Poo. It smells in here.'

'Well, stop eating Cheez Whizz then.'

Ellie wound down the window.

'Oh, God, what if Arthur doesn't come? That'll be crap.'

'I'm sure it'll be fine,' said Julia, a little stiffly. They set off on the poker-straight road.

'No, that's not what I meant,' said Ellie. 'I just . . . hate depriving him of his trip.'

'Perhaps you should have thought of that before you sent us five thousand miles off course.'

'Yeah, okay okay.'

Ellie fell silent. Why was it she never felt like she was doing something selfish until she'd actually done it and somebody pointed it out? It had been a mistake, okay? She hadn't meant to hurt anyone. She just had to find someone, that was all. Thinking about this led her uncomfortably to thinking of her mother. She shifted in her seat uneasily.

'What's the matter?'

'Nothing,' said Ellie. 'Just bog-standard contemporary alienation.'

'Oh, that.' Julia turned up the Cyndi Lauper tape they'd bought for $2.99 and Ellie stared wistfully out the window to 'Time after Time'.

From far in the distance a figure appeared by the side of the road.

'A hitchhiker!' said Ellie excitedly.

'Yeah, no way,' said Julia. They drew closer, and the road shimmered in the heat.

'It's like that Shania Twain video,' said Ellie. 'Look! It's a woman.'

Julia peered over the top of the steering wheel.

'It looks very tall to be a woman,' she said doubtfully.

'But she's got long pink hair,' said Ellie. Still doubtful, Julia slowed the car a little. The woman

219

waggled her hips energetically and kicked up a very high heel.

'Wow, it looks like she might be very *very* grateful if you picked her up,' said Ellie.

'Oh, look, I'm not going to.'

'You're going to leave a lone woman by the side of the road? Right on sister.'

'Argh.' Julia wrestled with herself.

'Oh, *please* can we pick her up?' begged Ellie. 'I've been feeling really guilty about . . . things . . . and this would be a good thing to do, wouldn't it?'

Making a Marge Simpson noise, Julia drew up by the exotic creature.

'HEY!' screamed the woman in a suspiciously deep voice. 'Thanks *so* much. Oh, get you two cuties! What are you, like, Spice Girls that have been left out in the rain?'

Julia looked at Ellie as the 'woman' laughed, dumped her leopard skin travelling case, folded up her endless and suspiciously slim legs and poured herself into the back.

'I'm Holly Wood,' she began conversationally, poking her head through the gap between the two front seats. 'And you're my new best friends!'

* * *

'So you don't think,' Ellie said, when Holly paused to let her get a word in edgeways, 'that being a seven-foot-tall transvestite dressed as a hooker isn't a bit of a dangerous way to go hitchhiking?'

'No, honey! I give those truckers the biggest thrill they ever saw.'

'I bet you do,' said Julia.

'Ooh, get you,' said Holly and Ellie at once.

'Where are you headed?' Ellie asked her.

'Well, I'm going to Toledo to pick up some chums . . . then we're off to NEW YORK. YAHH!'

'Ow,' said Julia, whose ear was rather close to Holly's massive carmine-painted mouth.

'We are too,' said Ellie, just as Julia shot her a warning look.

'Yeah? For the festival?'

'What festival?'

'The tranny festival, hon. End of the month. Where do you think I'm off to, Carnegie Hall? We're going to be dancing in the streets, hon. Don't you even THINK about missing it!'

Ellie looked at Julia suddenly.

'Do whatever you like,' said Julia. 'I'll be at the Guggenheim.'

'No!' said Ellie. 'Don't you see? I think I know how to re-enlist the third musketeer!'

* * *

'WARRRGH!'

'What's that?' said Arthur. 'I can't really hear you

221

this end. Colin and Big Bastard have turned the front room into an ice hockey rink. It would take too long to explain. Oh and by the way, Billy was round here. He says could you let him know if you're coming back to him or not before he gets a new tattoo.'

'Wow,' said Ellie. 'You know, I haven't thought about him at all.'

'I guess that means no,' said Arthur, worriedly. 'I'd better get on to him.'

Ellie told him about the International Transvestite Awards.

'You know transvestites and homosexuals aren't the same thing,' he said reprovingly. 'Oh God, Big Bastard's using the Hoover as a sleigh.'

'Yes, I *know* that,' said Ellie. 'I just thought you might like to know. In case you were reconsidering coming.'

'Hmm,' said Arthur. 'So, while you were out actor-hunting in the snow I'd have to put on a hula skirt and wiggle my butt around to disco music?'

'Not if you didn't want to . . .'

'See you in Kansas City!'

* * *

'Good luck, Holly Wood!' Ellie gave her a hug as they dropped her off in a quiet town in the middle of the Arizona desert.

'Hon, I don't need luck, I just need someone who

222

can sew a sequin on tight. So you'll come and see me in New York?'

'Definitely.'

'Okay! Have a good trip now y'all! And don't go picking up any strange men!'

'As if!' snorted Ellie and they pulled away.

* * *

'Oh God,' said Arthur, staring at his suitcase.

'I don't even *have* any jumpers.'

'Borrow some of his,' said Colin, who was perched on top of the bed wrapped up against the cold in an England rugby top fifteen sizes too big for him. 'I've already packed your hula skirt.'

'Absolutely not! I don't know where they've been. No, actually, I do know where they've been – underneath those armpits for a start.'

'Hey!' said Big Bastard, wandering in with a six-pack protectively tucked under his arm, and leaning against the doorway.

'By the way . . . which airline are you flying with, Arthur? British Gayerways? or Gay-roflot?'

Arthur turned round slowly.

'BB, how long did it take you to think of that?'

Big Bastard hung his head.

'Yeah, it was a slow day.'

'A whole day?'

Big Bastard shrugged.

'Well, I started yesterday. There's loads you know. Oh, and are you going to be cruising at 30,000 feet . . .'

'Yes, yes,' said Arthur, cutting him off. 'And anyway, what are you doing in here? The presence of hastily hidden Nancy Friday books would seem to indicate that it's not your room.'

'What the fuck are they when they're at home?'

'It's like porn, right, only for girls,' piped up Colin.

'Girls don't like porn!' scoffed Big Bastard dismissively.

'Big Bastard, you think girls don't like sex,' said Arthur.

'Neh, I've just had an unlucky run of frigid bitches. What's it like then? Is it all todgers and that? Do you two like it?'

'No, it's just writing,' said Colin, holding up a copy of *Women on Top*.

'Just writing? That sounds like it'll be complete crap,' said Big Bastard, picking it up and tucking it under his free arm nonetheless.

'When are you off? I'd give you a lift on my scooter. But I'm a bit busy.' He clutched the Nancy Friday book almost imperceptibly tighter.

'That's okay, Siobhan's coming over to drive me to the airport.'

'Middle of winter doesn't sound like a proper

fucking holiday. You should come with me and the boys from the club. We're going to Ibiza, right, to get lagered up and get off with those lasses you're always seeing on TV that're totally pissed up. They're up for anything, right, and they're wearing practically nothing. And they're pissed up! Fantastic. I suppose you'd have to try and get them to be sick *first* though,' he finished, almost to himself.

'Actually, I think I'd better just go and answer the door,' said Arthur, hopping off the bed.

'I suppose the trick would be to carry chewing gum, right . . .'

'Dammit,' said Siobhan, who was hopping about outside in the rain.

'I was going to use your loo, then I remembered this was Big Bastard's house. Last time I used it there was a toothbrush in it.'

'Quite right,' said Arthur. 'Thanks for this.'

'Not at all. I can pick up some bathroom fixtures in Slough on my way back. Oh, and I can throw a stone through his dad's greenhouse.'

'You wouldn't!'

'I know. I'm running out of ideas.'

'Colin!'

Colin scampered out carrying the suitcase and hopped into the back seat.

Arthur peered round the door one last time 'Bye Big Bastard . . .'

225

There was a muted grunt.

'He went into the bathroom with that book,' said Colin, hanging over the front seat. 'I don't think he's going to be out in a hurry.'

'Well, I'm glad I didn't even attempt it,' said Siobhan.

'Plus, we'll get to the airport quicker if your bladder's about to explode,' said Arthur.

* * *

Colin fell asleep before they'd even hit the Westway, and Siobhan took the opportunity to turn round. They were inching ahead in the traffic, and the windscreen wipers were working overtime.

'Arthur?'

Arthur raised his eyebrows. Siobhan sounded serious.

'Is he asleep?'

'Yeah, I would think so. He goes out like a light in cars. And night buses too. In fact, that's how we met.'

'You're so lucky to have a man like him.'

Arthur looked at him asleep. 'He is sweet, isn't he? Although of course I'm off to New York to be wild and crazy.'

'Can I talk to you about something?'

'Of course. Anything.'

'Can you keep it secret?'

226

'Probably. Unless it's against my own self-interest.'

Siobhan lowered her eyebrows at him.

'Just being honest! What if I was being tortured?'

'Arthur it's . . . it's Loxy.'

'What?' said Arthur. 'What about Loxy?'

'Well . . . more specifically, it's about Loxy and me.'

'WHAT?'

Taken off guard, Siobhan swerved the car almost into the path of the enormous truck coming up behind them.

'JESUS!!!' she screamed. The truck blew its horn loudly as the car slowly skidded back into position.

'MUM!!' Colin woke up with a start.

Siobhan rolled her eyes.

'What are you rolling your eyes at *me* for?' Arthur hissed. 'I can't believe . . .'

'You just nearly killed us! So shut up!' said Siobhan, putting on the radio loudly. Eminem came blaring out.

'I like him because he swears,' said Colin.

Arthur put his hands over his eyes and looked out of the window.

'It's not . . .' said Siobhan.

'What, serious? So, what – you're going to finish it when she comes home? Or maybe wait until the wedding?'

'*No.*'

'I can't believe you. You, of all people. Don't tell me: you've started ballet class.'

Siobhan pulled off the road next to a corner shop and handed Colin a pile of change.

'Go buy sweets.'

Colin's eyes widened.

'But none of that treacle toffee,' shouted Arthur after him. 'It sticks your teeth together and last time you cried, remember. And you,' he returned to Siobhan, 'I just can't believe you.'

'Yeah, you said that,' said Siobhan, turning on him, furious. 'Rather than wait two seconds to get the actual facts.'

'You're fucking your best friend's boyfriend. Hmm. You're right. There are many different and subtle shades of meaning I can take from that.'

Siobhan clenched her arms to stop herself hitting him.

'I AM NOT FUCKING HIM!'

Arthur looked at her.

She stared at the floor.

'OKAY? I've . . . I've just got a terrible crush on him. I wanted to tell you . . . expected some sympathy. But perhaps you'd rather cut off my hair, paint me red and parade me around town naked.'

'Oh Shiv, I am sorry.' Arthur reached out and touched her arm. 'Sorry, I just . . .'

'Jumped to conclusions the first second you could, you fucking drama queen.'

'I'm *sorry*.'

Siobhan sniffed unhappily then glanced at Arthur.

'So, I would guess you wouldn't approve?'

'I don't know,' said Arthur. 'I would *love* to see you bald and red and stomping about naked.'

'Oh, but Arthur, he's just so *sweet*. He's so handsome and loving and sexy and devoted . . .'

'Yeah, but not to you.'

'Yeah, but I've got a good imagination.'

'Has he made *any* move towards you at all?'

'No. He just comes round and moans. He really misses her.'

'And you were going to change this by taking your clothes off?'

'Oh, you make it sound so shabby.'

'No, you're right. That fake sympathy/clothes off tactic really is a pretty classy affair. Works on widowers as well, I've heard.'

'Okay, thank you. Thank you. What am I going to do?'

'What do you mean, what are you going to do? Don't you remember last year? I couldn't go outside on any Saturday *at all*.'

'Ehm . . . yes, I do remember now – which one was it again, Ant or Dec?'

'Oh, both of them. Unbearable. But then it passed. That's what crushes do. Then you wake up one day and say to yourself, "is that adorable puppy fat or is it actually a gut?" And then it's over and you can choose someone from *ER*.'

'So people get over their crushes then?'

'Yup. Yes they do.'

'And what is it Ellie is doing again . . . ?'

'Oh, here's Colin,' said Arthur abruptly. 'Col! Get in! We've got to get a move on!'

'Gmdppffhh,' said Colin.

'You better not have bought that treacle toffee.'

'Frnnggfff,' said Colin, shaking his head fiercely.

* * *

'Hum hum hum.' Arthur strolled through the airport with a light bag and customary panache. He was on his way to buy a bumper quantity of books and magazines in preparation for an open-ended stay at Kansas City airport, after his change at Atlanta. It was going to be a long fifteen hours plus Ellie unpredictability tax.

A cute steward passed by and caught his eye, winking at him. Arthur froze immediately as the steward shrugged and waltzed off, towing his little bag. Damn it! Arthur was a free man! It was his right to flirt. Sighing, he stalked on. He was, he had to admit, a bit worried about Colin. He was worried that Big Bastard wouldn't be seen out with him any more and wouldn't take him anywhere while Arthur was away. A threesome was fine, but apparently real men

230

never went to the pub in twos because it was a badge of gayness. He sighed, reached Smith's and turned in, managing to completely miss Colin's little pug face still pressed up against the airport window.

Dangerous Liaisons

Blancmange were playing 'Living on the Ceiling' which, Julia was beginning to believe, would be infinitely preferable to spending this much time in a car.

They had stayed two nights in the kinds of motels frequented by Mulder and Scully on the trail of flesh-sucking, incestuous tree people, and had been greeted with a variety of friendly, if deeply suspicious attitudes, particularly since Ellie had found an enormous polka dot bow and insisted on wearing it in her hair. Mile after mile after mile of dusty roads and endless, endless strips of the same signs – Transco, Wendy's, Tacobell, White Castle, Elf. Over and over again. Behind, great mountain ranges loomed and soared; ahead, huge yellow fields stretched out forever. Stuck in the rusty tin box of a Toyota, Julia had two straight lines etched on her eyeballs. Now it was hammering rain, harder than they'd ever seen before, battering the roof of the car as they puttered through Kansas.

Ellie, however, was finding it peaceful. Nobody could find her. There weren't any messages to return on her voicemail. No mobile. No e-mail. No fax. No commuters: hell, there were hardly any other cars; no news apart from supermarket tabloids. She hadn't seen a single Ikea, and the rhythm of the car and the hills and the days was lulling her.

'"Every Kansas farmer feeds seventy-five people,"' she read dreamily out loud as they entered the state. 'Is that seventy-five Americans or seventy-five ordinary people? There's a big difference. That's probably about three hundred ordinary people.' She returned to the guidebook. 'Kansas City – ooh! – Harry S. Truman was born here,' she continued. 'And it has a really big zoo.'

Four hours later she was still reading contentedly. But now the signs were saying, 'leaving Kansas'.

'Hedgehog,' said Julia, anxiously. 'Look at the map again please.'

'I have looked at the map,' said Ellie, eating a vast bag of something called Tater Tots, a revolting mix of Smarties and Pringles that she, however, didn't seem able to put down.

'We're heading towards Kansas City.'

'But we're *leaving Kansas*.'

Ellie turned the map upside down.

'Hmm. Are you sure you didn't turn one hundred and eighty degrees somewhere when I wasn't looking?'

'YES I'm sure. Look, there's the fucking state line!' It was rare to see Julia cross but then it's rare to spend days cooped up with someone who keeps dozing off on you while you have to do all the work. 'Where the fuck is your fucking city with its enormous fucking zoo??'

'Should be around here somewhere.'

The view for hundreds of miles in all directions was entirely flat.

'Oh, for CHRIST's sake, Hedgehog, why couldn't you just do your one tiny job – of getting us along a completely straight road. You just have completely NO fucking sense of responsibility.'

Ellie immediately sulked up.

'Yes I do, Miss Smarty Pants. It's got to be around here somewhere.'

They reached the state line.

'That's what bloody Captain Scott said!' yelled Julia. 'That's what they said when they were looking for the lost city of Atlantis. Give me that map!'

Ellie handed it over.

'FUCK! Hedgehog what the fuck are you thinking?'

The scale was about 1: 250,000.

'Oh, for fuck's sake!'

'WHAT?'

'We're two thousand miles bang in the middle of absolutely nowhere and we don't know what fucking *state* we're in and we don't know anyone and we have no fucking idea what we're doing and I wish I'd never fucking come . . .'

Julia did a squealing turn across an intersection.

'Right,' she said. 'We are going back across this state very, very slowly. And if you don't find it, you're going to walk in front of the car until you do.'

Ellie was silent for about fifteen seconds.

'Does this mean I don't get to say, "We're not in Kansas any more"?'

'It's not funny.'

They drove on in silence, back along the same route they had come, through the identical pounding rain. There didn't seem to be any signposts for anything. Suddenly Ellie shouted,

'Shit! Stop the car!'

'Yeah. Right. Like I am going to take my driving advice off you.'

'No, no, I mean – Shit! Okay – if you want some idea of where we're going, why don't you ask *him*!?'

They had whizzed past a solitary hitchhiker on the other side of the road, spraying him with water. The hitchhiker had turned round, and Ellie had checked him out through the back mirror.

'If you think I'm going back for another fucking hitchhiker, you're even more off your fucking head that I thought you already were,' said Julia, still white with anger. 'And that one's definitely a bloke.'

Ellie turned to look at her.

'You didn't read his sign then, did you?'

'*What?*'

Nevertheless, Julia slowed the car a little.

'Believe me. You want to pick up this one. Go back. You have to go back.'

'Hedge, I can't go back, we're on the freeway. What did it say?'

'Oh, how would I know? I was too busy over here being irresponsible. God, I haven't even cleaned my teeth for two days.'

Julia slowed to a stop on the hard shoulder.

'I swear to God, Hedge, if you're talking bullshit, I'm going to dump you on the road and leave you to fight it out with the hitchhiker.'

'Fine!' Ellie started singing 'Freeway of Love' softly to herself as Julia made a dangerous and illegal reversal back up the freeway through the rain. She stopped a short distance from the hitchhiker, who ran up as soon as he heard the sound of the car.

Julia peered forward through the car windshield,

trying to see through the rain and oncoming dusk. The drenched figure held up its arms and sign apologetically. Julia fumbled at the door and pushed it open, launching herself into the rain. Ellie shook her head and returned to the guidebook.

'What . . . what on *earth????*'

Andrew McCarthy II stood in the gravel at the side of the road laughing his head off. He held up his sign again. It said 'Looking for Andrew McCarthy'. The black marker had started to run.

'But what – how – what the *hell* are you doing here?'

'Calm down. You look like you've seen a ghost.'

'I'm not sure I just haven't. This kind of thing used to happen all the time in *Misty* magazine. I'm going to find out later you were killed in Los Angeles at exactly the same time . . .'

'Ssh,' he said, putting his finger to her mouth.

'But . . .'

'There's only one road into Kansas City,' he said. 'Figured you'd be along sooner or later, so I thought it would be funny to come and meet you this way. Of course, I wasn't planning on a good old Midwestern rain shower. Oh – and you're going the wrong way.'

'Yes, sorry, the car . . . oh, come and sit inside, you're soaked.'

They dashed to the car.

'Ellie, look who it is . . . !'

238

'Yes, I saw who it was, thanks. You may remember I pointed it out. Hi Andrew.'

'Eh, yeah, hi there.'

'How's Hatsie?'

'Fine thanks. Back in therapy.'

'Oh well, it was nice to see him come out of his shell.'

Andrew smiled. 'You look different.'

'Yes, thanks, I've stopped peeling off long strands of my skin.'

'Right. I just couldn't put my finger on it.'

'So, umm,' said Julia, turning round from the wheel as Andrew squeezed his long legs into the minuscule back seat, picking up various greasy wrappers and cardboard coffee containers from Ellie's side. 'I just can't believe you were there. Because we're lost.'

'Lost? I thought you were going to Kansas City.'

'Yes, we were . . . but we've been all round Kansas and . . .'

'Ohh.' Andrew's eyes sparkled. 'Ahh. Who thought of that?'

'The Hedgehog's idea.'

'Well, d'uh,' said Ellie, scarcely lifting her head from her guidebook.

'Not at all,' said Andrew. 'Mistake anyone could have made. Anyway, it's about ten miles away from here. And it's not really in Kansas.'

They both stared at him, open-mouthed.

'But . . . but that makes no sense at all,' stuttered Ellie, finally.

'Yeah? You're the ones who measure these things in millibillidecameters.'

'That's so STUPID.' Julia started up the car again, mindful of the encroaching dark and the fact that out there somewhere were very tall policemen with guns.

'Yeah? But Rhodesia was fine? Look, I'm sorry, calm down, you're nearly there now. Just you wait until you see their zoo.'

'Ahem!' said Ellie. 'Anyone called Julia want to apologize to me?'

'I've missed you two,' said Andrew. And although he felt Ellie briefly stroke his right arm, as if by accident, he pretended not to. But he did remember it.

* * *

Andrew directed them to a little hotel he'd found, and sure enough it was a hundred times nicer than anywhere they had stayed so far and scarcely more expensive. A large fire burned in the grate in the bar, and once they'd changed out of their wet clothes, they rendezvoused there and sipped large glasses of Jack Daniel's. The spirit went right through Julia, and she wasn't sure whether it was that, the fire, the drive, or the proximity of a certain tall, rugged-looking someone that was making her so woozy.

'I can't believe we're going to pick Arthur up on time,' said Ellie sleepily, examining the menu. 'Oh wow – it's weird to see a menu without cheeseburgers on it. I've forgotten what else there is to eat.'

'Or what else there is to wear,' said Julia, looking pointedly at the fourth day of Ellie's 'fat girl' jeans.

'I'm sure they'll make you up a burger if you really want one,' said Andrew. He was sitting with a large pad and different coloured markers and looked like he actually was going to be working on his film.

'Green salad please,' said Ellie grumpily.

'We're Not In Kansas City Any More,' suggested Andrew with a flourish.

'We've done that today. But I thought the dinosaurs *were* in Kansas City. That's the whole point. That's why they're eating people there and throwing meteors at them and stuff,' pointed out Ellie.

'Good point.'

'I thought it was good, though,' said Julia. Andrew smiled at her lazily. Ellie gulped her drink down and decided not to say anything else.

They were the only guests in the hotel, and had dinner served to them on small tables in front of the comfortable armchairs.

'Ah, how American,' said Ellie. 'Now all we need is the forty-inch TV drowning out all possibility of conversation.'

'Dinosty!' shouted Andrew suddenly. 'Hmm. I wonder if I can work in the enormous zoo.'

'Andrew, stop working for one tiny second,' said Julia, eyes heavy. 'Tell me – I mean, us – about yourself.'

'Well,' started Andrew, 'I was born in Northern California, and started surfing before I could walk, pretty much. Then my father moved to Los Angeles and became a lawyer, and as soon as I arrived I realized how much I wanted to be in the movie business, however, ehm, peripherally. So I hung out and went to UCLA and . . .'

Ellie glanced over at Julia, who after thirty-six hours on the road and four Jack Daniel's had passed out entirely.

'Ah,' she said tactfully. 'Well, I was enjoying it.'

Andrew looked crestfallen. 'Oh dear. Well, just as well I never got into any of my fratboy stories. Some of them would knock out a ferret on speed.'

'I'll put her to bed,' said Ellie.

'Okay . . . I'll stay here and keep working. Hmm. Do you think you could have a Kansasaurus?'

'Nope. Shame they're not doing it with kanga-roos.'

'It *is*.'

'Goodnight,' said Julia woozily. 'Oh,' she said, as they reached the room and Ellie started helping her get undressed. 'No, hang on . . . I didn't want to go

242

to bed yet . . . I wanted to stay up . . . I wanted to . . .
this is too early for . . . *God* I'm tired.'

'I know what you wanted,' said Ellie. 'Maybe think
it over in the morning, eh? Maybe phone Loxy.'

'Oh God,' said Julia. 'Remind me when the having
fun part starts again?'

* * *

Ellie crept back downstairs and examined Andrew's
fine profile from the hallway.

'Absolutely not,' she whispered to herself, but went
in anyway.

Andrew looked up and stared straight at her with
his clear blue eyes. She smiled.

'How is she?'

'Oh, she's fine. Just knackered, you know. Having
to put up with me.'

He smiled. 'Or me.'

They both looked into the fire.

'Actually, I'd say it's probably me,' said Ellie.

'Yeah, I would too . . . just trying to be nice.'

Ellie, too keyed up about his proximity to respond,
just smiled.

'Why do people call you Hedgehog?' he said,
looking at her.

'Isn't it obvious?'

'No – I don't know what a hedgehog is.'

'You're joking.'

'Nope.'

'Um . . . it's a very beautiful creature . . . like a mermaid . . . only with legs.'

'Oh.'

'It's a prickly pig that lives in the countryside.'

'But you don't live in the countryside.'

'Aha ha hah.'

'Seriously.'

'Seriously . . . I don't know. The world pisses me off a lot.'

'Why?'

'I don't know. It just never turned out quite how I wanted it.'

'What . . . covered in gold and naked film stars and Ben and Jerry's? Or like a John Hughes movie?'

'You think I'm stupid.'

'I don't think you're stupid. But, you know, the world never turns out the way you want it. I mean, look at me.' He held up his board. 'Writing one-liners, not movie scripts.'

'You could write movie scripts.'

'Yeah, but I'd need a concentration span of more than fifteen seconds.'

'Sorry, what did you say? I wasn't listening.'

He laughed and, casually, pushed a finger through one of Ellie's curls.

'I think you and I might have more in common than you think.'

244

Ellie instantly went puce.

'Umm . . .' She attempted to defuse the situation. 'Why, what's your favourite food?'

'Bananas.'

'Me too! How many do you think I could eat in one go?'

'Twelve?'

'No, double that, easy.'

He smiled. Ellie sighed.

'Something else we've got in common,' said Ellie. 'I think we both like my big blonde friend.'

He looked mildly surprised. 'Julia, you mean?'

'Uh huh.'

'Is she single? She's got settled down written all over her.'

'Really?'

'Um, well I don't want to seem nasty, but yeah. I mean, why does she keep playing with her ring finger every time she talks to a man?'

'Not all men.'

'Oh, really?' He twirled his drink around his glass.

'She really, really likes you,' blurted Ellie. 'Well, you know, in a very cool way . . .'

'I like her too. She's perfectly nice. But I have no wish to get beaten up by one of your skinny, yellow-toothed nautical countrymen, however devious and effete they may appear on celluloid.'

The fire was burning down as Ellie explained the situation.

'So, you see, if you wanted to have a fling . . . I wouldn't rat or anything.'

Andrew stared straight ahead. 'I don't think so, do you? Do you really think I'd solve her problem?'

'Maybe! She might realize how much she loves Loxy.'

'Oh, that makes me feel really good. Maybe I could be deliberately terrible in bed.'

Ellie looked at his long muscular body and squeezed her eyes tight shut.

'I think if it's on a different continent it doesn't count.'

'Hmm. No, hang on, we tried that in Vietnam . . .'
Ellie shrugged.

'Ehm, Hedgehog . . . *Ellie*. Look: I think there are enough lovely things in the world to go round, without having to poach someone else's, don't you?' he said meaningfully, looking at her with those clear blue eyes.

She gulped, but, knowing her history of unfortunate conclusion-jumping in these sets of circumstances, didn't say anything.

'What about you? Do you have someone?'
Yikes.

'Ehm . . . not as such . . . well, I've kind of got a saxophonist stalker . . . does that count?'

He shook his head and, slowly, extended his large, smooth hand over hers. Ellie felt herself trembling. The firelight continued to flicker around them as he gradually cupped her face and moved closer to her.

'I Kansas live . . . if living was without you . . .' he suggested.

'Ouch,' said Ellie. Then, 'Not ouch.'

* * *

'Ah,' said Loxy, when he came back into the tastefully decorated, Moroccan-influenced sitting room with two full mugs of tea. The rain continued to lash against the windows.

He managed not to drop the tea. 'Ah,' he said again. 'Ah, Siobhan, do you realize that you're completely naked?'

* * *

They kissed powerfully and deeply. Ellie shut her eyes and let her hands revel in his strong shoulders and long back. When they pulled apart, he was coiling her hair around his fingers.

'Wow,' he said. 'Black hair. God! Haven't seen that in a while. Must be a California thing.'

As if she'd been slapped, Ellie sat back suddenly.

'Oh my God.'

'Well, thank you.'

'No, I mean . . . I've just broken the Girl Code.'

'Really – will it be okay?'

She looked at his handsome profile outlined in the firelight.

'No, I mean . . . you just don't get off with someone else's fancied person. It's just not allowed.'

'But she's engaged. And we're both single.'

'That's not the point. What happens when you and Hatsie both meet someone . . .'

'Oh, Hatsie gets all the women. I'm used to it.'

'You're joking.'

He touched her lightly on the jaw. 'Hey,' he said softly. 'What about that different continent thing?'

Ellie's insides turned to water, both from how much she desperately wanted to kiss Andrew and how much she knew she couldn't let Julia down. Also struggling in the mix was the certain knowledge that Julia, with her smooth blonde hair and air of capability – Pamela Anderson crossed with Delia Smith – had always, always got her first pick of men. This felt like *her* turn, surely . . . A million things added up in her mind to justify grabbing that dirty blond hair . . .

Suddenly the door to the lodge flew open with abandon, and there was a cacophony of screaming and yells. Both of them jumped up guiltily, as fourteen or fifteen teenagers piled into the room, alternately screaming their heads off or barfing like dogs.

'Good God!' Ellie gaped at the scene in front of her. The girls all had hair made out of candyfloss, teased to Mr Whippy proportions. Their dresses were pastel colours, with tulle, net, taffeta and nasty fake versions of all three, ruched and low cut. The boys were in mullets and ill-fitting tuxes, with white and pale blue cummerbunds.

'We've been invaded by the Sorbet People!'

'HOW YOU DOIN' THERE?!' hollered one ample young madam, under the misapprehension she was being casually friendly. She was spilling out of what could have been a bridesmaid's dress (as long as it was a hooker wedding).

'Aw shit,' said Andrew. 'Just our luck. It's a prom.'

The teenagers were stumbling about, taking notice-ably clumsy sips from hip flasks. The restaurant waiter came to the kitchen door, raised his eyebrows and beat a hasty retreat.

'No, really?' said Ellie excited. 'They've just come from a prom?'

'No, in America proms start at eleven at night.'

'I *always* wanted a prom.'

'You're joking!'

'You don't joke about the *prom*. My God, isn't it, like the high point of your life?'

'Tammi-Lee! Tammi-Lee! Are you going to give Chip a handjob or am ah?'

Andrew shrugged. 'Well, I suspect it may be for

Chip,' he said, as a huge lad with a fat ass ambled off in search of the voice.

'Oh God . . . I mean, if you're not asked to the prom . . . your life is *over.*'

Ellie said this with such certainty that Andrew laughed.

'You know, it's only the high spot of your life if you never do anything else ever. If you go and work on your father's feed farm and marry Betty Sue.'

'Are you talking about my girlfriend, man?' said a boy in a frilly sky-blue shirt.

'No, no way.'

'Okay. Have you got any drugs?'

'!' Ellie was shocked.

'Oh yeah,' said Andrew, 'and I forgot to mention; it's also an excuse for them to get more fucked out of their tits than they ever do before or since.'

One of the girls started taking down her whale-boned top. Ellie hastened over and zipped it back up again.

'Really?'

'Oh yeah. It's just an excuse for everyone to lose their virginity.'

'Ah, so I see,' said Ellie, observing four legs making energetic motions behind a sofa.

'I scarcely remember my prom, I was so drunk.'

'Yeah? Did you lose your virginity?'

He laughed at her.

'No, actually. I've never met a woman before who does it for me like you do. I was hoping tonight would be the big night . . .'

'You're kidding.'

'Well, d'uh!'

'Aw, shit.' A boy jumped up from a particularly spit-filled and messy snog at the other side of the room. 'I *hate* it when you're necking with some ho, and she throws up on you.'

'Ooh, me too,' said Ellie, in fascinated horror. The boy dumped the girl on a chair and headed back into the centre of the room, wiping his mouth and looking for more victims. The girl's head lolled, and the ugly girl with the thick spectacles and the hairband bustled around and cleaned her up, for something to do.

'Don't worry, they're not normally this awful,' said Andrew. 'They get a lot of their teenage ghastliness out of the way all on one night. And you have to admit,' he said, as one hapless little weedy guy fell full forward over the carpet, landed on the wooden floor and stayed there, twitching like a frog, 'it's fun to watch.'

'If not to smell,' said Ellie. 'Oh, I am just so disappointed. I used to dream what I'd wear to my prom – if we had one. And not just a school disco as an excuse for all the boys to sit at one end of the gym and all the girls to sit at the other.

We wore Clockhouse. The boys wore their school uniform with their ties taken off. And cuff boots.' She sighed nostalgically. 'It was really, really terrible. Really awful. Except when we did "Double Dutch".'

'Huh?' said Andrew.

Ellie looked at the girls' long, flouncy dresses, so hopefully sexy and demure at the same time, and sighed. 'This is what I wanted,' she said, sitting back on the arm of the chair. 'Well, without the puke. I wanted a proper American prom, with a pink dress, and Andrew McCarthy to take me.'

'Hey,' Andrew put his arm around her shoulders. 'You know, I'm not sure they come without puke.'

'Might have known,' said Ellie.

She stood up. 'I'm sorry. I think I'd better go to bed.'

'What, and miss Truth or Dare?'

'It's late.'

One of the kids in the corner was setting up a stereo.

'C'mon,' said Andrew. He picked up a pink throw from the back of the sofa and tied it around her waist. 'Why don't you dance with me? Just one dance before you go to bed.'

Ellie laughed and coloured. 'Do you think they've got any Psychedelic Furs?' She stopped for a second, looking perturbed. 'Have I just realized this, or is that the worst name for a band of all time?'

Andrew drew her close to him and buried her face in his shoulder.

'From the country that brought us Orchestral Manoeuvres in the Dark . . .'

In the corner the tape recorder started up.

'FUCK PIGS AND HO'S!!!! FIRE ON THEM AT WILL WITH A MILLION GREAT BIG ENORMOUS GUNS!!!!! . . .'

Ellie's face fell in disappointment.

'Hang on!' said Andrew. He fought his way through the throng and took something out of his bag. He clicked the tape off, ignoring the howl of the disgruntled teenagers, and replaced it with one of his own. Suddenly there was a very familiar refrain and . . . yes, it was. The Psychedelic Furs!

Ellie grinned broadly and laid her head on his shoulder.

'Caroline hum . . . and it's humphy-humph humph . . .'

Andrew chuckled. 'Wow, you even know all the words!'

Ellie looked up at him in shock.

'You did this on *purpose*.'

He laughed. 'I do everything on purpose. And you are . . .' and they both joined in the chorus, 'Pretty in pink.'

And they stood there swaying in front of the fire,

ignoring the carnage around them, until the song finished and Ellie finally, reluctantly, tore herself away and went to bed.

* * *

'Oh God, I needed that,' said Julia, stretching her arms above her head. 'I can't believe I slept twelve hours.'

'Hmm.' Ellie drank her coffee quietly, reflecting that what was the point of doing the decent thing if you couldn't tell anyone about it because they'd give you a hard time anyway and not listen to you when you tried to explain.

'This room smells funny,' said Julia.

'Teenagers.'

'Oh, God, I *thought* I recognized it. You know, actually, it's quite sexy. It reminds me of that party . . .'

'That Kool and the Gang party! How could I forget? You were wearing your new Poison perfume. Nearly gassed the lot of us like badgers.'

'That's what it is,' said Julia, shaking her head. 'Bless 'em.'

Andrew came in, looking rather coy. Julia immediately brightened and turned towards him like a sunflower.

'Hello there! Did you stay up late last night?'

'Not really,' said Ellie and Andrew both at the same time. Then they looked at each other, which felt to Ellie, on the sensitive side, as tantamount to admitting extreme guilt – they might as well have said, 'yes, we went behind your back and did it up against the neo-colonial fireplace.'

At the thought of sex, Ellie realized she didn't want her grits, which meant she obviously fancied Andrew – she could never eat in front of anyone she liked. She sighed.

'Not hungry?' asked Julia, cheerfully. 'Maybe Hatsie got you pregnant. Maybe that's what happens when he takes his hat off.'

Ellie grunted and forced down some scrambled egg.

'So, Andrew . . . what are you doing today? We have to collect Arthur this afternoon.'

Andrew shrugged, 'Well, I have to pick up a bit of Missouri scenery to help me out with the slogan . . .'

'Oh, you've seen the way Ellie map-reads!'

'Ha ha ha,' said Ellie, a bit snuffily. 'I'll go and pack.'

'Okay,' said Julia, pleased to get some Andrew time to herself. 'Oh, and if you get confused – yours is the stuff strewn all over the floor.'

'Yes *Mom*.'

* * *

The airport was huge, empty and soulless. Amazingly,

they were early. After some awkward, waiting-for-someone-style banter, Julia walked past an international payphone and got a sudden tug of guilt. After all, here she was, flirting with this boy, and who knows . . . maybe this was completely wrong . . . maybe Loxy could convince her not to; convince her it was him she really loved.

She excused herself from the others and looped around to a phone well out of sight.

'Hello?'

'Um, hi there,' said Loxy. He sounded extremely taken aback. 'Ehm, how are you?'

'I'm fine,' said Julia. There was a long pause.

Then he said, coldly, 'Ehm . . . great. Well, I'm, you know, just . . . nothing, really.'

Julia winced. So. He obviously hadn't forgiven her for the little Heathrow fiasco.

'Okay,' she said, forcing levity into her voice. 'I've got to go now. I'll phone again soon.'

She peered round the phone. Andrew and Ellie were laughing at something and she suddenly realized that right at this moment she wanted to be where they were.

'Right! Bye then!' she said abruptly, and put the phone down.

'Okay,' said Loxy into an empty receiver.

* * *

Loxy put the phone down and slowly removed the hand he had covering Siobhan's mouth.

'I can't believe you were going to pick up my phone at this time of night.'

'I could have just popped over on my way home from work.'

'You *did* just pop over on your way home from work, Siobhan. That's still weird.'

Loxy was standing in Julia's dressing gown, which he'd been wearing since she left. Siobhan was wearing a business suit and high heels, however one of the shoulders of the business suit had been pulled down to show off an extremely expensive bra. Loxy was really starting to worry. He liked Siobhan and everything – actually, he'd tended in the past not to notice Julia's friends very much – but ever since he'd found her naked in his flat and gently moved her out (after coaxing her back into her clothes), things had gone a bit weird. He suspected she was turning into a bunny boiler.

'I just came round to see if you wanted any supper,' said Siobhan, tantalizingly waving a bottle of wine.

'No, thank you.' Loxy rubbed his eyes wearily.

'Okay, sweetheart . . . do you want me to bring you some breakfast on the way in tomorrow?'

'No, thanks, it's okay . . .'

But she was gone.

* * *

Loxy needed some male advice to help him sort this out. Unfortunately, since devoting his life to Julia, he no longer had quite so many options in that area.

'So, let me get this straight.' Big Bastard squinted into his pint. 'Let's just go over this one more time, because I'm not getting it. Okay. She wants to have sex with you and you're . . . not doing it. Sorry mate. I just don't understand. Explain it again.'

'I love Julia,' said Loxy desperately. 'I'm trying to stay faithful.'

'So, what – you think Siobhan might have a really stinking minge or something? Clap?'

'What's "clap"?' said Colin.

'It's what Arthur does when you manage to go three days without wetting the bed,' said Big Bastard. 'I mean, mate, really. Why don't you just shag her? Jules decided to piss off and leave you, didn't she?'

'Yes, on holiday. I'm not sure that's a random invitation for me to have a big fuckfest.'

'It might be. Women find it difficult to talk about these things, don't they?'

'Yes, well I'm sorry Big Bastard, but I still think, "I'm going on holiday," probably doesn't mean, "Have a big fuckfest."'

'Suit yourself,' said Big Bastard. 'What's her address?'

'39 Lavender . . .why?'

'No reason!'

'She's gagging for it,' said Big Bastard quietly to Colin. Colin, eyes wide, nodded, just for a quiet life.

'Do you want me to go round there and have a word with her, mate?' said Big Bastard, bluffly. 'Just get her to lay off a bit, yeah?'

'Ehm . . . I don't know – do you think that would help?'

'It would help *me*,' said Big Bastard. 'Bloody Carmel chucked me. Honestly. I mean, if you can't fart in your girlfriend's bed, where can you fart? And sometimes, when you fart, things just get broken, that's all.'

Colin and Loxy regarded him in amazement.

'You know. Anyway, it was only an old vase.'

'You farted and broke a *vase*?'

'Hey – I thought we were talking about your psychotic nymphomaniac stalker.'

Loxy got up and got another round in.

'Ehm,' said Colin, 'Big Bastard?'

'Uh-huh?'

'What's our – you know – what's the rota for cleaning up and things in the flat?'

Big Bastard put back his head and laughed.

'Okay little one. Here it is. Mondays, you clean everything. Tuesdays you clean everything. And Wednesdays, Thursdays and Fridays. And that way, I refrain from kicking your teeth in on Saturdays, okay?'

Colin nodded.

'Good. Now go and tell Loxy to get extra pork scratchings.'

* * *

Arthur started in surprise. It had taken him over eighteen hours to get to Kansas City, and, walking unoptimistically through the exit, leaning over his trolley in tiredness, he really hadn't expected to hear his name screeched out in harsh accents quite different to the soft murmurs that surrounded him. Waving frantically, Ellie and Julia jumped up and down, looking tanned and excitable. They were with a tall, extremely good-looking blond guy. Arthur raised his eyebrows.

'And this is Andrew . . .' said Julia rather propriet-arily, after the screeching and the hugging and the jumping up and down were finished with.

'Hi,' said Arthur warily, looking at Julia's flushed face. There's trouble, he thought. He eyed Andrew's muscular physique appreciatively, even though, as soon as he did so, he had a vision of Colin's beseeching little face.

Ellie was looking uncharacteristically chirpy.

'Hey, Hedgehog,' he said, draping an arm around her. 'How's the search for enlightenment going?'

'Pretty good actually,' Ellie said, surprising herself. 'Arthur, what do you think is worse – school discos or school proms?'

'They both sound equally revolting,' said Arthur. 'Why?'

'No, they *are*,' she said, sincerely. 'Good, isn't it?'

The four stood around awkwardly as Arthur picked up his baggage. 'So,' said Julia enthusiastically. 'What are we doing now? Enormous zoo?'

Andrew II shrugged. Arthur looked slightly perturbed. 'I thought I might . . . have a very long sleep in the back of a car heading towards NEW YORK? REMEMBER?'

'Oh,' said Julia, looking anxiously at Andrew II. Ellie managed to resist the urge to do precisely the same thing. 'Damn it,' she said to herself. 'This is going to be tortuous.' Half of her wanted Andrew to go, get away, to avoid all the complication. The other half wanted him to stay very, very much, as she eyed the long curve of his back.

'Um,' said Andrew II. He shuffled a bit.

'Guys?' said Julia desperately. 'We're going to stay here for a bit aren't we?'

'I don't know,' said Arthur sceptically. 'Where's the International Transvestite quarter?'

The awkward silences were gaining ground.

'Well, the Hedgehog wants to press on,' said Arthur, conscious of trying to make the decisions despite being there fifteen seconds.

'Umm,' said Ellie.

Nobody moved.

* * *

'Actually,' said Andrew II finally, and with deliberate carelessness, 'I haven't taken a trip to New York in a while. You know, driving it might be rather fun.'

'There you go,' thought Arthur ruefully, as he saw both the girls' faces light up, then the expressions being quickly hidden. 'Bingo.'

'Fantastic!' said Julia, a little too quickly.

'I'll just have to phone Hatsie, let him know what I'm doing,' said Andrew. 'Last time I went away he tried to freeze himself to death through leaving the chiffon curtains blowing open.'

'It's lucky that hats keep in eighty per cent of body heat,' said Ellie.

'. . . and we live in a place with three hundred and twenty days of sunshine a year,' agreed Andrew. 'And then I'll go and pick up a car. Meet you round the front.'

'We're going to need another car?' said Julia disappointedly before she could stop herself.

Andrew looked back at the Toyota. 'I think so. Unless we can do *Honey I Shrunk the American*.'

'Okay,' nodded Ellie and Andrew headed off towards the rental desk. The remaining three stood there looking slightly sheepish.

'So,' said Arthur. 'Um, how come I didn't get to hear about Adonis over there?'

The girls looked shifty.

'Is he good-looking?' said Ellie. 'I hadn't noticed.'

'Ehm, Arthur . . .' said Julia, carefully. 'Do you feel like doing a bit of driving? Only I've been going for days and . . .'

Ellie saw where this was going immediately.

'Oh, but you must be exhausted,' she said to Arthur.

'I am,' said Arthur.

'Well, you two go in one car and I'll go with Andrew in the other so you can stretch out.'

'But –!!' said Julia crossly. She gave Ellie a quick Paddington Bear. Surely they'd already got this sorted out. Ellie looked at the ceiling insouciantly.

They moved out across the concourse and stood on the kerb, waiting for the car.

'Andrew's car will probably be bigger,' said Julia, making a lunge for the lesser of two evils. 'Arthur could stretch out in that and the Hedgehog could come with me. The seat's moulded to the shape of your arse anyway.'

'Oh, I'm *sick* of us,' moaned Ellie.

'Actually,' said Arthur. 'Jules, you probably should come with me. I need to talk to you about Loxy.'

'What about Loxy?' Julia said hotly, as a gleaming silver Thunderbird drew up. They all ignored it at first, not used to being connected to such lovely cars.

'Who's Loxy?' said Andrew II casually, leaning out of the open window of the beautiful machine.

Julia was momentarily dumbstruck, and Ellie took the opportunity to run round to the other side of the Thunderbird and hop in, waving.

Big

Big Bastard swallowed hard and tugged at the tight collar round his big pink neck before ringing the bell. There was a long silence. He let the drips from the porch roof hit him on the head. Finally, he heard tentative footsteps on the stairs and a pale, washed out-looking Siobhan put her head round the door. She squinted at him for a long time. It was a grey and dreary evening.

'Uh . . . hello,' said Big Bastard.

She stared at him. 'Big Bastard? . . . Are those new sweat patches or are you just pleased to see me?'

'Can I come in?'

'For why?'

'Ehm . . . I need to talk to you about Loxy.'

'Oh, thank God for that.' Siobhan opened the door.

'For a moment I thought you'd come round on the off-chance of a shag.'

Big Bastard stuffed the box of Terry's All Gold back into his inside pocket.

* * *

'Ehm . . . About Last Night,' said Ellie, once they had finally hit the open road and she'd found a radio station that was playing 'Everybody Wants to Rule the World'.

'Changed your mind?' said Andrew with a grin.

'No,' said Ellie, staring at her hands. It had been easy to tell Billy to fuck off, because she'd wanted him to. Having to do it now with Andrew, purely out of altruism, was a complete pain in the bum.

'I didn't . . . I wanted to apologize.'

'For letting me come onto you?'

'No . . . yes . . . not sure.'

'Oh,' said Andrew. He attempted to look unperturbed, but his face took on a fixed expression.

'Sure. You're not going to sue me for sexual harassment are you? That's pretty normal in this country.'

'That's because it's mad,' said Ellie, looking at his tousled hair.

'We're mad? You're the ones that get four teams in the soccer world cup.'

They sat for a while staring ahead. Then he grinned at her and put his hand on her leg. She let it lie there.

'Oh, I think I've got your catch-phrase,' said Ellie suddenly, smiling.

'What's that?'

'"Missouring you already".'

He smiled back at her then, turned up the radio and put the hood down, so that their hair blew back in the wind and they couldn't hear each other speak as they sped through the endless golden cornfields of the Midwest, looking, Ellie thought in a pleased, private way, as much like 'Footloose' as she'd probably ever get.

* * *

'God, look at those two,' snorted Julia jealously, trying to see round the accumulated mound of luggage and junk that was cluttering up the tiny Toyota as it puttered along. The only way they were keeping up with the others was that Ellie and Andrew had to stop for petrol every fifteen minutes. Arthur had fallen asleep the second he had sat down.

'Who does she think she is: Lori Singer?'

'Huh?' said Arthur, snoozily. 'Oh . . . the boat's just come through the field – hello headmaster!'

'Arthur,' said Julia crossly. 'What was it you were going to tell me about Loxy?'

Arthur considered pretending to be asleep a little longer but decided not to prolong the agony.

He struggled up from his sunken position.

'Oh. Yeah,' he said. 'Well, it's more Siobhan, actually.'

And he told her what Siobhan had told him on the way to the airport. Julia listened without saying anything, although her grip tightened perceptibly on the steering wheel.

'Uh huh,' she said, when he had finished.

Arthur looked at her and crinkled up his nose.

'Well?'

She tutted. 'Oh, don't be ridiculous, Arthur,' she said finally. 'Loxy would never cheat on me. It's just not in his genes. Or his trousers. I feel more sorry for Siobhan, really.'

'Just out of interest,' said Arthur. 'How would you feel if anything happened?'

Julia shrugged, her mind completely and totally made up. 'It couldn't.'

* * *

Loxy was taking a walk past Julia's house. He had a key, but he didn't feel like going in – it felt too much like snooping. He gazed up at the carefully curtained windows and sighed. He needed something – some kind of sign. After all, if everything was fine why had she made just one desultory phone call? She'd hardly wanted to chat, even if he wasn't exactly in a perfect position. Not a letter, not even a postcard. He wasn't looking forward to her coming home. If only there was some way he could get in touch with her, show her how much she meant to him.

He got a brief image, suddenly, of Siobhan's pale left breast exposed underneath her business suit, and the combative look she'd worn.

* * *

'So?' said Siobhan, briskly.

Big Bastard rubbed the back of his neck. Really, he couldn't stand relationship things. However he realized his chances of getting a shag in were directly in proportion to how tactful he could be.

'You know Loxy, right?'

'Yes, I think I know who you mean.'

'He says, right . . .' he grappled for the right words. 'He reckons, right, that you're not leaving him alone and you're turning into a bit of a Bunny Boiler.'

'A *what*?'

'You know . . . a kind of hungry minge-type maniac.'

'A hungry minge-type maniac.' Siobhan repeated slowly. 'Ah, the language of love.'

'So he says, right, could you leave his chocolate soldier alone.'

'His *what?*'

'You know. His knob.'

'He has sent *you* to tell *me* that I'm bothering his knob?'

'Eh . . . yeah, kind of.'

Siobhan slumped down in the corner of the room. 'Great. Just when I think my life can't get any worse I find out that "worse" was a breeze compared to this. The day Patrick left me was, I now realize, a free day out at Alton Towers.'

'So you really were bothering his knob then?'

'Big Bastard, you couldn't possibly understand. And please take your hands out of your pockets while you're talking to me.'

'I might understand,' Big Bastard sat down next to her in the corner. 'Did you really get naked in his house?'

'Oh Christ!' said Siobhan. 'I can't believe he told you that. He's not even a gentleman.'

'Did you REALLY?' said Big Bastard. 'He never said a thing, I was just making a stab in the dark. Fucking brilliant. Were you completely naked, or were you wearing, like, boots?'

* * *

Colin was sitting in the flat watching the phone ring. Eventually, when it wouldn't stop — every time the ansaphone clicked in, the phone was put down, then it immediately started ringing again — he edged closer and closer to it, and finally picked it up.

'Hello?' he piped, nervously.

'Can I speak to Miss Ellie Eversholt,' said an officious voice.

'Um . . . she's not here at the moment – can I take a message?'

'No . . . no you can't take a message . . .'

* * *

'Biggest Pig in the World!' shouted Arthur sitting bolt upright out of his latest doze.

He had spent most of his first twenty-four hours in America unconscious, having sleepwalked to his room as soon as they had stopped at a motel the previous evening.

Julia, on the other hand, hadn't let Ellie and Andrew out of her sight, so they had been an uneasy threesome until they had all given up on their various agendas and gone (separately) to bed.

'Oh God – can't you get a dummy or something?' she said now, disgruntledly, from the front, where she'd been having to listen to 'Take My Breath Away' very quietly.

'No, no, I'm awake,' said Arthur, pointing to a big hand-painted sign. 'Look – Frosty. The biggest pig in the world. He's on display at the Indiana State Fair. We *have* to go.'

'Don't be silly Arthur,' said Julia patiently. 'We're not going to see the biggest pig in the world.'

'The *biggest*,' said Arthur. 'We could send Big Bastard a postcard from his relatives.'

'No!' said Julia.

From behind them, though, came a frantic honking. It was Ellie, clearly mouthing 'Biggest Pig in the World!' Andrew shot Julia a resigned look as the Thunderbird drew alongside them and both cars pulled over.

'So we can't go to the zoo but we are going to . . .'

Ellie and Arthur jumped up and down, nodding madly.

'We *have* to go to the state fair!' said Ellie. 'It's practically the law!'

Julia grunted. 'Maybe we can find a magical Far Eastern machine which isn't plugged in but manages to turn you into a grown-up.'

* * *

'I can't believe myself,' thought Siobhan, getting up first thing on Friday morning, after kicking Big Bastard repeatedly on the shins, thighs, buttocks and chest in a fruitless attempt to get him to wake up and move.

'I can't believe myself,' she thought, as she made one cup of tea in her lovely china for herself, and filled a glass with water to pour over Big Bastard if he didn't stop grunting into her high thread count Irish linen sheets.

'I can't believe myself.' She stared at herself in

the hall mirror, seeing an attractive, slim, slightly uptight-looking person staring back at her.

'If I was looking at me,' she thought, 'I would think I was the kind of person who didn't have a problem in the world. I'd look at this lovely flat and the nice clothes and think, "there goes an incredibly sorted woman. I bet she's not the type who tries to seduce their friends' blokes and jumps into bed with great big guys they don't even like."'

'Who happen,' she reflected to herself, 'to have dicks the size of washing-up liquid bottles.'

Big Bastard's big beefy head appeared round the door.

'Alright darling? Coming back to bed?'

'Yeah, alright,' she heard herself saying. Looking at herself in the mirror she shook her head in disbelief, then found herself phoning in late to work.

* * *

The Toyota and the Thunderbird bounced along smaller and smaller roads which were increasingly turning into dirt tracks. They'd also passed a few old wooden houses, but not a lot more.

'De de ding ding ding ding ding ding ding,' said Arthur, strumming the theme from *Deliverance* on his copy of *GQ*.

'I'm sure this really isn't a good idea,' grumbled Julia.

'But it's . . .'

'. . . the biggest pig in the world, I know.'

'Look!' Arthur pointed to a huge blimp in the distance, which had 'Bueller's Corn Feed' written on the side.

'Oh great,' said Julia. 'Fun with a really heavy agricultural slant!'

They came off the dirt track onto a single lane road which was busy with vehicles all going the same way. Mostly small trucks, some with enormous wheels; there wasn't a car there that looked like it did more than five miles to the gallon. Driving the Toyota felt even more like driving a pram than it usually did.

'Yikes,' said Julia, as a truck full of good ol' boys leaning out of the window started honking its horn at them. 'Are people really still wearing dungarees?'

More and more people were heading towards a massive field, which had a large Ferris wheel in it and was obviously rather more than just a pig-meeting place. Dusk was coming in across the massive plains, and they began to feel the familiar excitement of approaching a fair. The people here looked very different to the people in LA. The women didn't have hard, fiercely worked-out bodies, and they wore considerably less lycra, hot pink, and lip pencil. They favoured pinafores and florals. The men had nut-brown forearms and baseball caps. Children were everywhere; peachy, healthy-looking teenagers and enormously tall little boys with Norman Rockwell freckles. In the air was the hot dog smell and excited chatter of fairs everywhere.

They parked in a field larger than Balham and slowly crept out. Julia made a mental note of where the car was, but she needn't have bothered; it was the smallest vehicle around by a factor of about fifty.

Arthur started looking shifty as soon as they left the safety of the vehicle.

'What's up with you?' asked Julia.

'I don't know . . . nothing. Ehm, are you absolutely sure that none of these people are going to kill me?'

'Of course they aren't. Just . . . you know, don't get off with anyone.'

But they definitely felt distinctly conspicuous – much more so than in LA or even Nevada. They weren't just figures of curiosity; they were very foreign and very far from home.

Ellie bounced up, Andrew following behind.

'Hey – I know!' she called out. 'Let's not take part in any competitive shooting games.'

Suddenly, as if from nowhere, a clean-cut young man wearing a button-down shirt and suspiciously ironed-looking chinos materialized.

'Hi!' he said, with a wide grin that didn't reach his eyes. 'How y'all doin'?'

'We're fine thanks,' said Julia. 'We're looking for the biggest pig in the world.'

'Yeah? You come here for fun and gratification?'

'Eh?'

'Oh. Y'all foreign?'

'Yes, something like that.'

'Well, can I just ask y'all one thing?'

'I don't know – is it about the pig?'

'Have y'all found Jesus Christ as your personal saviour?'

They fell silent and stared at him. He smiled widely again, displaying rather too many extremely white teeth.

'Oh,' said Andrew II. 'Please excuse my fellow countryman.'

'As opposed to what?' said Ellie finally to the chinoed young man. 'General saviour? Umm . . . and anyway, aren't we all supposed to share him?'

'You know,' the strange man went on, relentlessly, 'since I found Jesus Christ as my personal saviour I've been a very happy man.'

'Maybe that's because he lets you come to funfairs all the time,' said Ellie.

'Young man.' He addressed Arthur 'Have you given up your life into the hands of our Lord?'

'No . . . although I once met a Lord with very nice hands . . .'

'THE WORLD IS A SODOM!' screeched the man suddenly. 'EVERYTHING FALLS INTO A VILE PIT OF EVIL AND DESTRUCTION! FOR

IT IS EASIER FOR THE CAMEL TO PASS THROUGH THE EYE OF A NEEDLE THAN IT IS FOR THE RICH MAN TO ENTER THE KINGDOM OF HEAVEN.'

'Well I'll be alright then,' said Ellie.

'YOU WORSHIP AT THE FALSE IDOLS OF FUN AND SEXUAL INCONTINENCE . . .'

'I wish,' thought Julia, but only to herself.

'BURGER KING AND IKEA!'

Ellie stopped short, her smile gone.

'What did he say?' she demanded.

'I'm sorry about all this,' said Andrew. 'Tends to be a bit of a feature around here.'

'I'm scared and I want to go home,' said Arthur.

'But . . .' Ellie shook her head fiercely. Julia, her current Hedgehog-pissed-offishness notwithstanding, took a step forward and touched her lightly on the elbow.

'But . . .' tried Ellie again. 'That's kind of exactly what I was thinking.'

Andrew took a step back. 'Oh, don't tell me you're going to run away and start handling rattlesnakes.'

Ellie stared straight ahead, thinking hard.

'AMERICA HAS LOST ITS WAY!' the man went on, inexorably.

'So have I,' thought Ellie.

'Don't worry,' said Julia.

'How can I not be worried?' said Ellie. 'If all this was just my problem, there might be a solution. If I share it with the whole of America, the odds go up a bit against ever solving it; this is the country that invented the electric nasal hair trimmer.'

'Dubose!' shouted a harsh woman's voice suddenly. 'What you doin' over there, Dubose?'

'I'm just spreading the Lord's word, Ferenza.' The young man pulled on his collar.

A tall, round woman with a grey bun of hair and a floral pinafore came stalking up.

'Is he bothering you?'

'Yes,' said Ellie.

'Don't worry about him. He's just trying to scare yis.'

She turned back to Dubose, who was now staring at the ground, all fire gone out, looking embarrassed.

'I'm just doin' what the reverend said, Ferenza.'

'Yeah, well you can do it without scaring folks half to death. Watch this.'

She turned back to them.

'Okay. Do you want to accept Jesus Christ as your personal saviour?'

'Does it have to be tonight? I was planning on holding off until fifteen minutes before I die and doing it the Catholic way,' said Arthur.

'Really, we just wanted to see the big pig and be on our way,' said Andrew.

'There you go,' said Ferenza. 'You're just bothering these fine folks.'

'I'm sorry,' said Dubose, looking contrite. The four breathed sighs of relief.

'Folks want to burn in hell, you've got to realize it's their *own affair.*' And she made as if to cuff him around the head.

* * *

The foursome walked on into the fair, Ellie quiet and slightly withdrawn.

'Come on,' said Arthur, slinging his arm around her shoulders. 'Big pig, remember?'

She attempted a half smile. 'Yes. Perhaps I could worship that instead.'

Julia used the opportunity to fall into step with Andrew II.

'How's the driving going?'

'Fine,' he said. 'As long as we keep the music up and the windows open.' He chuckled, but slightly awkwardly. They walked on, past a coconut shy. Spontaneously, Andrew picked up one of the small rubber balls and hurled it at a coconut. It hit full on.

'You wanna couple more of those for five bucks?' the greasy-looking carnie said.

'Sure,' said Andrew nonchalantly. Then, without drawing breath, he knocked down seven in a row. The others eyed each other in disbelief. He looked embarrassed.

'My dad liked shooting,' he offered by way of

explanation. The carnie leaned over and plucked out an enormous plush tiger from his display.

'Here you go then.'

Andrew, nonplussed, took the huge orange animal in his arms, not quite knowing what to do with it.

'Aww,' said Julia and Ellie at once. Andrew looked at the tiger and looked from one to the other of the girls.

* * *

They turned up at the door. Colin hadn't seen Big Bastard for forty-eight hours and hadn't a clue what to do. He let them in, then sat on the sofa kicking his feet, until they gleaned from him that he wasn't expecting Ellie Eversholt home any time soon. They looked at each other with worried expressions.

* * *

Ellie stared at Andrew, and made an almost imperceptible shake of the head. He gave her a slightly cross look, but slowly proffered the tiger to Julia.

'Fancy a quick tiger?' he said. She took it eagerly.

Ellie squeezed Arthur on the arm. 'Pig!' she said fiercely. 'Let's go see the pig!'

'I think I'll pass,' said Andrew. 'I've seen it. But it's huge, I promise.'

'Oh, me too,' said Julia. 'I need the fresh air. And my tiger has to forage for livestock.'

'Okay then.' Arthur and Ellie headed off towards the large old-fashioned tent, where a big painted board declared 'Inside – Frosty II, the Biggest Pig in the World.'

'I wonder what happened to the original Frosty?' remarked Ellie. She eyed the busy hot dog concession next to the tent. 'Never mind.'

'Hello there lovely ladies,' said the barker to them both. Arthur raised his eyebrows. 'Only five dollars to view one of the wonders of the modern world.'

'Or the pig,' muttered Arthur.

'Five dollars?' said Ellie. 'What does she do, tap dance?'

'Yes,' said the barker quickly.

Inside the tent it was dark and smelled of hay. Suddenly, a lantern flared and a hippopotamus loomed up in front of them. Frosty II was indeed monstrous. She was lying on her side and each of her eight teats looked like a porn star's nipples. She snuffed a bit and poked her snout in their direction.

'Fucking hell!' said Ellie.

They gazed at her for a bit in silence.

'What's the matter then, Hedgehog?' said Arthur, holding her hand. 'I have to say, you're not giving off "this is the best trip of my life, saying goodbye to my youth" vibes.'

'No,' said Ellie, a little sadly.

'You're not giving off "isn't fun the best thing to have?" vibes.'

'I know. I just . . . I mean, what if I don't find out anything? What if Andrew McCarthy can't help me any more than that mad religious guy can?'

Arthur shrugged. 'It's still a holiday though.'

'I don't know. I'm beginning to think the whole thing is pointless. And then I'm going to have to go home having tried everything and that really *is* frightening.'

He laughed. 'Well of *course* it is! Remember what we said about invisible problems? It's the crisis of Western capitalism. No spiritual direction.'

Ellie nodded. 'Except to keep heading East,' she said, thoughtfully. 'God. I'm going to turn into Caroline Lafayette and start wearing bloody Himalayan prayer bands.'

Then, 'Is there *nothing* left to believe in?'

Arthur shook his head slowly. Then he nudged her.

'It seems to me,' he said thoughtfully 'that you also have a problem that isn't quite invisible, don't you?'

Ellie shrugged and stared at the floor and didn't answer.

'He's very handsome.'

'Isn't he?'

Arthur nodded and waited for her to go on.

'Julia saw him first,' Ellie grumbled. 'Well, that's what she says. And she wants to have a mad fling before she gets married. So I'm not supposed to muscle in.'

'I think,' said Arthur, 'that religious nutter may have had a point about moral relativism.'

'But I really, really want to.'

Arthur squeezed her hand tightly. 'Friends are around for the longest time, sweetheart. Vodka's thicker than water, remember?'

Ellie nodded like a child.

'And Julia's been pretty good to you in the past, hasn't she?'

She nodded again.

'Well then. Believe in that. Maybe that's all that matters in the end.'

'I suppose,' said Ellie.

'There are lots of nice men out there that Julia will find revolting. Everyone you've been out with in history for starters. Try and stick to one of those.'

'Do you want to pet her?' said the barker.

'What *is* her?' said Ellie. 'Was her mother up to something with the local horse?'

The barker laughed. 'Jus' good breedin, that's all.'

'But she can't support her own weight!'

'Yis, but I takes her swimming a lot.'

Arthur was regarding the massive pink object with some distaste.

'Better not let a member of the royal family in here. They'd want to marry it.'

Frosty II made a large snuffly sound. Ellie reached out and scratched her comfortingly behind the ears. The pig whinnied in pleasure.

* * *

'Well, can you tell us when she'll be back?'

Colin stared at his Nikes and shrugged.

'And what about her landlord?'

Colin shrugged again. 'I don't know,' he said in despair. 'Arthur normally sorts everything out. But they're all away. Hedge . . . Ellie too.'

'Where are they?'

'America somewhere.'

The tall woman and the man in the cheap suit swapped looks and shook their heads.

'Do you want to get onto the consulate?'

* * *

Julia tucked her non-tiger-guarding arm through Andrew's as they wandered along looking at the stalls, feeling the warmth from his chest. Her heart was beating like a drum as she leaned into him more and more.

'It's so nice to have you with us,' she said, nuzzling into his long chambray shirt.

'Hmm? Uh huh,' he said. 'Well, it's nice to get away.'

She leaned in even further. 'It was great when you

came to meet us.' Then she stopped and looked up at him squarely. 'It was great when you came to meet me,' she said, smiling at him shyly. Then she stretched up and kissed him full on the mouth.

It took her a couple of seconds to realize that he wasn't kissing back, by which time she'd already tried to stick her tongue in his mouth. Acutely embarrassed, she bounced back on her toes in bewilderment.

'Julia,' said Andrew, softly, bracing her shoulders with his hands. 'What about Loxy?'

Julia turned all the colours of the humiliation rainbow: white for pain, red for embarrassment, purple for fury.

'She bloody TOLD you,' she said, furiously. 'I can't believe that cow bloody TOLD you.'

'Nobody told me anything,' Andrew said quietly. 'It wasn't that hard to guess.'

'Oh for *fuck's* sake. Fuck, fuck, FUCK.'

She turned and hurled the tiger away with unusual force. It passed over the heads of some disappointed small children and hit the bullseye on another shooting stall. The stall-holder picked it up and looked at it, bemused.

'Um . . . I guess you've won a small rubber ball?'

* * *

Big Bastard was pawing through Siobhan's shelves and grunting.

'Hey – this isn't food.'

'Yes it is. It's couscous.'

'It's cous-*crap*.' He laughed heartily at his own wit. 'Right. We're ordering in a biryani.'

'It's eleven o'clock in the morning.'

'So?'

Siobhan thought about it then shrugged.

'I'll just nip out to buy some beer,' he said, kissing her firmly on the mouth. 'And when I get back, can we do it again?'

'Yeah,' said Siobhan, trying to work out when her mind had been taken over by shape-shifting aliens. 'Everyone says you're crap at sex,' she said, almost by accident.

'Huh,' Big Bastard grunted again. 'Nancy Friday, innit.'

'Well, well,' Siobhan thought to herself. 'Okay. Ehm, shouldn't you check up on Colin? You promised Arthur you'd keep an eye on him.'

'Yes,' explained Big Bastard patiently. 'But if I do what I want to do I get a curry and a shag, and if I go and look after him then I don't get either of those two things. Well, I suppose I could pick up some curry on the way home.'

'It's okay,' said Siobhan firmly, putting her hand on his trousers. 'I'm sure he knows how to dial 999.'

* * *

Julia stalked back to the door of the pig tent, Andrew following her mildly.

'How was it?' he enquired when Arthur and Ellie emerged, hoping that no-one would notice anything amiss.

'It wasn't as much fun as I thought it would be,' said Ellie. 'Although I don't know. Do you think it's fun just lying around all day and eating straw in the dark?'

'Have you started job hunting?' said Arthur. 'Because if you are, that sounds exactly like what my sister does in the civil service.'

'We should press on,' said Julia, stony-faced.

'Oh!' said Ellie. 'I wanted to go on the Ferris!'

Julia ignored her. 'Arthur, you come with me.'

And she turned and stalked out of the park. Arthur made a face then followed her. Ellie and Andrew looked at each other.

* * *

'She's gone looking for *who*?' said the man in the cheap suit.

'Umm . . . Andrew . . . Andrew McCarthy,' said Colin, who hadn't taken his eyes off his feet in the last half hour. 'I'm hungry.'

'Oh God – I used to *love* him,' said the woman. Then she put her hand to her mouth. 'I mean, oh, I see.'

'Maybe we can work it out from there,' said the man.

'Oh, I'll take that on,' said the woman, too quickly. 'I'll get in touch with him and see if she's been in contact . . .' She went puce.

* * *

Loxy was kicking at stones. This was, after all, ridiculous. You didn't go travelling away from someone you truly loved and barely phone them. Never even send them a postcard. That *was* like sending them a postcard – a postcard saying 'I don't give a flying toss about you'. That was what that was like.

Why should he wait for the inevitable? What should he do; go stand in the airport and wait for her? He felt tears welling up as he imagined her face coming out of arrivals. Compassionate, tender, *sorry*. Oh God. 'Purple Rain' was playing on his personal stereo and falling on his head.

He wasn't going to stand for this. He was a man, wasn't he? Well, wasn't he? And you don't let your woman kick you around like a complete fucking idiot. She was obviously up to it all over the place and he wasn't going to give her the satisfaction of winning the whole damn thing and blowing him off when she felt like it.

Although with all his heart, deep down, he didn't really want to, he set course towards Siobhan's house.

* * *

'Ten dollars for the Lord's work, ma'am?' asked Ferenza as Ellie and Andrew walked out of the park, the dark bringing the first hint of autumn chill they'd felt since they got there.

'I think not,' said Ellie sceptically.

Ferenza looked downcast. 'I actually meant, ten dollars so that Dubose and I can get a whopper?'

'Oh,' said Ellie, and handed over the money. 'I thought whoppers were evil.'

Ferenza smiled, showing not-great teeth for an American. 'Yeah, but nobody's looking.'

Ellie sighed. 'I thought not.'

* * *

Finally they were gone. Colin stuffed half a packet of Monster Munch into his mouth and, exhaling crumbs, staggered around the flat looking for Arthur's address book and the *A to Z*. Carefully, he sat down and plotted the route to Siobhan's house, his tongue protruding from the corner of his mouth. Then he picked up the map and crept out.

* * *

Loxy stood in the doorway brandishing the flowers and bottle of wine rather awkwardly. Dammit. Well, he'd show her. She wasn't going to come back from America with some cowboy on her arm, while he was sitting there with a ring in his pocket like a complete

289

prick. He rang the bell, with a sinking heart.

Siobhan opened the door, clad only in a Japanese kimono dressing gown. At seven o'clock in the evening. She looked extremely confused to see him.

'Hi,' said Loxy, holding out the flowers stiffly. 'Thought I'd pop by.'

She looked at him for a long second.

'Oh, fuck,' said Siobhan.

Big Bastard lumbered out of the back room, a towel almost but not quite making it round his waist.

'I knew it!' he yelled, grinning broadly. '*Everyone* likes getting their cock bothered. Well, you're too late. While the cat's away, the mouse has been shagging. Or perhaps that should be *tiger*, eh darlin'?'

Siobhan buried her head in her hands and wished herself somewhere, anywhere, else. Maybe she should have gone to America with the rest of them? Then she could be stuffing herself on cheeseburgers and arguing with the Hedgehog at this very moment, rather than standing here in this bloody awkward *ménage à trois*.

'Shame it's all over with that Julia though,' went on Big Bastard inexorably. 'She were right tasty. And I thought you were going to get married and everything.'

Loxy visibly slumped until his whole body seemed to be pointing at the ground, including the flowers.

'Sorry,' he said gruffly. Which he was.

'That's okay,' said Siobhan, feeling like the proverbial tart with a heart of gold.

'Yeah, you missed out mate,' said Big Bastard. Siobhan cringed and wondered how much of this kind of thing she was going to have to put up with, and what kind of person it made her when it turned her on.

'I'd better be off, then.'

'Can we have that bottle of wine?' said Big Bastard. Loxy handed it over without a struggle and turned to walk away. As he did, a small figure came belting up the hill towards them. They watched it.

'Isn't that Colin?' said Loxy, finally.

'What's he up to?' said Siobhan. 'Training for the egg and spoon?'

Colin's face was creased with exhaustion by the time he reached them.

'I have . . . I have . . .' he puffed.

'Calm down,' said Siobhan. 'What is it?'

'It's pfff . . . it's . . . people came and . . . wouldn't let me have any food and . . .' His bottom lip began to wobble uncontrollably. Siobhan looked around nervously wondering how she must appear to her neighbours.

'Look. Colin. Do you want to come in and tell us what's the matter?'

Colin nodded vehemently. He came through and

Big Bastard and Siobhan turned into the house. After a moment's pause, Loxy followed them in. Inside, Colin stared at Siobhan with wide eyes as she opened the wine.

'You've got no clothes on!' he said, pointing.

'Yes I do, Colin, this is a dressing gown. Now, what is it?'

But he continued to stare, until she sighed, jumped up and went off to change into a T-shirt and jeans.

'Now, what is it?'

Colin looked up at them, his large round eyes damp with tears.

'These people came round . . .'

'Yes?'

'Was there a big detector van thingy outside?' said Big Bastard.

Colin shook his head, then after a pause he choked, 'It's the Hedgehog . . . it's her dad. Her dad. Her dad died. And they don't know where she is.'

He burst into loud sobs. There was a long silence.

'Aw, don't cry for Christ's sake,' said Big Bastard finally, welling up. 'It makes you look like a top of the roofter.'

* * *

'It's a beautiful evening,' said Ellie, before she got back in the car, gazing behind them to the huge sunset throwing its rays across the fields.

'Isn't it,' said Andrew, looking at Ellie.

The horn in front of them blew abruptly and they followed the little Toyota out onto the dusty road again.

Licence to Drive

Loxy, Siobhan and Big Bastard were staring at Colin in horror as they all sat cross-legged on the floor.

'Just tell us everything the police said,' Siobhan was saying. She'd poured everyone a medicinal whisky and begged Big Bastard not to sit in a towel with his legs open – to no avail.

Colin hadn't quite regained control of himself, and sniffed loudly.

'Something . . . something about getting her tonsils out.'

'Her *tonsils* out?'

'But the Hedgehog's already had her tonsils out,' said Siobhan, thinking back to college. 'That's when she first moved to a primarily ice-cream based diet.'

'That's what the man said,' sniffed Colin. 'They

had to get in touch with getting her tonsils out. In America.'

'Colin,' said Loxy, calmly. 'Is there a chance the policeman said, "consulate"?'

'Maybe,' he sniffed.

'Okay. And what else?'

'They wanted to know if we'd heard from them. And where they were. But I didn't know.'

'Loxy, where did they phone from the other day?'

Loxy shrugged. 'Sorry, but I was trying to stop you from taking your clothes off at the time. I don't even remember.'

'Christ,' said Siobhan. 'When did this happen?'

'A few days ago,' said Colin, miserably. 'They've been phoning and things.'

'What a mess,' said Loxy shaking his head. 'Oh God. Poor Hedgehog. You know, this means she doesn't have a soul in the world.'

They stared at the floor. 'What . . . I mean, where is her dad?' asked Siobhan. Colin shrugged and handed over the policewoman's card.

'I told them what they were doing and they're going to get in touch with Andrew McCarthy to say that if he sees them . . .'

'God. What a fucking mess,' said Loxy again. 'What should we do?'

'I'm going to go and get them,' said Colin in a small voice.

'What?'

'Someone needs to find her. I think, if an American policeman found her, that would be bad.'

'Colin, don't be silly. You can't go to America on your own.'

'I can! I've seen *Sleepless in Seattle*.'

'You don't even know where they are!'

'I'll find them,' he said sullenly. 'I'm the one who has to give the news.'

The others looked at each other in dismay. Then Loxy stood up.

'You're right,' he said. 'Somebody should go. I'll go. Hedge shouldn't have to hear this from strangers, in a foreign country. And I need to see Julia anyway.' His voice trailed off. 'I really, really need to see her.'

Siobhan nodded sadly. 'Yes, you do.'

'No!' said Colin, his face creasing up. 'It's my news. I should go. And I really need to see Arthur.'

'Well I don't want to go,' sulked Big Bastard sticking out his bottom lip. 'I want to stay here and have sex with Siobhan.'

'You can do that too,' said Siobhan. 'I'll speak to the police from this end. Christ. Oh my God, it's such a lot to sort out.' She jumped up and started pacing around the living room.

'I WANT TO GO,' said Colin, sticking out his bottom lip.

'Look, it's okay, I'll do it,' said Loxy.

'Can't you take him with you?' asked Siobhan.

'No! It'll be fine!'

'Don't you like gay people?' sniffed Colin. The other two waited expectantly.

'Of course I do! Don't be ridiculous!'

'Well why can't I go?'

Loxy raised his eyes to heaven.

'Can't you take him?' said Siobhan finally. 'I'm already looking after one enormous baby.'

Loxy screwed up his eyes to think of another excuse but couldn't manage one.

'I suppose so,' he said sullenly.

'Woo hoo!' said Colin. 'Mickey Mouse!' Everyone looked at him. 'And very, very sad news.'

'Okay,' said Loxy, getting up. 'I'll go and pack a bag and we'll head to the airport. My mobile works abroad anyway, so as soon as you hear anything from them, you just phone me right away and we'll get to where they are. Don't say anything to them over the phone.'

'What about work?'

'I haven't been going to work. I'd already booked this time off to go away with Julia. I've been keeping myself busy by moping around.'

'Okay. What about you, little guy?'

'I'll get my mum to write me a note,' said Colin. Everyone started getting up and bustling around. The news was terribly sad, but the urge for action was strangely exciting.

'Okay. Colin, are you alright for money?'

'You know, seeing you being so bossy and assertive is turning me on,' said Big Bastard. 'When are they leaving?'

The room fell silent as everyone tried to avoid looking at Big Bastard's towel.

'Yes,' said Colin finally. 'I don't have any.'

Siobhan sighed, paused, then reached for her wallet and took out a gold company credit card. She closed her eyes briefly, then handed it to Colin, along with the PIN number scribbled on a scrap of paper.

'He doesn't know I've still got this one,' she said.

'Jesus,' said Big Bastard. 'Excuse me everyone.' He disappeared into the bedroom. 'Hurry up,' he shouted.

Siobhan ignored him. 'And remember, when you get there, you give it to *Julia*, okay? Not the Hedge-hog.'

'Not the Hedgehog,' Colin repeated dutifully, staring at the card as if it was made of real gold. Loxy touched Siobhan on the arm in gratitude.

'Nice to have something good come of it,' said Siobhan, looking down.

'Did someone say something about good come?' shouted Big Bastard loudly from the other side of the wall.

* * *

Ellie stared out of the window as they passed into Ohio the day after the fair. When Andrew put his arm around her shoulders, she gently shrugged it away. He looked at her with concern.

Ellie's heart was heavy. Suddenly, what had started out as her great idea felt completely stupid. She had been right – everyone did feel like she did, at least to a certain extent. But what was looking increasingly the case was that emptiness was a by-product; the balance on the scales that allowed her to upgrade her computer every six months. In the eighties, when people got rich for the first time, this had felt like fun. But now they were too jaded, too spoilt. They'd been there, done that, picked up the Phillip Starck toaster and were so busy looking for the next thing to ram in their maws they couldn't even settle down and look after their own families. She thought of her dad suddenly, and a tear ran down her cheek. Any other age, any other culture wouldn't leave him at the other end of town to eat pies and drink whisky. He needed looking after. He needed her.

That was what she was going to have to do. Quest over. Everything important couldn't be found. Rather, it was all around her, all the time, like straw around Frosty. She made a decision. They would have a wonderful time in New York. She would explain to Julia what had – hadn't – happened, and they could sort that out and everyone would be happy again.

Then she would go home and move back in with her dad. Back to her old bedroom, with the faded postcards and the Strawberry Shortbread doll; the little red mini hi-fi; the Howard Jones twelve inches and her pink and black stripy duvet.

After all, it would be cheaper too if she was job-hunting. And it would be right, even if she did wake up in the cold mornings dreaming of golden hair reflecting the late autumn sun as they drove through plains as big as the world.

'Are you okay?' Andrew asked her gently.

'I'm fine,' she said quietly, but sadly.

* * *

'She's dead,' Julia was saying. 'She *knew* what the gameplan was. So she just ignores it completely . . .'

'Calm down,' said Arthur. 'She spoke to me about him. She does like him, but she's not going near him for you.'

'WHAT!' Julia was white. 'That's WORSE. How noble of her. Fuck it.'

'I don't think it's Ellie you're cross about,' said Arthur.

'It is,' said Julia, sticking out her bottom lip.

* * *

Andrew looked at Ellie, unsure as to why he was getting such mixed signals. Although of course she was a woman, however unusual. He took a deep breath.

'I really like you, you know,' he said quietly.

Ellie was shaken out of her self-pitying reverie.

'Really?' she said with a slightly wicked grin. 'Enough to let me drive the car?'

* * *

'So, with Arthur, right . . .'

Loxy and Colin made an awkward-looking couple sitting on the Heathrow Express, particularly with Colin's Bart Simpson rucksack.

'Uh huh?' said Colin. His eyes were wide with excitement; he'd never been further than High Wycombe in his life.

'When you're off fixing telephone kiosks and things and you don't see Arthur for a bit, do you ever think about other people?'

'Oh no,' said Colin. 'But then, I love Arthur very much.'

'Uh huh,' said Loxy, staring out the window. 'So where should we start looking for them.'

'If I know them,' said Colin, 'they'll be in Disneyland.'

* * *

'How much driving experience have you had in America?' said Andrew, looking at the dashboard of the Thunderbird worriedly.

302

'Oh, loads,' said Ellie. 'Come on, pull over.'

'*What* are they up to now?' said Julia behind them. 'They're pulling in. To have sex, presumably.'

Arthur looked up from his copy of *On the Road*, which he was finding impossible to finish. (He didn't know that no-one in the history of the world has actually finished it and the last one hundred pages of most editions are left blank to save on printer's ink. Nobody has ever seen the end of the film either.) 'You're obsessed.'

Nonetheless the car was definitely pulling over. They drew up behind it, just in time to see Ellie jump out at the speed of light and dash around to the other side.

'WHAT!?' said Julia. They stared at the vehicle in front. Then Julia started honking the horn.

* * *

'What are they honking the horn at us for?' said Ellie innocently, examining the dashboard and trying to work out where the stop/go buttons were. She'd heard American driving was a piece of piss.

'Okay,' she said, spotting the keys. 'You're about to experience a *real* driver.'

'You're sure your definition of "*real*" doesn't mean "profoundly nasty"?' said Andrew II. 'Like "realpolitik".'

'Now, let's see . . . mirror, signal, manoeuvre . . .'

'Oh Christ,' said Julia, continuing to honk madly.

'I can't believe this. How can he be letting her do this? She's going to kill them both!'

Ellie moved relatively smoothly into the left hand lane.

'Nothing to it!' she breezed. 'No wonder you can pass your test here just by remembering what colour your car is.'

'Hedgehog, why don't you get out of the passing lane?' said Andrew.

'The what?'

'The fast lane. Let's just get out of this particular lane.'

'Okey dokey,' said Ellie, squealing over to the right. 'Oh, look. Thirty miles an hour!'

'You can probably go a little bit faster than this.'

'I've never been this fast before.'

He looked at her then.

'You do . . . you do have your driver's licence don't you?'

'Ish,' said Ellie.

Andrew closed his eyes.

'Don't shut your eyes! I'm relying on you to tell me where we're going.'

'Oh God,' he said.

'Kids in American movies drive all the time,' said Ellie. 'It's clearly easy.' The car jumped a couple of times, but continued lurching on.

'Fuck,' said Andrew, putting his head in his hands.

'Okay. Keep calm. And KEEP IN A STRAIGHT LINE! Okay. Between those two lines. You know, you only have to constantly move your hands on the steering wheel like that if you're a cartoon character. Right.' He took a deep breath. 'We're going to come slowly into the side of the road. SLOWLY!'

'I'm doing fine!' said Ellie.

'SLOWER!'

The Toyota veered beside them on the narrow lane.

'SHE CAN'T DRIVE,' screamed Julia out of the open window.

'I KNOW!' said Andrew. 'I'M TRYING TO GET HER TO STOP.'

'I'm fine!' said Ellie.

The massed hysterical shouting from the other three convinced her that perhaps she wasn't. Not only that, but there was a nasty big hill coming up ahead and her hand was flailing around, looking for a gearstick.

'Okay, maybe I will stop!' said Ellie. She inadvertently hit the accelerator.

'Oh Shit!' she yelled as the two cars veered dangerously close together.

* * *

Police Constable Saria Millstone was feeling stupid. She wasn't used to feeling stupid, she was used to feeling pretty damn cool as long as she had her uniform on, but this was just dumb. She had tried phoning Andrew McCarthy's agents in Los Angeles several times, only to be constantly put on hold and made to feel pretty foolish, particularly when she attempted to describe who she was looking for.

'We don't represent a Miss Eversholt,' she had already heard several times.

'I know that,' she had patiently tried to explain. 'I need to speak to Andrew McCarthy.'

'What would that be in connection with?'

'I need to know if he's come in contact with a Ellie Eversholt.'

'We don't represent a Miss Eversholt, ma'am.'

She knew she should let Interpol or the consulate deal with this, but there was a little teenaged foolish part of her which couldn't help hoping against hope that she'd be put through to him and he wouldn't be able to resist an English accent and . . . she sighed at her own stupidity and looked at her dumpy figure in the mirror.

'Stop being such an idiot,' she said to herself.

She was going to hand this over immediately. Just as soon as . . . she suddenly thought of something, and took herself off to the reference library.

* * *

A huge lorry appeared over the brow of the hill. It was

306

taller than a double-decker bus. Julia was still leaning halfway out the window, with one hand on the wheel, trying to flag Ellie and Andrew over. Andrew started screaming at her to get back in – they were taking up both sides of the road – but with all the shouting, the general cacophony was too loud to let individual voices be heard.

When it happened, it happened very quickly. Ellie saw the truck and lost all power of movement.

'Shit! Groundhog day,' she thought, staring at the massive load bearing down on them and instinctively letting go of the steering wheel.

Arthur flailed over and grabbed Julia back from the window, in time for her to see the danger and brake back down behind the Thunderbird.

Andrew II leaned across Ellie in the rapidly drifting car and tried to seize the steering wheel. There was suddenly a deadly silence, then an almighty crump.

* * *

'Hello there,' said the stewardess. 'Would you like a colouring-in pack?'

'No,' said Colin seriously. 'We're going to find some very sad friends of ours.'

'He's fine,' said Loxy anxiously. 'Just coffee will be fine. Decaff for him if you've got it.'

'No problem,' said the stewardess. 'Is this your first time flying?'

'Yes!' said Colin. 'I think it's great.'

'Well, maybe later on you'd like to come up to the cockpit and meet the captain?'

Colin turned to Loxy, his eyes shining. Given the gravity of their mission, Loxy was inclined to say no, but he had always longed to see it anyway.

'You never know, we might be able to see them on the ground from up here,' said Colin.

'You never know,' said Loxy.

* * *

'HHOOONNNNNKKKKKKKKK!' The truck let out an almighty blow of its steam horn and passed on its way without stopping.

'Bloody hell!' Julia said. The Toyota had come to a stop ahead of the Thunderbird. She was white and shaking.

'Oh God. Oh God. Oh God,' Arthur was muttering under his breath. They instinctively gripped hands, then very slowly got out of the car to see what was waiting for them on the road behind them.

The Thunderbird had crumpled some of its gleaming front bonnet into a tree by the side of the road, but it was still upright. Inside, belted in but wild-eyed were Ellie and Andrew, seemingly all in one piece.

'Christ!' Julia flew over to them. 'Is everyone okay?'

'Uh huh,' said Ellie very slowly. 'Uh oh.'

'Uh oh is right,' said Julia, glaring at her.

Arthur put his arm around Julia. 'Umm, also, I think you should get out of the car before it explodes.'

Ellie and Andrew fumbled with the buttons on the doors for a nightmare few seconds until they could throw themselves out onto the grass verge.

'Is it going to explode?' said Ellie, scrambling down the bank.

'I don't know,' said Arthur. 'They always do in films.'

From a vantage point of twenty feet away they all crouched, watching the car, which appeared disinclined to burst into flame.

Ellie stared at the ground, white and shaking. Nobody put an arm around her.

'Congratulations,' said Julia, her voice cold and furious. 'I thought you'd fucked this trip up before. But now you've managed it properly.'

* * *

Police Constable Millstone leaned over the telephone, still feeling absolutely ridiculous. They taught you how to brush off abuse at Hendon. But they didn't tell you what to do if you were the one making yourself feel a prat. Checking there was no-one close by in the open-plan office, she started to dial 9 . . . 00 . . . 1 . . . 562 . . .

* * *

'It looked easy in the films!' Ellie was yelling.

'EVERYTHING looks easy in the films. You stupid, stupid girl! You could have killed all of us!'

'I'm SORRY okay? I thought . . .'

'You didn't think anything,' hollered Julia. 'You never do. That's why we're all here on this ridiculous wild goose chase.'

'I had been thinking actually,' said Ellie, petulantly. 'I was giving it all up to try and make you happy.'

'By crashing a car. I see.'

'NO. I was . . . I was going to give up this quest actually and try and make everyone have a good time.'

Julia looked at her.

'Yeah right.'

Then she said something under her breath.

'What did you say?' asked Ellie dangerously.

'Nothing.' Arthur started forward protectively.

'WHAT DID YOU SAY?'

'I SAID, WE'RE JUST ALL SICK OF HAVING TO MOTHER YOU, OKAY?'

There was a terrible deadly silence. Ellie turned and ran off into the trees. The others followed more slowly.

'I didn't mean to say that,' said Julia sulkily. Arthur shot her a sharp look.

* * *

'Are you the actor Andrew McCarthy?' the voice asked. It was sensible-sounding, although he thought he detected a bit of a wobble.

'Ngnff,' said Hatsie, warily. Whoever this was, it wasn't someone that knew enough about showbiz to go through his agents.

'Do you know where I might be able to find that actor?'

'Just because they have the same *name*?' thought Hatsie.

'I'm sorry Sir. I'm phoning from the Metropolitan Police in London and we're trying to follow up some leads to find . . .'

'Ellie unghf Julia.'

The voice was beyond surprised.

'You've met Ellie Eversholt, Sir?'

'Nuh huh. Nofor ghel truF?'

'No Sir, she's not in any trouble. We just have to find her, that's all. We just need to, to contact them about a situation back here at home.'

With difficulty, Hatsie managed to communicate as much as he knew about the duo's intended path.

* * *

Officer Millstone spoke to her superior.

'Sir, we've got leads.'

'Okay, inform the FBI. Christ, I can't believe there's this much fuss for one missing person.'

311

'She's the only living kin Sir.'

'Hmpf.' He thought about this for a second. 'Well, it's going to help our figures, I suppose.'

'Yes Sir.'

'Well done.'

'I'd still better warn the actor, Sir. Just in case we miss her.'

* * *

Ellie sat on a tree stump, shaking furiously. Of everything, this was the most unforgivable. Of course, she had been stupid thinking she could drive the car – although she genuinely had thought it would be easy – but they were never going to believe now that after her pig epiphany she had been planning on turning over a new leaf. They would, in fact, think she'd bumped her head in the crash.

Julia was feeling equally terrible. Of course she must have been partly in shock to say such an awful thing but, she suspected, there might be just a *tad* of jealousy mixed in there . . .

'I'm sooo sorry,' she said as she approached. 'Hedge-hog, I'm sorry. I'm sorry. I didn't mean it.'

Ellie turned, in tears. 'But I'm *trying* to be a grown-up. Why do you think I'm out here? I'm *trying* to find out how to do things properly and not cock things up. I'd even decided to go back and look after my dad and everything. Then sometimes I just do stupid things to fuck it up, but I did think it would be okay.'

'Nobody's hurt,' said Julia. 'It could have been funny really.'

'Not really,' said Ellie.

'Well, okay, not funny as such. But it's okay.'

'I'm sorry,' said Ellie.

'No, I am,' said Julia. 'I've been a cow. I'm sorry.'

Ellie stood up and they embraced for a long time.

'So . . . you and Andrew eh?' said Julia gruffly, pulling apart. 'That's . . . great.'

Ellie stared at her like she was daft.

'But I was leaving him for you!' she said. 'That's what I've been trying to explain! You can have him: I was going to be far too grown-up to let him come between our friendship!'

Andrew II pushed himself off the trunk he'd been leaning against.

'What?' he said. The girls had completely forgotten he was there.

'WHAT?' he said again. 'So I'm . . . I'm some kind of competition to you?'

His blue eyes were flashing. He was clearly furious.

'No,' said Ellie in a small voice.

'Jesus. I thought you were different, you know, interesting. Not fucking whacko.'

He surveyed the two of them.

'Some kind of spot the foreigner competition. Little "shagging" of the locals? Well, I'm in no particular mood to be colonized today, okay? And if the car's all right, I'm going to – what the hell is it you bloody British say – bid you fine ladies "bye-bye".'

And he stormed furiously off.

* * *

Police Constable Saria Millstone was feeling odd – i.e. she'd acted on a completely dumb idea but something good had come of it. Now, however, she was stuck back on the phone to the agency in California.

After being put on hold for the ninth time, she was amazed finally to hear a voice on the other end of the line. Of course, it was only voicemail. She stared at her reflection in the partition once again and admitted to herself that perhaps Andrew McCarthy wasn't going to fall in love with her over the phone after all.

'Hello – this is Police Constable Millstone from the Metropolitan Police in London. We have reason to believe that there are two women, Ellie Eversholt and Julia Denford, who are trying to contact your client, Andrew McCarthy. It is imperative if your client comes across these women that you contact us

314

immediately. My number is 01 44 20 7555 7628 . . . thank you.'

She replaced the phone, thinking, one, those fancy LA folks are going to completely ignore that, and two, dammit, dammit, dammit. She wished she were looking for him too.

* * *

It was bad luck that Andrew McCarthy's agent was on holiday. And that the messages were being picked up by the temp. Who was on her first placement in a legitimate film business operation ever since coming to LA to try and make it in the dog grooming world after seeing *The Accidental Tourist* as a child.

'Oh my GAWD,' she squealed, then listened to the message for the third time. Then she pressed through to her supervisor.

'Marcia?' she breathed. 'I think we got ourselves a stalker situation!'

'Great,' said Marcia. 'This is going to make him *such* hot property!'

* * *

Ellie sat back down on the tree stump and burst into tears as they heard the Thunderbird sputter a little, then head off into the distance.

Arthur was freaked. Two crazy women on his

hands, one car and night was drawing in. He sighed and decided that for the rest of the trip they were going to concentrate on hot baths, cocktails and not a hell of a lot else.

'Come on,' he said, to no-one in particular. 'Pull yourself together.'

* * *

'No way,' said Loxy. 'This is not happening.'

'It's the only place I can afford,' whined Colin.

'I don't care. I'm absolutely not staying there.'

'Are you going to leave me?' said Colin, widening his eyes.

'Look, for Christ's sake . . . I'm sure we'd be able to find a cheap hotel.'

'Ain't no cheap hotels in New Yoik,' said the cab driver, chuckling.

'Oh, for fuck's sake.'

Loxy stared fiercely out of the window as the cab drew to a halt.

'Here you go, gennlemen. The YMCA.'

'You can get a good meal,' he added, cheer-fully.

* * *

'I'm sorry,' said Julia, again.

'No, I am,' said Ellie, sniffing mightily.

'I love you,' said Julia.

'I love you too,' said Ellie. Arthur joined them for a group hug.

'Just as well,' he said over Ellie's shoulder, 'Because here come the police.'

* * *

The cops were circling the vehicle, kicking the tyres. When they saw three tear-stained and grubby-looking people hanging around the trees, they straightened up and looked suspicious.

'Great big guns!' whispered Ellie, squeezing Julia's hand. Julia squeezed back.

'Is this your vehicle?'

Arthur bit back the urge to say no, they'd just hiked a thousand miles through the woods in sandshoes.

'Yes,' they said.

'It shouldn't be stopped here. Could you step over to the vehicle please?'

'Strip search!' whispered Julia in horror. One member of the party, who shall remain nameless, experienced a quick flash of sexiness momentarily overtaking their fear.

'Who is the driver of this vehicle?'

'Should I be grown-up and explain everything?' said Ellie, dropping both their hands and heading out of the trees.

'NO!' said Julia and Arthur in a loud whisper simultaneously. 'Not that we don't trust you,' added Julia.

317

'We just don't trust you not to go to prison,' said Arthur. He held on tightly to Ellie.

'It's me, Officer,' said Julia, leaving them behind. She went up and stood squarely in front of them.

'Okay,' said the taller of the two officers, who looked to have a slight squint. 'I'm Officer Frog. And this is also Officer Frog. We're brothers,' he added quickly.

Ellie's eyes widened. Even in her emotional state – particularly in her emotional state – Arthur had to pinch her hard to stop her from breaking out in hysterics.

'Can we see your licence and registration, m'am?'

Julia opened the door and fumbled in the glove compartment.

'Have you any idea how dangerous it is to be stopped here?'

'Sorry . . . it was an accident. We thought we saw an animal on the road . . .'

'Wow, look at this Edgar.' The smaller one picked up the passport. 'A little pink passport.'

'Sorry ma'am,' said Edgar. 'He's never seen one of those before.'

'A British passport?'

'Any passport.'

'Well, like I say, we really didn't mean it . . .'

'Have you been drinking?' demanded the younger cop.

318

'Nope.'

'Would you mind touching your nose with your index finger please.'

'*What?*'

'Yes ma'am. It's to check you haven't been drinking.'

'Why don't you just breathalyse me?'

The younger one squinted uncomfortably.

'Are you refusing to comply ma'am?'

'Ohh no,' said Julia.

'Go easy on 'em, Allen,' said the elder. 'They're strangers in these parts.'

Ellie and Arthur looked on confused, as Julia touched her nose, watching the policemen very carefully.

'That's okay,' said the policeman.

'Really? I thought it would mean I was drunk if I was stupid enough to do what you just asked me.'

'Can you walk toe over toe in a straight line just here?'

'This is so much more *fun* that at home,' said Ellie to Arthur. 'Why don't they do it this way? Drink driving need not be miserable.'

Edgar leaned over and peered very closely into Julia's eyes.

'Mm,' said Arthur. 'Strip search!'

'So, ma'am. You tell us *what* jumped out in front of you?'

Julia looked helplessly at Ellie.

'Well it *looked* like . . .'

'. . . a groundhog?' said Ellie helplessly.

'A what now?'

'Kind of . . . half badger, half monkey . . . ?' Julia was nodding along feverishly.

'I don't think we get many of them round here now do we Edgar?'

'Did it have a striped tail?'

'Yes!' said Julia.

'Woodchuck,' said Edgar. Allen nodded mournfully. 'We'd better get on to the Woodchuck Commission.'

'Why?'

'No reason,' he said mysteriously. 'And we're going to have to write you up a ticket.'

'She should tell him she'll do *anything* not to get a ticket,' whispered Arthur to Ellie, who nodded.

'Oh no, really?' said Julia. 'We are just having the *worst* run of luck.'

'What's your purpose here ma'am?'

Nobody said anything for the longest time.

'We were looking for Andrew McCarthy!' said Ellie. 'But it went a bit wrong.'

'You're looking for *who*?'

'Andrew McCarthy,' said Ellie again, rather shame-facedly. 'The movie star.'

'No shit!' said Edgar. The brothers looked at each other and laughed.

320

'What's so funny?' said Julia. Ellie moved further forward.

'A couple of years back, Allen and I . . . we were kind of stuck in a rut. And we thought, who's the best person to help us with all this? And so we went to LA . . .'

'And met Ally Sheedy!' piped up Allen.

'What? Why?' said Julia in amazement.

'Well, you know, just to see if she had any advice for us, that kind of thing.'

'Oh. Right,' said Julia.

'Was she helpful?' asked Ellie.

'Was she ever!' said Allen.

'Yeah, you know. She was just really wise. We sat and talked through our lives with her, and you know, just her perspective on things . . . she really showed us the way.'

'What?' Ellie's mouth was hanging open.

'She certainly turned our lives around,' said Edgar.

Allen nodded in agreement.

'Oh my God,' said Ellie, trying to take it in.

Julia leaned over.

'Ehm . . . seeing as we're kind of doing the same thing . . . any chance you can let us off that ticket?'

'No ma'am. If there's one thing Ally taught us, it's that you've always got to be honest.'

'Okay then.'

Julia took the outstretched docket as Arthur and Ellie piled into the car.

'Incidentally,' said Ellie, sticking her head out of the window, 'what jobs did you used to have before Ally Sheedy changed your life?'

Allen twitched. 'It was mixed up in the supernatural ma'am.'

'We don't really talk about it,' said Edgar, shooting his brother a warning glance.

'Okay then.' Julia swung into the car and started up the engine carefully. The cops stood and waved them out of sight as they limped off to the nearest motel, dreaming of warm baths, fluffy towels and, in the case of at least one of the car's occupants, big hairy policemen. Allen and Edgar stomped back to their car, having narrowly missed an all-points bulletin to be on the lookout for a silver Toyota.

Adventures in Babysitting

Loxy was looking ahead as he walked. Colin had craned his neck back to vertical and was staring at the sky with his mouth open. If it started to rain, he would drown.

'Colin, do you want to try and look less like a tourist?' said Loxy anxiously. 'We're here working.'

'I am working,' said Colin without dropping his head. 'I'm looking, aren't I?'

Manhattan was brisk and chilly. People walked incredibly quickly wrapped in scarves with matching gloves. Quite a few of them were treading on Colin.

'Now I reckon we should start with hotels,' said Loxy. 'Find the cheaper hotels and ask if anyone by their names has made a booking.'

'Boring,' said Colin. 'Why can't we just find the film star?'

'Oh!' he said, as they approached Central Park. 'We could look for him in a horse and cart.'

'This is hopeless,' said Loxy, looking around at the teeming crowds. 'We're never going to find them.'

'Yes we will,' said Colin decisively. 'If we just stood here, I bet we'd see them sooner or later.'

'Statistically speaking, I suppose so,' said Loxy. 'In an infinite number of years. Okay. How about we start with the theatrical agencies?'

* * *

'Well, at least we weren't actually *thrown* out,' said Loxy three hours later, as they were rearranging their collars. The security guard shot them a filthy look and headed back into the building.

'That wasn't as bad as the place where they thought he was a member of N'Sync,' said Colin thoughtfully.

'Hmm.'

'I don't get it,' said Colin. 'Why do you think they don't want to give out celebrities' home addresses? Weirdos.'

* * *

New York phoned LA.

'We had two men in here today looking for one of the clients.'

'Oh God!' gasped LA. 'Were they definitely men? Because we've got reports of two women this end.'

'This is New York. Our transvestite detectors are unparalleled. Definitely men.'

'Something's going on. There's obviously a huge revival about to take place.'

'God. I really hope they don't hassle the guy. Do you want to . . .'

'Write the press release? No problem.'

'Great! Movin' on up . . .'

* * *

'Oh *hi*,' said Siobhan, suddenly conscious that it was two o'clock in the afternoon and she hadn't been dressed for three days. Big Bastard managed to belch and scratch his arse simultaneously in his sleep. She watched him fondly.

'No. No, they haven't phoned. I haven't heard from them.'

'Yes, I know New York's a big place . . . look, Lox, I don't know what you can do until they get there. I'm sure they'll phone then. Why don't you just take Colin and try and get some sightseeing in?'

'Ooh yes please,' could be heard down the line.

'I don't know . . . it doesn't seem respectful somehow.'

'You can't worry about that,' said Siobhan practically. 'You're doing the best you can, and you didn't know Ellie's dad, so you might as well have some fun. And if you can't have fun in New York you're technically dead. Oh! It's a wonderful place.'

'You're very full of the joys,' said Loxy.

'I've certainly been feeling very full,' said Siobhan, giggling. Then there was an extremely awkward silence.

* * *

Ellie was back in the back seat and keeping very quiet. The radio was playing 'Missing You' by John Waites. To cover for her, Julia and Arthur were keeping up high decibel jollity rather in the manner of parents trying to keep their offspring's mind off the fact that their hamster was last seen three days ago in the vicinity of the back of the fridge.

'Hey!' Julia was yelling.

'Look!'

Ahead of them was the first signpost to New York City.

'Hooray!'

'Oh my God!' said Julia. 'I don't know what I'm going to do when we don't have to drive all day long. What do people do?'

'Eat sandwiches?' said Arthur. 'Build cathedrals?'

'I see,' Julia nodded her head. 'Oh my God. Do you think we're going to make it today?'

'It's possible,' said Arthur. 'As long as no-one, you know, crashes into anything.'

'Sssh.'

Ellie hadn't noticed.

'Start spreading the news . . .' started Arthur.

'Oh no you don't,' said Julia. 'Of all the car games we could play, I'm getting really sick of "Sing the Town on the Signpost".'

This was unsurprising: so far Julia had sat glumly through 'Sweet Home Alabama', 'Nashville', 'Georgia on my Mind', 'Chatanooga Choo Choo' and 'Nutbush City Limits', which had also prompted loud discussions of whether or not it was the actual same Nutbush. All hollered out by Arthur's tuneless voice, which tended to jump up or down an octave line by line. Still at least Ellie wasn't playing, with her habit of inserting made-up words to bits she didn't know. In fact Julia hoped she didn't cheer up by New York as, despite being a lifelong fan of Simon and Garfunkel, Ellie still tended to get a 'come on from the horse on seventh avenue'.

'Hmm,' said Arthur considering the alternatives. 'My mum used to make me and my sisters play "Spot the Diplomatic Plates".'

'That sounds very snooty,' said Julia.

'Quite the opposite. It was a desperate struggle to keep us quiet. Do you know how many diplomatic plates I used to see between Sheffield and Newquay?'

'Yes, that's the kind of thing I would know about you,' said Julia.

'NONE. Not once. Ever. In five years.'

'Let's not play that then.'

'And you got one thousand points for no number plate at all, which means that the queen's driving. Bloody stupid car game.' He sighed and looked out the window.

'What about "Botticelli"?' said Julia. 'What about that, Ellie?'

'Huh?' said Ellie listlessly. 'What the hell is that? Is this the kind of thing I missed out on by being an only child?'

'Yes,' said Arthur. 'Along with getting stabbed in the bum with a set of compasses and having someone to beat up the football team for you.'

'Stephanie did that for you?' asked Julia.

'Many, many times.'

'I always wanted a big brother,' said Ellie dreamily. 'To bring home lots of his good-looking mates for me to get off with.'

'What you've done there,' said Julia, 'is you've confused the concept of "brother" with the concept of "pimp".'

'What's "Botticelli" then?'

'Okay, think of a famous person and give us their initial.'

'A,' said Ellie promptly.

328

'Maybe we should do famous historical figures,' said Arthur.

'Still A,' said Ellie.

'Actually, does anyone know any songs about Virginia? And its plains?' said Julia, indicating the next signpost.

Ellie slumped back. 'Actually, it was Aristophanes,' she said to nobody in particular.

* * *

Loxy wandered back from the phone with a shrug.

'She doesn't know either,' he said.

'Hmm,' said Colin. 'You know, I've always wanted to go on Space Mountain.'

'That's in Florida,' said Loxy.

'Oh. Can we go there for the afternoon while we're waiting for them to phone?'

'No! For goodness' sake. What are they teaching in geography class these days?'

'Post-modern cultural relativism and interwoven reference points,' said Colin gloomily. 'Can I have another doughnut?'

'No.'

'D'oh!'

They wandered south on Broadway, taking in ridiculously familiar sights. A man crossed the road pushing a rackful of clothing. Steam came up through a subway vent. A stupidly well-dressed woman walked a stupidly tiny dog. New York, reflected Loxy, was a lot more of a film set than Disneyland would ever be.

Pasted up on a wall raked with fire escapes was a flyer that made Colin stop short.

'A NIGHT OUT IN ADVENTURETOWN!' screamed the ads.

'Loxy!' Colin grabbed him by the arm. 'Look! Adventuretown!'

Loxy squinted hard at the posters. There were various unidentifiable bits of muscular tanned skin covered in tattoos, rubbing up against other bits covered in black leather. All the bits were male.

'Uhm, Colin. I'm not sure this is the kind of theme park you're after.'

Colin came and looked more closely.

'It looks good to me,' he said.

'Oh no,' said Loxy. 'Definitely not.'

Colin turned the puppy-dog peepers on.

'Are you sure you like gay people, Loxy?'

'What! Don't be ridiculous! That's absolute crap!' Loxy blustered. 'I just don't think that . . . you and me together . . . I just don't think we should . . .'

'But I've got a boyfriend,' said Colin. 'They're not going to think anything. Really. Are you frightened of us? Do you think we've all got AIDS?'

'No!' Loxy's PC heart was cut to the core. Honestly speaking, he was indeed a little bit worried about going as apparently part of a couple to a gay club. Not that he was unsure of his own sexuality, but . . . well, it was just force of habit, that was all. It would be something very different . . . but he steeled himself not to be offensive. After all, Julia didn't mind in the least coming to the clubs he grew up with in Streatham. This was the same thing, he told himself. He was abroad. He should be opening himself up to new experiences. Well, not literally of course.

Loxy scratched the back of his neck uncomfortably.

'Okay,' he said finally. 'Do you really want to go? We can go.'

'Hooray!' said Colin. 'I wonder if they've heard of Geri Halliwell here yet.'

Too late, Loxy remembered the good old 'But I Hate the Music' defence.

* * *

Big Bastard stood on the street corner in front of the alleyway whistling quietly and trying not to look like as much of a plank as he felt. He kept out from under the main streetlights and hoped none of his pals would walk past. It was after eleven o'clock, and freezing, but the streets of Covent Garden were still heaving. He turned up the collar of his jacket and pretended to be Humphrey Bogart.

Finally, at about twenty past, he saw what he was looking for. He stepped out into the pavement.

'Yes, ex*cuse* me,' said the drippy-looking man, skinny in his Prada overcoat. He snorted at his emaciated companion, who looked up at Big Bastard with enormous, starving eyes. If she was pregnant, it didn't show.

'Patrick Cousins?' barked Big Bastard.

'What?' said the man, startled. He tried to push onwards, but Big Bastard held up one enormous meaty hand and rested it menacingly against his shoulder. It was like trying to walk into a force ten gale. Patrick's eyes suddenly filled with fear.

'Come with me, son.'

Big Bastard pushed him into the alleyway. Then he punched him on the nose.

The ballerina gasped as if she was going to faint, and leaned against the side of the alley wanly. Patrick lay on the floor staring upwards and clasping his hands to his nose. He was entirely white, apart from the blood starting to make its way through his fingers.

'What the FUCK!' he said. 'Oh God. Please don't kill me. Please. I'll do anything. Here. Why don't you take her. She's got more money than me, I promise. Please.'

The dancer perked up remarkably quickly and vanished into the night.

'That's for shaggin' around on my bird,' said Big Bastard. Patrick curled himself into a ball, clasped his hands over his head and started to cry. Big Bastard opened his wallet and pulled out a twenty-pound note. He handed it to Patrick with a grin.

'And that's for shaggin' around on my bird. Beer's on me, mate; I'm glad to have her. And I tell you what, I bet she's a damn sight foxier in the sack than that skinny little bonehead you've got going on.' He stood back. 'Now, stand up, stop crying, and fuck off, you snivelling little shithead.'

Big Bastard watched, arms folded, grinning broadly and pretending to be Vinnie Jones as Patrick picked himself up, looking at the ground, brushed off what he could of the muddy puddles, cigarette butts and old hamburger that had pretty much done for his Prada raincoat and limped off into the night. He paused just once, to cast one incredulous glance backwards – as if to check Big Bastard was indeed as enormous as he'd looked from the ground. Then he scarpered.

From her hiding place behind the bins, Siobhan squeezed her legs together and moaned.

'Andrea Dworkin will *hate* me,' she thought. 'And I just don't care.' She poked her head out.

'Fancy doing it behind the bins?'

'That's my *favourite* place for doing it. Reminds me of my happy childhood.'

* * *

Loxy discarded yet another shirt. Colin was wearing a muscle vest, despite the fact that the temperature had dropped considerably and it was only about four degrees outside. He was very excited.

'This will be the first time I've ever done something before Arthur,' he reflected with pleasure. 'Apart from the Pokemon tournament. And he didn't seem to care about that at *all*.'

'Well done,' said Loxy, shrugging on a checked shirt from the Gap. 'Okay. I didn't want to have to ask you this, but I'm going to. Do you think I look gay in this? I'm sorry, I just don't want to waste anyone's time by looking like I'm up for it.'

Colin examined him critically. 'No. No, you don't.'

'Okay then.'

'You look more like . . . you know, sexy trucker or woodcutter or something. Mmm.'

'Oh God,' said Loxy. 'Okay. Look, if I really hate it, can we leave again?'

'You won't hate it,' said Colin. 'They have coloured lights that flash on and off in time with the music.'

* * *

Andrew II headed the car out West, feeling a complete fool. It had been a long time – in fact, never – since he'd chased after a girl in that way. But something about Ellie had really got to him: her complete inability to not say exactly what she felt at all times, and her general cheekiness. So different from the ubiquitous blondes he came across every day. But not that different after all. They'd been punting him about like a piece of meat, a little stateside diversion. He squirmed uncomfortably in his seat and pushed the speedometer up a little.

His mobile rang, and he listened for a long time. Then he pulled over.

'Oh no,' he said. 'Oh, no. Poor Hedgehog.'

Hatsie snuffled some more. 'Okay. You've got his address? I think I'll try and get there before the police do'

He scribbled it down then sat in the car for a long time, staring straight ahead, realizing just exactly how much he was missing this daffy curly haired girl, and how much he wanted to protect her from what was coming.

Saddened – and, deep down, excited about seeing her again – he turned the car around and, facing back towards the East, started pushing out the Thunderbird to see how quickly it could go.

* * *

Everything out of the window was colder now, Ellie had noticed numbly, and whiter. She was trying to plan out how much fun they could have in New York – the transvestite parade for starters – but her thoughts kept slipping and sliding – to afterwards. Her imagination was working overtime – what was she going to do? Now the quest was definitely, definitely over. She tried to scoff when she thought of how daft it had been really, but she couldn't quite, particularly when she saw the Frog Brothers' faces in front of her. Perhaps, she thought, I could just pop into a couple of places. Just keep my eyes open. She looked at the two in front now eagerly discussing the Guggenheim. No, she thought to herself. Go with the flow. She wasn't going to find any answers; she'd been right all along. Isn't fun the best thing to have?

'This quest is *so* over!' she said out loud.

'Good,' chorused the other two.

God, she missed him.

* * *

The bouncer's flesh shone with oil or sweat – Loxy assumed it was oil, as he could see the breath in front of his face, it had become so cold. He hustled them through without questioning them, or giving Loxy any mysterious looks he didn't understand.

'Welcome to the meat packing district,' he said.

'*What?*'

'That's just the area we're in,' said Colin importantly. 'Isn't it?'

'Sure, kiddo.'

They were in a cavern underneath a warehouse. The

walls were curved, and brick, and covered in sweat. Everywhere were men of all shapes and sizes dancing, snogging or just generally hanging out. Some looked extremely camp and bizarre, some looked utterly normal, including one, Loxy noticed with a gulp, the spit of his old French teacher. There were a couple of women in the place, looking overweight and a bit awkward, desperately trying to seem as if they were fully taking part in conversations when they clearly weren't. The place was heaving. Colin was bouncing up and down with excitement.

'Dancy dancy!' he shrieked. 'Come dance with me.'

'Sorry,' said Loxy. 'But there is no way on earth that I am dancing to "I Know Him So Well".'

'Not even when it's being mimed by two eight-foot-tall drag artistes?'

'Oh, *that's* what those are. I thought they were holding the roof up.'

'Bringing the house down, honey,' said one of them, pushing past Loxy to replace his suspender belt.

'This is great,' said Colin, looking around, his eyes shining. 'This is the best place I've ever been.'

'Uh huh,' said Loxy. 'Do you want a beer?'

'Nope! I want a Manhattan!'

Loxy left him spinning around on the dance floor

and leaned on the bar. A burly man with a crew cut leaned over.

'What can I get you?'

'A Coors and a Manhattan, thanks.'

'So, who are you buying for tonight?'

Loxy indicated Colin, who was now dancing with everyone on the dance floor.

'Ooh, cute. Known him long? Oh no – he hasn't been out the womb that long.'

'I'm babysitting him for a friend, actually.'

'You *are* a naughty boy.'

'No, it's not like that. Actually, I'm not gay.'

'You'd be amazed how often I hear that.'

'I'm sure. But I'm really not. We're just . . .' he debated whether to explain his visit then decided against it. 'I'm in America to meet my girlfriend.'

'Ha! Well, I doubt you'll find her in here.'

Loxy took the drinks but decided against plunging into the mêlée. Everyone seemed to be bumping bits with everyone else. He sipped his beer and looked at his watch.

'Saving that for anyone?'

The voice sounded like Harvey Fierstein with a bad cold after a heavy night.

'Uh, yes,' said Loxy.

'Oh well, he won't mind if I just have a little sip will he?'

The man was about five foot four and entirely

covered in grey hair – his shoulders, his back, everything. His shoulders and his back were visible because he was wearing a holey aertex vest. The effect was of Teenwolf, gone quite remarkably to seed.

'Eh . . . yes, I think he would actually,' said Loxy, picking up the cocktail anxiously.

'Ooh, you are a big grizzly bear aren't you?'

'No,' said Loxy, desperately. 'Colin!'

Colin looked up briefly from his shimmying and shimmied over.

'I'm very happy,' he announced.

'Good, good, I'm glad,' said Loxy, desperately hoping he would stay.

'Hello little chicken,' said the older man. Colin looked at him for a second.

'He's frightening me,' he announced to Loxy, then turned away and disappeared back into the throng.

'So,' said the man, leaning in and resting his arm on the bar. 'Looks like you're by yourself now. Here for the festival?'

Loxy backed into the bar, feeling ridiculously torn between trying not to offend anyone and wrenching, gut-churning dread. He cursed himself for not taking out his earring.

'Is this man bothering you?'

Thank God. It was the beefy barman.

'Umm . . .'

'Beat it, DeLorean.'

'Aw, come on. I'm not doing nothing.'

'You're annoying the customers. AGAIN. Now, scram.'

The grey fuzzy man shrugged and plunged back into the near darkness.

'Thanks,' said Loxy, feeling stupid.

The barman shrugged. 'I used to work in a straight bar. The women used to get someone like him every five minutes.' He continued to rub his glasses dry. 'God, it must be crap being a woman. All that messiness, and you have to sleep with the really unattractive guys too.'

'It's probably alright really,' said Loxy.

'Yeah, yeah. I think our way's easier, don't you?'

'I'm not . . . Yeah. Sure.'

The barman grinned, and Loxy turned back to the dance floor where Colin was burning it up to 'Spinning Around'.

'Come over here and DANCE,' shrieked Colin.

'Okay, okay,' said Lox, and joined him.

* * *

They stumbled out into the freezing air at 3am, giggling their heads off. It was threatening to snow.

'I can't believe I know what it's like to be Kylie Minogue,' Loxy said, throwing his hands out in the air, a gesture not entirely disassociated with his seven Manhattans (and one beer).

340

'They *loved* you,' agreed Colin.

'That is because I am the best dancer of ALL TIME,' said Lox, whose tastes normally ran to R'n'B and who certainly hadn't got it on to the Bee Gees in living memory. 'Oh my God. And I could not be *happier* about my old French teacher. *Repete toi* indeed. *Fellate toi!*'

He giggled again.

'That scary grey man looked like you,' said Colin, skipping ahead.

'What? What are you talking about, Col?'

'I mean, he looked like you when you talk to Julia.'

'What do you mean?'

'All bending over and things. Like a big wolf.'

'That's not how I talk to Julia.'

'Like, if she wanted to move away from talking to you, you'd bite her really hard.'

'That is *not* . . .'

'Grrrrr! Grrrr.'

'Shut up,' said Loxy, his good mood evaporating like the steam from his breath as three Shirley Basseys staggered past them, blowing kisses.

* * *

'Hedgehog?'

'Snfrgh?'

Ellie was in the middle of a dream involving

Andrew McCarthy. Only, this time, she couldn't tell which one. Her dress was still pink; they were still kissing, but the faces kept dissolving into one another.

'Hedgehog . . . wake up.'

Arthur was shaking her gently. The car had stopped.

'Oh.' She sat up, shaking her head, feeling slightly displaced, as you do when your dreams are rather better than waking up crouched on a filthy Toyota back seat. 'Where are we?'

She hadn't meant to fall asleep, but had just drifted off. Now she realized she was freezing, and it was nearly dark.

'Ssh,' said Arthur, and beckoned her out of the car. Julia had already left, and was standing a little distance away.

They were at the top of a hill, with the sun setting behind them. In the foreground, in a ball park, there was a bunch of small children playing baseball. Behind them were fields, then water. And behind that was Manhattan, looming out of the river like Kryptonite, reflecting itself off the water like a giant shiny machine.

'Oh my God!' breathed Ellie.

'We thought you might want to see this bit.'

'*Oh* yes.'

She stood on the top of the hill looking across, then moved towards Julia and linked arms with her.

Julia patted her on the hand, as the first snowflake fluttered down.

'There's our destination,' Julia said.

'I'd rather hoped it might have been the start,' said Ellie a little sadly. She put her arm around Julia and squeezed her tightly.

The Lost Boys

Loxy and Colin were sitting in the All Flavor donut shop. Colin was on caramel cream and banana. Loxy was finding it difficult to conceal his nausea while continuing to eat, and looked green around the gills. They were en route to the Empire State Building clutching their hangovers. Despite his, Colin was still his usual chirpy self, which was reminding Loxy woefully of the difference between being thirty and still holding a young person's railcard.

'I want to throw a piece of paper off the top and see if it will really guillotine someone,' Colin was saying.

'Well you can't,' said Loxy, who had been impressed by the coolness with which he'd managed to retrieve a newspaper from the oddly shaped box on the street corner, particularly as he'd had to hold Colin back from taking all of them, and was now buried in it. Then he saw it, stuck on an inside page:

80s Movie Star in Stalker Drama.

Brat Pack star Andrew McCarthy (36) has been targeted by several stalkers, it was revealed today. The one-time teen actor, who has also had several successes on Broadway, was said to be concerned by the fact that he is being obsessively followed by fans from all over the world.

'Oh my God,' said Loxy. 'That guy they're looking for – it turns out he's being stalked!'

'Oh no,' said Colin. 'Poor guy.'

'Speaking from his chic apartment in New York's trendy SoHo . . .'

'Great!' said Loxy. 'That's where he is! Let's go!'

Colin looked at him wide-eyed and sticky-mouthed. 'But . . . the Empire State Building!'

'What's more important? The Empire State Building or your friends?'

Colin looked at his plate. 'What about the Empire State Building and my doughnuts against my friends?' His face creased until it looked like he might cry.

'The answer is "your friends",' said Loxy, dragging him up. 'You can eat doughnuts any time.'

'Yes, but not with maple syrup and figs . . .'

Loxy pulled him onto the sidewalk.

* * *

'Do you think it's really there, or is it just going to shimmer in a mirage and we're never going to hit it?' asked Ellie. They had spent, they hoped, their last night in a motel, and were up bright and early and ready for action. However the fifty-mile tailback into Manhattan didn't seem to have moved in any perceptible fashion for the last two hours. 'I wish I'd brought my own ice-skates.'

'I'm going to have to drop the car off,' said Julia moodily, staring at the map. 'Well. It's not like we'll miss it.'

'Oh, I don't know,' said Arthur. 'The way the vinyl retains sweat and odour.'

They limped in eventually and crawled under a tunnel which Ellie thought, rather nervously, she'd seen blown up in a movie before. Then suddenly New York burst upon them, and their entire world became vertical.

'Hey hey!' said Arthur.

'Yikes!' said Julia, as a suicidal bike messenger bore down on her out of nowhere. 'I thought London couriers were bad.'

'Not that bad,' said Arthur. 'I had one once. Went like the clappers.'

'Really?'

'Yeah, it was great. You could phone him up and order him like pizza.'

'That's not good for you, you know,' said Julia reprovingly.

'Hey – it wasn't *real* pizza.'

'Do you think if you could get married to Colin you would?' speculated Ellie.

'Don't be gross,' said Arthur, shivering in disgust. 'Have you ever been to a non-tacky wedding? God no. If I could show him at *Crufts* I would.'

'I think you're a bit hard on him.'

'Oh, stop it – I really miss being hard on him.'

They crawled along the busy street. Snow had fallen in the night, but on the streets it was drizzly and grey. People pushed their way to work, looking angry at the world.

'If I lived in New York, I'd be happy all the time,' said Ellie, looking at them in wonderment. 'With a lovely American boy.'

'I'm sure it's just like London,' said Arthur. 'With shiny molars.'

'It's nothing like London!' said Ellie scornfully. 'Nobody and nothing in it is the faintest bit like London.'

'Oh God,' said Julia.

'What?'

'Nothing. The funniest thing. Must have been away

from home for too long. Only, I could have sworn I saw . . .'

'Who?'

'Oh, no. Just two people that looked a lot like Loxy and Colin, that's all. Isn't it weird when that happens?'

* * *

The surly man in the courier booth didn't even look up at them when they turned the car in.

'Any problems?' he grunted.

'Nope.' said Julia.

'Ha. If only he knew,' said Ellie.

'Huh,' he grunted, and kept reading his magazine as they shouldered their bags and walked out, heavily burdened, into the freezing afternoon.

Thus it took him about ten minutes to identify the figures when the cops came in half an hour later, chasing the car.

'Hell no,' he said. 'Hardly noticed them. But hey – if they're vicious murderers, I'll be expecting a cheque from the NYPD for the cleaning bill.'

'Yeah, right . . . sue your own ass,' said the cop, noting the amount of litter in the back of the car. They weren't going to get too far leaving this much evidence kicking around the place. No rope though. Plus, they were limeys, so he didn't think they'd be carrying guns. He checked back into his radio, told them to look out for two Caucasian females, one male. Christ. That should narrow it down in a town of ten million.

* * *

They dumped their bags somewhere which appeared to be a very small hotel room or a broom cupboard, but by the price of it was actually a semi-detached house in Hounslow.

'Okay,' said Arthur. 'The parade is just starting. So I say we go see that, then ice skating in Central Park like in *Splash*, then Bloomingdales like in *Mannequin*, then plan to end up absolutely anywhere from *Bright Lights, Big City*.'

Ellie sat rather disconsolately on the tiny bed.

'I guess,' she said.

'Oh, come on,' said Julia, sitting down beside her. 'Isn't this what we decided?'

'Look at the alternatives,' said Arthur. 'Are you really just going to go piling out into . . .' he indicated the freezing cold and the wind outside. 'I thought we were all going to stick together here.'

'This is it, isn't it?' said Julia, in an encouraging tone of voice. 'Didn't we decide that? That us all being together was all that mattered?'

'Yes,' said Ellie staring at the floor. The last thing she felt like doing now was abandoning all the Andrews in her life and going out to the world's biggest transvestite awards. Then she thought again of what she'd decided in the aftermath of the crash and remembered her new found commitment to duty, even if it was duty fun. She shook herself briskly. 'Yes, it is. I bloody owe you guys a good time!'

'Not in the sexual sense I hope,' said Arthur.

'Nope!' said Ellie stalwartly. 'Come on! I am putting on my ra-ra skirt and we are HITTING THIS TOWN.'

* * *

New York crackled with icicles and excitement. Ellie linked one arm through Julia's and one through Arthur's and they shivered their way north along Lexington Avenue. The streets were very busy, and every so often they would see a feather head-dress or a man in stilts over the top of the crowd, which would make Arthur hop with excitement and Julia exclaim. Ellie held onto both of them tightly and pretended the wind was making her face as sad as it was.

'Quick, this way,' said Julia, pulling out the map. They craned over it to try and work out where they were. 'We cross Sixth and turn into 48th Street.' Arthur poked his head up.

'Over here!' he said. 'Oops. Walk or Don't walk; there doesn't seem to be a flashing man option. Shame.'

'It is *freezing*,' said Julia.

They reached the cross street and turned the corner, then Ellie really did freeze with her mouth hanging open.

* * *

The street was entirely full up. Yellow cabs were stopped in the middle of the road. Somewhere, someone had set up a gigantic stereo system that was pumping out pop music, and the whole street was dancing – transvestites of all shapes and sizes together with quite a lot of ordinary-looking kids.

'Oh my God,' said Ellie, extending her finger slowly. Set in the stone behind the dancers was a fine old Manhattan building proudly proclaiming 'High School For Professional Performing Arts'.

Two people jumped on top of one of the yellow taxis and started frugging furiously. The cab driver only laughed and shouted at someone to turn the music up.

Arthur and Julia stared at the scene, smiling broadly at the silliness of it.

Ellie wasn't smiling.

'It's a sign,' said Ellie suddenly. 'It's a SIGN!'

And she took off at a run and disappeared into the crowd.

* * *

'HEY!' shouted Julia and Arthur. They took off after

her, but before they'd gone two yards, Julia was nearly felled by a huge hug from a seven-foot black Marilyn Monroe.

'*HON!*' said Holly Wood. 'I KNEW you'd come. How did you manage to change your messy friend into something so cute?' She shot Arthur a look.

Julia scanned the crowds, but Ellie had gone.

'Oh, hi Holly Wood,' she said with a sigh. '*Weird Science*. Anyway. *You* look fantastic.'

'Hand sewn,' said Holly, shaking some decidedly anxious-looking sequins. 'So, come dance.'

'We've got to look for our friend.'

'Oh,' said Arthur, hips already shaking of their own accord. 'She'll turn up again when she's hungry.' And he shimmied into the throng, dragging Julia with him.

Ninety-nine red balloons went by.

* * *

Once past the crowds, Ellie slowed down, panting. No-one was behind her. But she knew now. She had to go looking. She was here. She had to. Otherwise, she'd never know.

She was in a slightly quieter seedier street now, and looked around nervously, wondering where to start. It began to snow. She set her head against the wind and went on.

* * *

Okay. Where would actors hang out? Where would he be likely to go? Second-hand bookshops and old black and white movie theatres, that seemed like his style. She kept heading south, away from the parade and the tourist sites, and pushed along the endless blocks down into midtown and from then, freezing, on to SoHo, glancing at every face and in every shop window.

* * *

Andrew II stared at the piece of paper with the address Hatsie had given him, and up at the elegant brownstone. Well, depending on their powers of deduction – which, frankly, he didn't rate that highly – they were going to hopefully make it here sooner or later. Hanging around seemed like a dumb idea, but then every time he remembered Ellie, and the awful news hanging over her, he couldn't bear the thought of going anywhere else.

* * *

'Hmm,' said Loxy, looking around. 'I think we need some strategy here.'

'Excuse me,' Colin was asking a bag lady on a bench. 'Have you seen my friends Arthur and Ellie and Julia?'

The bag lady grunted at him and put out her hand. Loxy pulled him away before he put more than five dollars in it.

'Okay,' said Colin. 'We're in the right bit. Why don't we just shout?'

'What?'

'Andrew!' shouted Colin. 'Andrew!'

'Maybe he'll be passing on his way to the shops,' Colin whispered to Loxy. 'And he'll hear us and come over.'

'Oh,' said Loxy. He thought it over.

'Andrew!' he joined in.

'Calling all units,' said the cop on the corner, quietly into his radio.

* * *

Four hours later, Ellie was still on the street. All the faces had started to look the same to her. As on the London Underground, the eyes flicked away sharply, apart from those of some of the more dodgy-looking men, which made her feel even more uncomfortable. She wandered in and out of antique shops, of cinemas, of chichi delis. 'This isn't even looking for a needle in a haystack,' she began to think. 'This is looking for a needle in Wales. A really small needle.' For the eight billionth time she wondered what Arthur and Julia were up to.

She tripped over a tiny dog.

'Hey!' yelled a voice. 'Get the fuck oudda it!'

'Sorry!' She stumbled on, laddering her tights and tripping down into a subway station. The millions of hard-faced commuters and travellers down there in the semi-darkness seemed to loom in front of her and she became short of breath, realizing the impossibility of picking out one person from the multitude.

Up top again it was more freezing than ever. She pushed against the wind again and went on, but now she was entirely without direction, plodding forward up the endless, endless streets. The thought 'this is stupid, this is stupid, this is all stupid,' swirled round and round her head. Tears pricking her eyelids were whisked away by the breeze. Although it was only early afternoon it already felt dark, with the heavy snow-filled clouds touching the tops of the skyscrapers. Her feet were agony.

Finally, feeling miserable and defeated, and soaked through from the tears on her face to her sodden toes, she fell into the first coffee shop she came to.

* * *

'Well, hello y'all,' said a familiar voice. 'What happened to your friend? She ran away, di'n't she? Can't say I'm surprised.'

Ellie staggered back and clasped onto the back of a chair.

'Oh. My. God!'

'Ehm, yeah well, God or whatever,' said the waitress from LA. 'I mean, do you want a priest or do you want some pancakes?'

356

'Pancakes!' said Ellie, recovering from her shock and discovering a broad grin plastered across her face.

'Okay then.' The waitress filled up her coffee cup without being asked.

'So what brought you here then?' said Ellie, cupping the mug with both hands and inhaling the steam. 'Oh, that smells good.'

'Well, you know . . . I got a big part in a movie. I'm playing a waitress. I'm not actually working, I'm method acting.'

'Seriously!'

'Well, durr. No! Some stupid guy.' She shrugged. 'With a big mouth and small pants. A three-day wonder, as it turned out.'

'Yeah?'

'So I'm stuck here with lousy weather and this crazy East Coast inability to distinguish between "apartment rental" and "extortion".'

'Yeah.'

'Still, there's Off-Broadway . . . hey, what's the matter? You haven't cheeked me once since you got in here!'

Ellie shrugged.

'Did you find that fella you came looking for – who was it again? Oh, wasn't it Rob Lowe? Did you boff him?'

'No,' shrugged Ellie. 'It was Andrew McCarthy.

And,' she took a deep breath, 'I am *genuinely* not looking for him any more.'

'Andrew McCarthy! Of course!' the waitress sat down opposite her. 'Of *course*. Why the hell didn't I put two and two together? Oh, apart from the fact that I didn't think I was ever going to see *you* again. Andrew McCarthy. Little sweet-faced fella, right?'

'Yeah?' said Ellie.

'Yeah, I think he lives round here . . . comes in for his coffee most days.'

* * *

Ellie attempted to stop choking on her own tongue.

'You . . . you're kidding, aren't you?'

'Still looking for him, huh?'

'Yuh . . . yuh *huh*.'

'Well, there you go. Hang around here long enough and you might get lucky.'

'Can I . . . can I use your phone . . .' burbled Ellie.

'Sure.'

Ellie left a completely garbled message back at the hotel hollering for the others to join her, then sat back and ordered enough pancakes for a long day. Which, if you're Ellie, is an awful lot of pancakes.

* * *

'Excuse me, Sir?'

Loxy turned round, embarrassed. He became less embarrassed when he realized he was standing in front of a cop. A bit less embarrassed and a bit more utterly terrified.

'Uhm, yes?'

'Can I ask why you're shouting out "Andrew" now?'

'Umm.'

Loxy pondered how to explain this to a cop. He was rather more used to policemen than the others, not only through his work, but also because he drove quite a nice car and was used to getting pulled over to have it searched for anything else he wasn't supposed to be able to afford. And he was never cheeky and he never lied, having realized long ago that these things just made the whole process take a lot longer.

'We're looking for the actor Andrew McCarthy, Sir.'

The cop looked him up and down and slowly pulled his handcuffs off his belt.

'Sir, I'm arresting you . . .'

'What!?' said Loxy, genuinely stunned.

'. . . for Stalking in the Fourth Degree. You have the right to remain silent. Anything you say may be used against you in a court of law. Do you understand?'

'Not in the slightest,' said Loxy, holding out his hands nevertheless.

'Is that minor with you?'

The cop was indicating Colin, who was watching the proceedings with wonder, rather than fear.

'Ehm, yes . . . and he's not a minor.'

'Really? And is he also "*looking*" for your actor friend, eh buddy?' The cop shoved him nastily on the arm.

'Yes.'

'Shall I run away?' piped up Colin directly to Loxy.

'*Noo*,' groaned Loxy. 'Although once we're out of this, I'd recommend running *very* quickly away from me.'

* * *

After dancing frenziedly for half an hour, Arthur and Julia had escaped, giggling, into the calm and serenity of the Guggenheim Museum.

'Holly was *definitely* after you,' said Julia.

'Yeah,' said Arthur, gazing fixedly at the pictures. 'Just not my type, I guess.'

'I thought *everyone* was meant to be your type,' said Julia teasingly.

Arthur reddened and smiled at the ground. Julia nudged him.

'Give it up,' she said.

'Give what up?'

'You know . . . admit to the world that you're an old pipe and slippers gent at heart.'

'I am *not*.'

'Uh huh.'

They wandered up the spiral walkway. Arthur looked at her.

'Well, you give it up.'

'Give what up?'

'Pretending that you don't know the answer to your own question.'

Julia stared into the atrium.

'You know.' She took a deep breath. 'Until a couple of days ago . . . when Ellie crashed the car and kind of came to her senses . . . well, you know, I hadn't actually finally given up all hope of meeting Andrew McCarthy. And there was a tiny – the *tiniest* bit of me thought he might be able to help. I know it sounds stupid. But I feel like I've given up all hope of ever really knowing what to do about Loxy.'

'Uh huh,' said Arthur, studying a particularly elongated nude.

'What do you mean by *that* particular *uh huh*? And I don't think you're meant to touch that bit.'

'But it's so *long* . . . well, I mean, come on Jules. Fair enough to expect a space cadet like the Hedgehog to want to get her life advice from an actor, but I didn't think it of you.'

Stung, Julia walked on.

'Well, it wasn't advice *as such* . . . just . . .'

'I mean, how many good, loyal, faithful, interesting, trustworthy guys with nice arses are going to ask you to marry them anyway?'

'Not many,' said the attendant. 'Sir, would you mind not touching that? It makes it all shiny.'

'Exactly,' said Arthur. 'To both things.'

'I know. I know. I know,' said Julia. 'It's just . . . he's such a wimp . . .'

* * *

'Can you get us a brief?' Loxy was saying in his best Prisoner's Advocate voice as they walked through the precinct door.

'And I'll need a phone call. And then you can tell us what this damned stupid charge actually is, and then we can explain it and you can send us on our way. Okay?'

'I love your accent,' said the cop.

* * *

'. . . and he's all over me all the time, like he just can't leave me alone . . .'

* * *

'Colin, don't make me come over there. I'm only telling you once.'

Colin was attempting to imitate the 'Wanted' posters on the wall.

'Right, let's get this sorted out. Best start with me.'

* * *

'Is that the worst you can think of to say about him?' said the attendant. 'What's his number? I'll have him. And Sir, I won't tell you again.'

They passed into a room covered in Pollocks that seemed to jump crazily from one canvas to another.

Julia stood stock still in the middle of the room for thirty seconds.

'Arthur,' she said suddenly, turning round, her eyes full of tears. 'Have I been a complete and utter wombat?'

Arthur came up to her gently and put his arm around her.

'Of course you have,' he said, squeezing her tight.

'But . . . what if it's too late?'

'I think if he's been crazy about you for two years, a few weeks isn't going to make a difference.'

'Oh my God – *what* if I'd got off with that stupid surfer boy?'

'Well, don't worry about it, because you didn't. Anyway, you just couldn't bear the thought of anyone not fancying you for a change.'

'Christ, yeah.' She looked embarrassed. 'Well, they normally do.'

'I know. But, one day you just have to say, "let 'em. I've got mine".'

'Oh Arthur.' She wiped her nose. 'Oh God, sorry . . . was that your sleeve?'

'Again, don't worry about it,' said Arthur, mentally allowing himself three free angel points.

'I have to go and phone him right away.' She pulled away agitatedly, and started rummaging in her pockets for change. 'I can get him on the mobile, even if he's at the prison. I just phone the British number and . . .'

'Okay.'

She stopped faffing suddenly and looked up.

'Oh my God – you know what this means? I'm getting MARRIED!'

'I know!'

'I'M GETTING MARRIED!'

She jumped up and down and Arthur spun her around in a hug.

'Don't they make the *loveliest* couple,' said one of the other attendants.

* * *

'Oh Jesus,' said Siobhan. 'Lox, why did you phone *me?*'

'Well, I don't know, do I? You're the only person who knows where I am. And why I'm here. Because I, personally, have pretty much forgotten why I'm here.'

'You should have phoned the consul.'

'What for? You're acting like I've got four pounds of heroin up my jacksie. Which I *haven't* –' he glanced crossly at the duty sergeant, who was trying to pretend not to eavesdrop.

'But Lox, they haven't phoned – I don't know where they are. I'm so sorry, I just don't know what to do . . . ugh . . .'

'Hang on a second – are you having *sex?*'

'Loxy, I . . .'

'I'm going to prison and you're having *sex???*'

'I don't think I could help you any more if I wasn't . . .'

But he had already hung up.

* * *

'Come on then Sir.'

Loxy wearily started taking off his coat and indicated to Colin that he should do the same. Suddenly, his mobile rang.

The desk sergeant reached inside the coat, picked it out and pressed the 'on' switch.

'Yes! Yes! Yes!' could be heard distinctly around the precinct lobby.

'I think,' he said, passing it back to Loxy, 'it's your friend that's having sex again.'

* * *

'We're all clear for now,' the officer in SoHo heard on his radio. 'Keep an eye on him, but I don't think the girls will prove so much of a problem. I think he's got a message to them anyway; there's certainly a lot of screaming going on.'

Andrew II noticed all the police and wondered what the hell was going on. This was getting stranger and stranger. He hoped the girls remembered that American policemen had guns.

* * *

'You're in *New York*!!!' Julia was so over the moon she didn't even stop to question whether it might not be to see her.

'I've got to see you.'

'Ah,' said Loxy. 'That might be a problem. You see, we've been arrested.'

'Oh my God.'

Arthur held Julia up while she went weak at the knees.

'Who's "we"?' he whispered, urgently.

'Who's with you?' said Julia. 'Oh my God. Why have you been arrested? What have you done!?'

Loxy tried as well as he could to explain, interrupted

366

by Julia's 'oh my god's.

'They think you're *stalking him?* But that's what *we* were doing.'

'You may want to have said that a little quieter.'

The cops were gathered around the phone.

'It doesn't matter. We're coming to get you anyway. We can explain it all then. I'm sure they'll understand.'

Loxy sighed and held up his hands.

'Don't worry,' yelled Colin, 'I can pay for bail with Siobhan's gold card.'

* * *

'We've got them all,' said the police radio. 'You don't need to keep him under surveillance any more.'

'They've got them all!' said the women at the agency. 'Quick! Get the photographers down to the precinct immediately. And stand by to phone him for quotes. If you can't get any, just come straight back to me. This is a BUST!'

* * *

Andrew II, feeling increasingly stupid, waited till the police were out of sight, and the door to the building had opened and closed. Unsure of whether to follow the policemen or the actor, he decided on the latter, bearing in mind the whole who had a gun issue.

Some Kind of Wonderful

The slightly-built man in the smart grey overcoat paused on his way for coffee, shook his head at the rather ridiculous events of his last couple of days, then pushed his way onwards through the biting wind.

Ellie sat nursing her fifth cup. The waitress had moved her onto decaffeinated very early on. Her stomach was churning nonetheless. She thought over all the questions she would have asked him in her bedroom, but they seemed so stupid now – all, 'should I keep my brace in at night or secretly take it out?' or, 'should I be using both hands for this?' I mean, what was he going to think, confronted with her, thirty years old, freezing, wet through, a complete stranger in a shop asking him to sort her life out? She groaned in anticipated embarrassment, then got up to go and check herself in the bathroom.

Her wild curly hair had turned frizzy in the wet, and she pulled it back with a large scrunchie. Her cheeks were also very pink from the sudden change in temperature, and the knowledge of what was coming, but that didn't look too bad – it made her look younger, at least. She wiped away the mascara debris from underneath her eyes, reapplied it and whacked on some cherry-coloured lipstick. She'd looked a lot worse. She'd looked a lot better.

'Hey, what's the big deal?' said the waitress coming past. 'You're just going to say hello, right? Take a photo, get him to sign an autograph. It'll be fine.'

Ellie searched with panic for her camera and found it bumping away at the bottom of her bag along with the remains of at least fifteen assorted packets of chewing gum.

'Will you take the picture?' she said.

'Sure.' The waitress popped the camera into her belt.

'What's he like?'

The waitress shrugged. 'Double espresso. Always tips. Nice, then.'

'Huh. But you never spoke to him?'

'To tell him what: beware of demented British girls? Nope. Guess I should have done, huh?'

Ellie stuck her tongue out at her.

'See! You're feeling better already.'

* * *

The detectives and the duty sergeant watched as the pretty blonde girl rushed over to the cell door.

'Lox!' she shrieked, scarcely able to breathe.

'Julia!' he said, and, suddenly, quite without realizing he was doing it, he burst into tears. 'Oh, Julia, you don't know . . . it's all gone really, really wrong.'

'What?' she said, thinking instantly that he must have changed his mind about her. 'What is it? What's happened?'

'Oh God, it's . . . I don't know how to say this . . .' he looked up. Julia's heart was racing.

'Where's Ellie?' he said.

* * *

By three-thirty the lunch crowd had left and the early evening crowd hadn't yet descended. Ellie sat all by herself in the corner, her face a picture of misery. The owner had glanced at her once or twice, but the waitress had reassured him. She'd been here less than a week, but had a face like the first day of spring and a body like the fourth of July, so he wasn't about to argue.

At twenty to four the door of the shop tinged.

* * *

The cops summoned them in right away.

'Seems to me,' said the detective, surveying them all, 'that you people couldn't stalk a turtle with three legs.'

'No Sir,' they shook their heads vigorously. Julia was welded to Loxy's side, and could hear his anxious heart beating. Arthur and Colin were standing a little apart.

'So all you wanted was an autograph?'

'Yup,' said Julia, crossing her fingers.

'Why couldn't you have sent from home for that?'

'Well, it's more of a holiday really.'

'Uh huh. So what are these two boys doing here?'

Julia and Arthur looked up as expectantly as the policemen did.

'Umm,' said Loxy. He rubbed the back of his neck and stared at the floor.

'The Hedgehog's dad died,' said Colin very clearly.

The room fell silent.

'Oh . . . oh,' said Julia. She sat down heavily on the table behind her.

'Oh God, poor thing, poor thing.'

'Hang on, who's this Hedgehog now?' said the cop.

'Our friend we're travelling with; her real name's Ellie,' said Julia, looking white and sick.

'Wait a minute – *you're* not Ellie?'

'No, I'm Julia.'

The cop looked at his charge sheet.

'Sheesh. Ellie Eversholt – that's the name of the girl we're looking for that's following Andrew McCarthy – we just assumed that was you.'

Julia shook her head.

'I don't know where Hedge . . . where Ellie is. She went off on her own this morning.'

'Christ,' said the cop. He thrust the folder at the nearest uniformed policeman.

'Bunch of fucking ass clowns this is going to make us look in front of Interpol.'

Julia looked at Loxy. 'Oh my God – you came all this way to tell her!'

Loxy shrugged. 'It was . . .'

'It was my idea,' said Colin. 'I thought it would be better if we were here.'

'God,' said Julia, shaking her head. 'You know, I've known him nearly as long as I've known my own dad.'

'When do dads die?' asked Colin.

'When they're old and they eat too many sausages.'

'Oh. My dad's forty. That's pretty old.'

'That is NOT,' they all said.

* * *

The waitress was making ridiculous wobbling eyebrow motions at her, but Ellie couldn't move. She sat there, petrified, shaking her head.

'Hi there. Double espresso please.'

'How you doing today?'

'Oh, not too bad . . . been a bit strange.'

'Yeah?'

She poured the coffee. Ellie covered her face with her hands. He was ten feet away from her and she couldn't move. *Certainly* couldn't talk. She desperately tried to swallow the lump in her throat but couldn't.

'Listen,' the waitress said. 'I hate to hassle you and everything, but there's a friend of mine who's come an awful long way to meet you.'

Andrew McCarthy picked up his coffee cup and glanced around the shop. His eyes lighted on Ellie, who whimpered. He half-smiled.

'*Tell* me she's not English,' he said.

'Well, yes she is,' said the waitress. 'But she's not too weird, honestly.'

'I've been told to be on the lookout for crazy English stalkers.'

He'd spoken loudly enough so that Ellie could hear.

'But I reckon I could take her on now, don't you?'

'I hear she scratches,' said the waitress.

'I'll be certain to watch out for that.'

He walked slowly towards Ellie, whose heart was stopping, pulled a chair out from the next table along and sat down on it back to front, facing her.

'Well then. I guess . . . hello there.'

* * *

'Okay, I think it's about time to get this little circus on the road,' said the detective. 'I'm very sorry about your friend, but I don't think I can really be bothered to charge any of you, huh?'

'Thank you,' said Loxy. He looked at Julia, who was hovering nervously next to the door, watching him with trepidation in her eyes.

'Oh, and by the way, I think you'll find . . .' the cop opened the swing doors with a flourish.

As they stepped out they were confronted with three or four news cameras.

'We're *news*?' said Loxy, holding up his hand instinctively.

'Very, very local,' assured the policeman. 'Plus one or two sent along by the agency. They like it when stuff happens to their clients. When their clients don't actually get hurt of course. Well, I *think* they prefer it when the client isn't hurt. Not necessarily.'

Julia was staring around wide-eyed. 'Oh God. I can't believe this.' She turned to Loxy. 'And I can't believe you're here. And I can't believe it about the poor Hedgehog.'

'Uh huh,' Loxy said carefully.

Colin couldn't resist pouting a little and sticking out his tongue, until Arthur cuffed him down the steps.

'Why were you stalking Andrew McCarthy?' shouted a bossy New Yawk voice.

'Um, well, it's a long story,' said Loxy, trying to look for a cab. 'Really, we're here . . .'

Julia silenced him, sent him to flag down a cab she'd spotted, then leaned over to the microphone.

'Because he's great,' she said, solemnly. 'But we promise not to do it any more.'

Then, with the journalists shouting more questions at them, they all piled into the cab as quickly as they could and drove away.

* * *

'Eh, hi there.' Ellie took a gulp from the glass of water the waitress had been kind enough to place at her side and willed herself to shift her eyes from the checked plastic tablecloth.

'You look exactly the same,' she whispered.

'Well, so do you, I'm sure.'

She smiled for the first time.

'My agent didn't quite get this straight but . . . have you come all the way over from Britain to find me?'

Ellie nodded.

'Well, that hasn't happened in a while . . . though you'd be amazed at the loyalty of some of the Japanese women I run into.'

'Uh huh,' said Ellie grainily, not having anything

trenchant to add on the subject of being pursued by devoted Japanese ladies. Then she realized to herself that she was buggering this up and being ridiculous, and pinched herself hard on the thigh.

'Andrew,' she forced herself to say.

'Yup? Can I get you another coffee by the way?'

'No, I'm fine. Andrew.'

'Still here.'

He flashed her his famous grin.

'Umm . . . well I guess I'm just going to ask you straight out . . . Okay.' She took a deep breath. 'Look. Do you ever feel that things aren't working out the way you wanted them to? That somehow stuff isn't being part of the plan?'

He paused and took a long sip of his coffee.

'Wow . . . are you sure you don't just want to know what happened to the bra and panties from *Class?*'

Ellie shook her head.

'No, of course you don't. Well,' he shrugged, 'what makes you think there's a plan to be a part of?'

'Just your own plan. You know, your own idea of what something is going to be like.'

'Hmm. Well, has anything in your life ever turned out the way *you* planned it?'

Ellie screwed up her eyes for a second.

'Um. Well, I made a chocolate cake once.'

'Uh huh.'

'It was revolting.'

377

'There you go. And do you beat yourself up about it?'

'My father nearly did. There was a raw egg in it.'

'Exactly my point. Don't make plans. Just keep rolling on and accept that life isn't ever going to be like it is in an *actual* movie, is it?'

Ellie grimaced a little in disappointment.

'Is that absolutely definitely not going to be like it is in a movie thing really, really true?'

'Yes, of course it is. I mean, God, it would be like . . . I mean, life isn't like you're walking down the street and by coincidence just bump into someone and it all turns out for the best.'

Ellie was quiet for a second.

'No,' she said. 'I guess it isn't.'

* * *

Julia, Arthur, Loxy and Colin raced into the hotel off Fifth Avenue.

'Did Ellie Eversholt check back in?' gasped Julia.

'No,' said the clerk, as they all looked upset. 'But she left a message.' He slowly handed them the piece of paper.

'Quick,' said Loxy, and they jumped straight back into another cab. Inside the taxi they found themselves all holding hands.

'Do I still tell her?' said Colin quietly.

'No,' said Julia, thinking all the way back to the

insouciant little girl poking her hard in the leg with a pencil in Year One. 'No, Colin, I think I'd better tell her.'

The others nodded their agreement.

'I wish Siobhan were here.'

Arthur looked at Loxy, who shook his head vigorously, and shot Arthur back a warning look.

'There's news about Siobhan,' said Loxy. 'But I think it'll keep for now.'

The cab crawled through the traffic.

* * *

'It's impossible to make plans anyway. We understand about one per cent of what's going on in our brains, and all the brains in the world understand about one billionth of what's going on in the universe. It's a logical impossibility to attempt to place order on something you have no chance of coming close to conceiving the nature of.'

'Uh huh,' said Ellie.

'I mean, metaphysics already deals with the realms of the unknowable, and it looks like real world physics is going the same way.'

'I knew you were the right person to choose,' said Ellie quietly.

'So, you know, I reckon the best thing you can do is try and trust your animal impulses and try not to do things that actively make you unhappy. Like, look at me. I hated LA. I love it here. I hated being a movie star.'

'Really? But you still are one.'

'Yeah. Honestly. I mean it. After the first fifteen minutes it gets really boring. You know how stars always say the best part of being famous is getting tables in restaurants?'

'Yup.'

'That's because the rest of it is so shitty. And your TV dinner at home on your own still tastes exactly the same. But I love being a movie actor and I love being a stage actor – I *really* love that – so that's what I do. I, personally, don't trust my brain to come up with anything much better.'

'And you don't feel disappointed?'

'Disappointed about what – not having to take sixteen security guards with me everywhere I go? Only having the one house?'

'You're doing a lot better than me,' said Ellie.

'I'm sure that's not true. You look like you're doing all right.'

Ellie shrugged. 'I just . . . I just tend to feel disappointed.'

'Yeah? Hey! You're in New York and it's snowing!'

'Oh, New York isn't disappointing. New York is great.'

'Follow those animal instincts.' He cupped his chin in his palm and grinned at her.

'I just . . . feel my world is a bit, you know, blearrgh.'

He nodded. 'That blearrgh will be in the ninety-nine per cent of the brain nobody understands. Soon as your brain's got its food and clothing and shelter issues sorted out it moves directly onto blearrgh. But, we don't understand that part yet.'

Ellie nodded. 'I think I'm beginning to catch on.'

'Well, what have you got? Know any nice guys?'

'I did meet one,' said Ellie. 'I've got his telephone number. Then I really fucked him off.'

'Really?' he said, sounding concerned. 'Having someone to love is kind of the most important bit.'

Ellie nodded.

'But you've got his telephone number, right?'

'Uh huh.'

'Well, that's something. What about the rest of your life?'

'Well, I gave up my job to come here.'

He looked shocked.

'Tell me you didn't.'

'Yup. I needed the money and they gave me redundancy. Eventually.'

He ran his fingers through his hair and looked worried.

'Sorry – please tell me you didn't quit your job just to come and find me.'

'Oh! No. Don't think of it like that.'

'I told you,' said the waitress, who'd been valiantly eavesdropping. 'She's crazy.'

'But unarmed,' said Ellie quickly. 'And actually, you know, now I think about it, I didn't give up the job for you. I gave up the job because it sucked and I sucked at it. Sucked big time.'

'Really?'

'Yes. The only person who had anything to do with it was me.'

'Thank God. I thought for a moment I was going to have to foster you or something.'

'Nope. I followed my instincts.'

'That's the plan! Remember: we humans understand nothing. Okay. What about your friends?'

'They're fantastic,' she said, smiling. 'They're the best.'

'There you go. Hold onto them. I diagnose no real requirement for blearghh whatsoever.'

'I suppose not. And I'm going home to take care of my dad.'

He smiled at her.

'Well, then. You didn't need to come and see me at all. That is, I assume, that you're not about to tie me up, dump me in your trunk and chop me into bits.'

'No. Unless you'd like that.'

'Okay, hang on.'

He put his hand to his head.

'Okay. My instincts are saying no, no, no.'

'Well, alrighty then.'

Suddenly, his pager buzzed.

'Oy,' he said, reading it. 'I'm afraid I have to go and give a press conference – about you of all people.'

'No, really?' said Ellie.

'Yup. You're my famous stalker, didn't you know?'

'No, I did not know that.'

'Well, I guess you'd better not come with me unless you want to get arrested.'

'Can't I come?'

'I don't know . . . what do your instincts tell you about getting arrested?'

She shrugged. 'Blearggh?'

'You got it.'

He stood up.

'I think it is time for me to go to work, and for you to go and try to get the random piece of incomprehensible flotsam in this universe that may or may not make you happy depending on a, you know, whole set of infinitely multiplying parameters that we'd never understand in a billion lifetimes.'

He smiled at her. She smiled back.

'Thank you. I mean it.'

'Well! Hey. My work here is done.'

Her eyes followed him as he went to go.

'See you again Marilu.'

'No problem,' said the waitress.

'Oh!' he said, as he was nearly at the door. He

turned back to Ellie. 'I nearly forgot something. You know, it's my birthday today.'

'It's November 29th? Of *course* it is,' said Ellie.

His eyes sparkled. 'Want to give me a birthday kiss?'

'Tongues?' Ellie couldn't help herself.

'*No.* That's for zero ended birthdays.'

She went towards him slowly, and he put his arm around her very gently and kissed her briefly on the mouth, so softly and sweetly that it was like the only kiss she'd ever wanted – at least, the only kiss she'd ever wanted when she was thirteen years old.

'Bye,' he said softly. 'Good luck.' He disappeared out into the drizzly snow. Ellie stood and watched him go.

'I loved you,' she said quietly to herself. Then she crumpled back into her seat and had a little cathartic weep.

* * *

Andrew II straightened up from his hiding place when the original left the coffee house. He had glimpsed Ellie inside, but didn't want to burst in and rain on her parade. Now, however, he started to stride across the square.

A cab pulled up abruptly outside the shop and four people jumped out quickly, with worried expressions.

He recognized Julia immediately and was about to call out her name when he noticed the ashen look on her face. He stood back as they walked in and over to the girl he knew sitting alone at a table.

* * *

Ellie's face went through nine levels of shock when the four of them walked into the shop.

'Oh my . . .'

When they didn't smile, she squinted at them even harder.

'You guys . . . you guys . . . what are you guys all doing here?'

They all sat down.

Julia swallowed heavily, and reached over and took Ellie's hand.

'I met him! Did you see him? He was here and we kissed and . . .'

'Ssh,' said Julia. Ellie scanned their anxious faces then stood up abruptly. Everyone was quiet. She knew at once, but couldn't say it.

'What?'

'Sit down,' said Julia, not letting go of her hand. 'Just sit down.'

Arthur asked the waitress for some tea.

Inside Ellie it was like an iceberg calving off and breaking her in two. She couldn't breathe.

'It's my dad, isn't it? It's my dad?'

Julia nodded slowly. Colin stifled a sob and buried his head in Arthur's greatcoat.

'Is he . . . did he . . . is he okay?'

Julia shook her head. Without thinking, Ellie took a swallow of scalding hot tea and didn't even flinch.

'He's dead. Okay. Right. I see. Thanks for telling me.'

'It was a heart attack,' said Julia, stroking her arm and continuing to talk in a low, calm voice. 'It was very quick.'

'Quick! Great. Lovely . . .'

She was staring into space. Arthur came and stood behind her and rested his strong hands on her shoulders.

'We'll book you your ticket home, we'll sort that out right away, get everything organized . . .'

'Yes,' said Ellie, bewildered. 'Yes of course.'

'And then you'll have to come and stay with my mother,' said Julia. 'She'd love to have you for a couple of weeks.'

'Yes,' said Ellie again. 'Thank you. I'm sure that will be lovely.'

Then, 'He died all on his own.'

'I thought everybody died on their own,' said Colin suddenly. Arthur hushed him.

Ellie turned her face to the wall.

* * *

They sat that way, not knowing what to do, for some time. Suddenly Ellie pushed the chair away and stood up.

'I was going to look after him, you know.'

'We know,' said Arthur, putting his hand on her arm.

'I was going to make sure he ate properly and I was going to make up for everything and . . .' She dissolved. 'And he never knew.'

'I'm sure he does now,' said Arthur.

'Of course he doesn't!' she stood up. 'I'm . . . I'm off,' she said. 'I'm . . . going . . .'

'Don't dash off again,' said Arthur. 'Please. Let us stay with you.'

'I have to be on my own. For once, I have to be on my own. Okay?'

They nodded and watched as she went up to the waitress and hugged her, then left the store, leaving the others staring after her, aghast.

* * *

It had started to snow again and was getting dark. Ellie went through the crowds, finally catching a taxi when she realized how far it was to walk. Her brain was trying to process rather too much information, her feet were aching and it was everything she could do to choke out a destination to the cab driver.

'Sure. Havin' a good day?' he asked her.

Ellie stared out the window and ignored him.

* * *

The ice rink in Central Park was busy, and she had to queue to hire skates, passing her own sneakers over blindly. She sat down on the damp wooden benches to lace the skates on. Around her she could hear the shrieks and cries of excited children – with, no doubt, both mothers *and* fathers. Oh. It started to hit her. Her stupid, stupid dad. All those bloody sausages. All that bloody whisky. All her fault. All her mum's fault. Then her fault. And her dad's fault. She shook her head to try and clear it.

After a wobble or two, she glided off, the sense memory of her father's hand in hers very strong now. The music playing was 'Whistle Down the Wind', by Nick Heyward.

Ellie avoided the other skaters almost without seeing them and took on a contemplative look, like someone making their way through a railway station at rush hour. Her thoughts felt curiously detached.

Well, she was definitely the grown-up now, that much was for certain. The last line of defence had gone. And now what?

She looked up at the stars beginning to twinkle over Manhattan and thought about it.

What was left? She described a slow lazy figure of eight in the ice.

At home: no dad. No job. Big Bastard. Billy, she supposed. Nothing to make her happy.

Here . . .

She pulled up suddenly against the side of the rink. What the hell was she thinking about, 'here'? There was no 'here'. This was a trip, a vacation.

She realized she'd just thought the word 'vacation', instead of 'holiday', and took another thoughtful tour around the ice. Her eyes had started to take on a slightly wild expression, and people were being careful not to get in her way.

I mean, it wasn't like she didn't know anyone. Okay, so she didn't know anyone . . . but she'd have a bit of money now. Not a lot, but there was the house, she supposed. She could stay for a bit, punt around some more . . . maybe learn to drive. Properly.

She could waitress, couldn't she?

And she wouldn't have to go anywhere with people feeling sorry for her all the time. It had happened to her when she was fourteen, she didn't think she could bear it happening all over again. People indulging her, letting her do things, behave worse and worse until they got pissed off with her.

Here, nobody knew who she was. She was mysterious, foreign. Travelling. Different. Herself.

She spun around again. And, hell, if she hated it she could always go home. And if she liked it she could always stay. Well. Maybe. She could marry somebody gay or something. That happened all the time.

She hugged herself tight. The world was full of possibilities. Follow your instincts. Andrew had said that. The world made no sense. Well, now she had had that proven in a fairly dramatic fashion. And if it was going to be a world without her dad in it, she supposed she better make the most of what was left over. Feeling her dad's hands in hers she started to spin, slowly at first then quicker and quicker as the momentum picked up, as he'd taught her. He just wanted her to be happy. It wasn't Ikea's fault. It wasn't the world's fault that she didn't quite fit it. She thought of her mother, for once without rancour. Maybe she'd just been born to run. Maybe, if she did it now, she wouldn't catch anyone else in the crossfire. Born to run.

The ice shard in her heart felt as if it was on fire now; her chest felt like it would burst. The music sounded louder and louder. She spun until someone bumped into her.

'Hey!'

'Sorry!' she said, jumping around, trying to sound normal, although her eyes and her heart were aflame.

'No, I'm sorry,' said Andrew II, his dirty blond hair protruding from underneath a checked hat. 'It's just, I haven't done this in a while.'

Ellie stood stock still, breathing hard, and stared

at him. The other skaters swerved to avoid them, with the traditional array of colourful New York epithets.

'Oh,' she said. 'Oh. Oh. Now. Where the hell did you come from?'

'Well, I was born in Northern California . . . no, hang on, don't go to sleep, you'll fall over and hurt yourself. I'll skip the middle bit until we get to "and then I followed you here from the coffee shop".'

'You are somebody whose timing could not possibly be worse.'

'Yeah, that's what kept me out of cheerleading.' He stopped trying to gentle her along.

'I know.' He reached out and held her hand. 'Oh, darling. They phoned the house looking for you. I'm so, so sorry.'

She looked up at him, and her voice cracked. 'Me too.'

'I'm so sorry you were away.'

Andrew II led her to the wooden slats at the side of the rink and sat her down. After a second Ellie put her head on his shoulder and wept and wept and wept as the cold stars came out over Manhattan.

* * *

He patted her on the arm, soothed her and kissed her curls, ignoring the curious glances of the other skaters, and they sat that way until it was fully dark.

391

Eventually she sat up again.

'I'd better . . . I'd better get going.'

'Of course. I'll take you back to the hotel.'

'No, it's okay. The others will be there. They'll look after me. Honestly, I'll be fine.'

'Well . . .'

'I'd rather you didn't. I don't want to have to explain.'

'Okay. If you're sure.'

They stood up, facing each other awkwardly. Ellie rubbed hard at her eyes.

'I'm coming back to the States anyway. Once everything's sorted out. I think. For a bit longer.' Ellie tried to say this carelessly to try it out on her tongue.

'Really? Huh!' said Andrew II. He was looking at her and smiling.

'You know. Just to hang out and stuff. A new start. Maybe.'

'Yeah. Well. Hey. That's great I guess.'

He started to help her back across the ice to the hire desk.

'Are you going to look me up?'

She tried a shaky smile. 'God. At the moment I'm concentrating on putting one foot in front of the other. Or, one skate in front of the other. Which, thank God, is easier.'

He slowed.

'Did your daddy teach you to skate?'

'He taught me a lot of things.' Ellie sniffed a little.

'Well, looks like he didn't do too bad a job.'

'You think?' she asked.

'I think,' he said seriously.

She relaxed a little and let him take her hand, and they took one last tour around the ice not wanting to let go; they seemed for all the world like any other couple looking for magic in Manhattan.

'I . . . it would be really great if you felt like calling me some time if you ever got back to LA,' he said. 'I mean it. It would be really cool.'

She smiled at him

'Well, I know where to find you.'

'Yeah . . . LA. Right. Sure. Whatever.' He sighed.

'No, I mean, you're in the book.'

'Oh.' His face relaxed into a smile. 'Oh yes. I'm in the book.'

Andrew II leaned down and cupped Ellie's chin in his hand.

'This is going to happen, okay? I really want this to happen.'

She swallowed heavily.

'That's definitely a line from *Pretty in Pink*.'

'Endured just for you, okay? And yes, it is. But it's also a line from me.'

He leaned down and kissed her firmly on her pouty little mouth.

'One of these days I would like to do a *little* bit

more than just kiss you, Ellie Eversholt.'

'Thank you,' she said. 'It helps a lot to know that, it really does.'

She clasped his hands tightly then let them go.

'Well, I'd better head.'

'Yeah . . . me too. Better be getting back to Hatsie.'

'Sure . . . who knows what he could be up to?'

'Stealing his father's Ferrari . . . maybe converting it into a time machine . . .'

'That kind of thing.'

He skated – clumsily – backwards to the side of the rink, and she waved and watched him go, treasuring and nestling the tiny kernel of warmth he had brought somewhere deep inside, to be taken out and re-examined on a better day.

'Hey!' he yelled from the other side of the rink. 'You are going to be alright, Ellie Eversholt.'

'Yes I am,' she said to herself, swallowing hard. 'Yes, I am.'

* * *

Arthur and Colin were going back to the hotel to pack up Ellie's stuff and try to get her and, if possible, all of them on a flight that evening, so Julia and Loxy found themselves alone together for the first time. It felt slightly strange, and they were both picking up on the tension.

'God,' said Julia. 'What a day.'

'Yuh,' said Lox, looking down at the street and kicking away a flyer.

'Do you think she really did meet Andrew McCarthy? God. That would have been weird. I'd have been fucked off to miss it if she did. Especially after I did all the driving.'

Loxy shrugged his shoulders.

'Dunno.'

'It was amazing of you to come all this way.'

'Well, it couldn't wait – she's the only next of kin they could find.'

'God, her mother was such a selfish bitch . . .'

Loxy shrugged.

'Oh, Lox,' she put her hand on his sleeve, 'I don't know how she'd have coped not hearing it from us.'

'Yuh.'

'And . . .' she stopped and turned to face him. 'Something else. I really missed you, Loxy. I really, really did. All the time. Well, nearly all the time. I thought about us and I thought maybe we were doing the wrong thing and then I thought maybe I should see other people and then I couldn't and then I saw you walk in and I thought, it doesn't matter if we're doing the wrong thing or not I just want . . .'

'Julia.' His commanding voice made her stop suddenly. It wasn't a tone she had ever heard him use. 'Ssh a minute. I just wanted to say I'm sorry.'

'What? What? Sorry for what?' Suddenly a panic

gripped at Julia's heart. He was going to tell her it was over wasn't he? She'd turned him down once – twice maybe, if you counted that time at the airport. He was a proud man. He wasn't going to stand for this. Oh no. Oh no.

'Look,' he said. His face was serious. She didn't like the sound of that 'look'.

'I realize I've been a bit much. All over you. I was too hasty and too much and . . . I'm sorry. I really am. I'm sorry I pushed you. I wouldn't give you any space, and that's why you had to come away, and I see that now. From now on, I promise, I'm going to be a completely casual boyfriend and never pressure you . . . that is, if you still want me at all and . . . fucking hell!'

He made the last remark as Julia launched herself at him and he nearly fell over backwards into a puddle. She leapt up with her arms around his neck and her legs around his waist until he was pushed against the side of a shop.

'Oh, thank God!' she said, staring deep into his eyes. 'I love you so very much.'

His face creased into an enormous grin and he crushed her body to his. She finally broke free for long enough to look at him again.

'Oh – and . . . wasn't there something you wanted to ask me?'

* * *

Arthur put his arm around Colin as, from a short distance away, they watched the other two leaping around the street. Loxy pulled something triumphantly out of his inner coat pocket.

'What are they doing?' asked Colin.

Arthur drew him closer.

'Nothing,' he said. 'Well. Things other people do. Not us. We just have fun.'

'Isn't fun the best thing to have?' said Colin.

'Oh yes,' said Arthur, kissing him hard on the forehead. 'Oh yes.'

Epilogue

'Jesus Christ!'

They had decided to hold the wedding in a big stately house rather than a church, much to the disgruntlement of both sides of the family, even though it was a beautiful place near Box Hill. And they decided not to have a bride's side or a groom's side either, because otherwise it looked ridiculously segregated: 'You might as well just draw a set of railtracks down the aisle,' as Julia had pointed out.

However, Loxy's aunties had insisted on bringing their gospel choir, which was doing a lot to dispel the secular atmosphere, even if it was being accompanied by a rather unpleasantly wailing saxophone.

Outside it was a glorious June day, and inside there was a lot of bride-waiting-around and fanning with programmes going on. Loxy was hopping from one foot to the other and looked like he was doing a very slow tap dance. Colin, however, his rather unexpected choice of best man – 'You mean flower girl, surely,' had been Julia's outraged reaction – was standing very seriously, staring straight ahead and mouthing his speech to himself.

Upstairs in the bridal suite, a pretty, large, slightly frilly room with two beautiful sash windows overlooking the grounds, Julia, in understated ivory silk, was pacing back and forward furiously. She was waiting to go downstairs for what was a pretty bloody important day in her life, but she couldn't go and retouch her lip gloss for the last time because the door to her powder room was locked and she strongly suspected there were people rutting in it.

'Christ! Big Bastard!' She hammered the door heavily. 'I really do *not* want this to be my last view as a single woman.'

'Eh – how about I'm only having a shit?' came the yell, punctuated by Siobhan's muffled giggling.

'This really is my special day, isn't it?' sighed Julia. 'Get the *fuck* – oh, I don't want to swear in this dress. Get the FUDGE out of there. Loxy's waiting.'

'Are you sure you don't want me to do you just once for luck? It's your last chance ever.'

'Yeah, because after he did you I'd chew off his entire reproductive apparatus,' growled Siobhan.

'Get OUT the both of you. Or I'm taking the brown sauce away from the buffet.'

A couple of seconds later they emerged, smirking and looking red in the face. She shooed them out of the suite, then took one last look around. Suddenly everything was quiet. Her father was waiting downstairs, she knew, and she could picture every detail of Loxy's shaky face from here. Arthur too, right behind him, ready to read the poem they'd chosen, which he would do beautifully, naturally. He'd already offered to be an honorary uncle to the first baby, given how much practice he'd had. She twirled quickly in the three-way mirror, but scarcely needed to glance to know that she looked as lovely as she could. She looked as beautiful as a garden.

No Hedgehog of course. They hadn't seen her since the funeral, and she'd been quiet enough then. Julia shivered when she remembered the long cold trip home, the horrible fussing and sorting, and custard creams and dry, curled-up catered sandwiches. Ellie's mother hadn't bothered to show up, unsurprisingly. A subdued Christmas with Julia's family had followed, then, out of the blue on the 2nd of January, Ellie had picked up her battered old rucksack and disappeared, leaving a rather confused note that said something about going to look for the New Jersey Turnpoke.

Since then, correspondence had been sporadic to say the least. In one 5am phone call, they'd finally got her to discover e-mail, but at the moment it tended to be the last line of what had clearly been very long letters, followed by strings of swear words and abrupt cuttings off. Julia picked up the picture she'd brought along to use as a stand-in – she'd discovered it in Ellie's camera about a month before, when she'd decided to develop the film and see what was there.

What had been there was: two blurry shots of the carpet of the Ritz hotel; one of her looking pallid and Ellie looking scarlet against the first little Toyota with the Hollywood sign just visible in the background haze; a giant cockroach next to a bottle of tequila; Julia sitting exhaustedly on a kerb in the sunshine in the middle of God knows where; Andrew II and Hatsie, Andrew clearly laughing his head off at something Hatsie had just said; a big silver Thunderbird; someone who might have been the back of Arthur's head emerging from Arrivals; an underexposed very large pig in the dark; Julia standing next to a sign that said 'Julia 25 miles'; some blurry trees through a car window; Ellie very late at night reflected in a motel bathroom mirror; New York from a distance, Arthur's knees; New York a bit closer up. The last one she couldn't even remember being taken. It was a little blurry, shot inside a coffee shop on a very grey day, but once you'd looked at it closely, it definitely appeared to show Ellie kissing someone who looked *spookily* like Andrew McCarthy.

Julia shook her head and propped the last photograph up on the mantelpiece. Then she began to make her way across the room to pick up her bouquet, making very, very sure that her train didn't get caught on any of the spikes of the five-foot-tall cactus plant which had arrived that morning with an enormous bow around it, and which was now absurdly dwarfing all the other gifts spread around the room. The return address was simply the *poste restante* in some tiny little town in Arizona. The message said, 'With all my love, the Hedgehog. A sends love too.'

Julia wondered who 'A' was. It couldn't be, could it? No, surely not. *Surely*. She smiled and shrugged to herself.

The morning sun was picking up the motes of dust through the windows. Downstairs, the choir started up a spiritual version of 'Together in Electric Dreams', which was Julia's cue. She picked up the bouquet, and, on a whim, carefully plucked out a couple of cactus spikes. Sprinkling them on the top of the flowers for luck, she pushed on forwards through the open door.

Talking to Addison

Jenny Colgan

Holly is a frustrated florist whose life doesn't exactly seem to be coming up roses . . .

Fleeing the houseshare from hell, she moves in with Josh, a nice rich boy with a terminal case of sexual confusion; Kate, a city high-flyer with talons to match; and the gorgeous Addison, who spends his day communicating only with his computer and those who worship at the altar of Captain Jean-Luc Picard.

Holly's desperate to have a one-to-one with Addison, but can she drag him away from his monstrously ugly, not to say jealous internet 'girlfriend' Claudia, or will they just continually get their wires crosses?

ISBN 0 00 653177 6